Inkslingers Ball

A Claudia Rose Novel

Sheila Lowe

Write Choice Ink

ISBN-10-1970181060
ISBN-13-978-1970181098
ASIN- B08WWXYGDX (EPUB)
This book is a work of fiction. Names, characters, businesses, organizations, places, events, incidents are the product of the author's imagination or are used fictitiously. Any resemblance to actual events, locals, or persons, living or dead, is coincidental.

Cover Design: Jane Dixon Smith

Printed in the United States of America

PUBLISHING HISTORY

Write Choice Ink Ventura, California, 2026
Suspense Publishing, Print and Digital Copy, 2016
NAL/Penguin Group, Print and Digital Copy, September 2008

www.sheilalowebooks.com

Praise for Sheila Lowe

"Lowe expertly delivers a solid criminal investigation while guiding her readers into a unique culture where tattooing and the murder of a young girl come together on the autopsy table. Hit the lights and siren because this is one fast ride from beginning to end."

— Lee Lofland, Author of "Police Procedure and Investigation" and founder and director of the Writers' Police Academy

"Sheila Lowe's writing is fast-paced and suspenseful and made believable by her own background as a forensic handwriting expert. Yet another page-turner for Claudia Rose fans."

— Rick Reed, Author of the Jack Murphy Crime Series

"Inkslingers Ball is the perfect novel for an afternoon by the pool. With vivid characters, smooth writing, and a twisty plot, Sheila Lowe has crafted a mystery that will keep you guessing to the very end."

— Boyd Morrison, International bestselling author

"Sheila Lowe's Inkslingers Ball is a reminder of every parent's nightmare. Lowe drags us into the underworld of street mobsters who destroy reputable businesses through shakedowns, torching, and murder, luring naïve youth into their employ. A deadly dance orchestrated by the lowest forms of life."

— Sandra Brannan, Author of the acclaimed Liv Bergen Mysteries

ALSO BY SHEILA LOWE

CLAUDIA ROSE NOVELS

Poison Pen
Written In Blood
Dead Write
Last Writes
Inkslingers Ball
Outside The Lines
Written Off
Dead Letters
Maximum Pressure

BEYOND THE VEIL NOVELS

What She Saw
Proof Of Life
The Last Door

MEMOIR

Growing From the Ashes

NONFICTION

Reading Between the Lines: Decoding Handwriting
Advanced Studies in Handwriting Psychology
Personality & Anxiety Disorders
Succeeding in the Business of Handwriting Analysis
Improve Your Life with Graphotherapy
Handwriting of the Famous & Infamous
The Complete Idiot's Guide to Handwriting Analysis
Sheila Lowe's Handwriting Analyzer software

Inkslingers Ball

one

Early Wednesday morning

It started with a late-night phone call.

The familiar ringtone was never a good way to be woken up, especially when the phone belonged to a homicide detective—unless you were already in the middle of a nightmare. Curled on her side in the darkness, Claudia was grateful to have been jarred out of her sleep—to escape the dream.

She knew the phone would be in Joel's hand even before he rolled out of bed. He'd press the answer button and wait until he was in the bathroom with the door shut before acknowledging the caller.

Still, his low voice filtered through the wall. The words were indistinct, but the clipped tone told her this was something other than a routine homicide callout.

If any homicide could be thought of as routine.

Fragments of the nightmare clung. She'd been running barefoot through the forsaken rooms of a derelict house, her feet not quite touching the floor in the odd way things worked in dreams. The sense of long, predatory fingers stretching for her as she fled. The memory left her unsettled, though she wasn't sure why. She reached for the blanket crumpled at the foot of the bed and drew it over her bare shoulders.

The sound of water beating against the wall came a minute later. Three minutes in and out of the shower—water running in the sink—brushing his teeth, a hurried shave.

Before re-entering the bedroom, Joel switched off the bathroom light, still doing his best not to disturb her as he made his way across the room to the closet. And yet, Claudia knew from the snap of the security clasp precisely when he holstered his Glock; from the whisper of cotton against acetate when he shrugged into his suit coat. She knew, too, from the muttered curse under his breath when he stumbled against the sharp corner of the bed frame while hunting for his shoes.

The red numbers on the bedside clock glowed 2:33.

"Where is it?" she asked, her voice still thick with the remnants of the dream.

"Shhh. Go back to sleep."

"Tell me."

Joel hesitated, then loosed a sigh. "Venice Beach."

Normally she would not push him, but something in his reluctance made her persist. Propped on an elbow, Claudia sought him through the shadows. "Is it bad?"

Already halfway through the bedroom door, he paused and turned back, chilling her with his words.

"It's a kid."

two

The previous Friday

The Venice Boardwalk was an adult theme park where the attractions were the various wack jobs doing their thing. Weed shops, tattoo parlors, Rose the body painter. Crazy Guitar Dude on roller blades, amp strapped to his back, singing as he swept past. Amateur rappers hawking their latest album. Old guy wearing nothing but a Speedo—everyone said he'd been there forever. A haze of weed thick enough to give everyone within a block a contact high.

The crazies fascinated fifteen-year-old Annabelle Giordano and stirred her curiosity—she wanted to know what made them do what they did. She started toward the dude with the "Kick me in the balls for $1" sign to ask him, but Monica grabbed her by the arm and dragged her away before she could, afraid she'd catch rabies or maybe something worse.

Monica was Annabelle's BFF, which was totally weird because two girls could not have been more unalike. Monica's aunt Claudia said they reminded her of Snow White and Rose Red, like the two sisters in the fairytale.

Annabelle's raven-colored hair and olive skin were gifts from her father. She wasn't exactly pretty, but even she knew there was something appealing about her exotic looks. At least, when she forgot to paste on her sullen face and curl her cupid's bow lips into a sneer, there was.

Monica, on the other hand, was conventionally cute, with the curly blonde hair of a baby doll and china blue eyes that got big and anxious when she was out of her comfort zone. Like now, when conscience was beginning to get the better of her.

"I hope my dad doesn't call me," she said.

Annabelle eyes were fixed on the painted men dancing like robots, and the rapping acrobats. "Why would he call you when he thinks we're at the mall?"

"You know how he is."

"Yeah. He's obsessed with keeping you a child." Annabelle let out a huff of irritation. For sure Pete Bennett would have never given permission for his daughter to go to the Boardwalk if she'd told the truth about where they were going. "He should let you be more independent. That's how you learn what to do if something bad happens."

Annabelle knew a lot about bad things happening.

"You know it's because of my mom," Monica said softly.

Annabelle could tell her friend was regretting the little white lie she'd told her father. She tore her gaze away from a weight lifter who was getting his photo taken with a girl in a bikini—he charged ten bucks for the privilege. "Your mom getting killed by a drunk driver doesn't mean he has to keep you wrapped up like a big burrito for the rest of your life," she said.

That was something they shared. Annabelle's own mother had died in a car accident, too. She changed the subject. "I might get a piercing. Maybe my tongue." She stuck it out for effect.

Monica snorted. "Not while you're staying at my aunt's. She'd freak."

"You think so? She's usually pretty cool."

"She just wants us to think she's cool. *Inside* she's freaking. Remember when she caught you with those cigarettes? I heard her talking with my dad. She was pretty upset about it."

Annabelle grinned. "Duh. I didn't even smoke them; I'm not that stupid. I was just carrying them in my backpack so my homies wouldn't think I was a total loser."

"Well, Auntie C told my dad that he'd better keep an eye on you when you're over at our house."

"Everyone says I'm a bad influence on you."

"It's not that...well, maybe it is. But you know she loves you anyway."

Annabelle didn't answer. It would have sounded pitiful to say that nobody loved her, even if that's how it felt a lot of the time. Deep in her heart, she knew it wasn't true. But after believing it for so long, the habit was hard to break.

Annabelle had been fourteen when Monica's aunt Claudia came into her life. She'd been motherless for eight of those years. Practically fatherless, too. The man who raised her had given her his name, and far more material things than she could ever wish for, but a name and material things were not what she hankered after.

Discovering that Nicholas Giordano was not her father was like having a big icky spiderweb peeled off her. She had always felt it in her bones—isn't that what people said when they knew something with their whole entire self? That's how strongly she had known something was wrong with the way Nick—she had come to think of him as her fake father—had looked at her, like she was something gross he'd picked out of his nose. When he even bothered to look.

Before Claudia and Monica had come into her life, Annabelle had tried every way she could think of to get his attention, from jacking up the sound of her favorite metal bands to a gazillion decibels, to involving herself with a very bad crew. But it was always the same. Nick's voice reverberating through the big house in the hills above Malibu Beach, screaming at whatever dildo was directing the latest movie his studio was producing, demanding to know why they were over budget and behind schedule. Nothing Annabelle did mattered.

Finally, she had given in to her loneliness and desperation to be loved. She'd stolen a bottle of expensive vodka from Nick's wet bar and took it down to the beach in the middle of the night. She'd forced down as much of the booze as she could tolerate, then smashed the bottle on the rocks and dragged a thick shard of the broken glass across her wrists.

She had no memory of it, but later, in the hospital psych ward, they told her that a guy walking his dog had found her before it was too late. She'd wished he had let her die.

Nick had stood over her hospital bed and yelled at her for making him look bad. He sent her to the Sorensen Academy, a school where rich parents sent their troublesome daughters when they didn't know what else to do with them, or just didn't want to bother. Annabelle thought of it as Juvie with fake glitter. She had been to real Juvie, so she knew.

Meeting Claudia Rose had been the start of her new life.

Claudia had come to Sorensen and talked to the student body about their handwriting and what it said about their personalities. Later, she had shown Annabelle something called 'graphotherapy,' which was exercises she was supposed to do while some funky special music played in the background.

Claudia said the exercises would help her deal with her feelings appropriately, instead of stuffing them inside until they erupted all at once. At first, Annabelle had pretended not to be interested, but deep down she was totally over constantly getting in trouble for her behavior. So, she pushed her skepticism aside and agreed to try the program. After a while, she was surprised to discover that she was actually starting to feel better.

Meeting Monica was another awesome event in her life. The instant feeling of sisterhood was foreign to Annabelle, but despite—or maybe because of—their differences, the two girls quickly formed a bond that had deepened as their friendship evolved.

Annabelle was older by only a few weeks, but Monica, who had been sheltered by a loving father and aunt since the death of her mother, seemed much younger. Tender-hearted Monica had been hurt when she learned how Annabelle had pretty much raised herself, and had burst into tears at her tales of smoking dope at thirteen and cruising with gangbangers in the cars they stole. Annabelle decided she had better not tell her the part about getting passed around for sex.

Suddenly, Monica's impatience filtered through the memories and brought her back to the boardwalk. "Anna, are you even listening to me? You can't get a piercing!"

"Chill, Mon, don't be so extra. I'm just *thinking* about it. Maybe I'll get a tattoo instead."

"What kind would you get?" Monica asked, a tiny bit wistful. "I'd put a little flower on my ankle—maybe a rose." She sighed. "I'll have to wait 'til I'm around a hundred. My dad would never let me do it."

"Truth. He's like the witch in that *Rapunzel* movie. You might as well be locked up in some old tower, growing your hair a thousand feet long."

"So now I'm a burrito, *and* Rapunzel?"

Annabelle grinned. "A big burrito with really long hair."

"What*ever*. Anyway, what would you get?"

Annabelle stopped walking and thought about it for a minute. "A mermaid, maybe. I'd have it someplace no one could see it."

"Why?"

"Because it's nobody's business."

"Well, what's the point, if nobody can see it?"

"*I* would know it's there. It would be *my* secret."

Monica giggled. "Unless you had a boyfriend. He would know."

"Shut *up*. I—"

"Hey, Anna*B*. Hey, home skillet, wait up."

Annabelle swung around in surprise.

"*Angel?*"

She had recognized the voice, but it took a moment to match her memory to the girl calling out to her. The silky chestnut hair she'd worn when they'd gone to school together was now dyed white blonde and teased out like straw. Thick black mascara outlined her eyelids like pictures Annabelle had seen of Cleopatra. In her tiny stretch shorts and hi-top sneakers, she looked like a baby hooker.

Angel and the girl with her crossed the sidewalk to them.

"Hey, this is Angel," Annabelle said to Monica. "We used to hang out in jail—I mean at Sorensen Acad."

Angel jerked her head at the other girl. "That's Jamie."

"Hey." Annabelle nodded back, thinking that Jamie, whose face was masked behind a pair of enormous shades, must have gotten her strategically torn jeans and tight T-shirt off the same tacky rack as Angel.

"So, whatup, AnnaB? It's been like forever." They all stood in the middle of the crowded boardwalk, ignoring the beachgoers who flowed around them, some throwing annoyed glances at the four girls blocking their path.

"I know, huh? We gotta talk." A strong whiff of barbecued meat wafted past and made Annabelle's stomach rumble loud enough to be heard in Santa Monica. Everyone on the boardwalk seemed to have food in their hands: mangoes with chili powder, hotdogs, churros.

"Let's go to Figtree's and get some food," she suggested.

Angel nodded. "I wanna hear what you been up to since the great escape."

Fanning out across the boardwalk, the girls turned as a group. A small boy licking a mile-high ice cream crashed into them and nearly dropped his cone. His father shot them a dirty look and muttered something about stupid teenagers as he walked away with his family.

"Fuck you, asshat," Jamie yelled after him, and Angel laughed. Monica blushed bright crimson. Embarrassed even though for once it wasn't she who had done something wrong, Annabelle grabbed Monica's arm and started walking faster toward the café.

They got a table on the patio and ordered burgers and Cokes, except for Monica, who was trying out vegetarian and asked for a veggie and tofu sandwich. Across the boardwalk, three shirtless dudes with guitars and a bass were singing for donations. They sounded better than they looked.

Angel leaned forward in her white plastic chair, bony elbows on the table. "So, tell me, AnnaB, what happened after I left that fucked up school? Did that skank Jordan Riley get herself pregnant? All those times she sneaked out at night; I know she was too dumb to take care of herself."

Her old friend looked like she'd had the flu and was just getting over it, but Annabelle recognized her sallow skin for what it was—bad diet and drug use. She shrugged. "Didn't you hear, the school got shut down? It wasn't all that long after you left."

Monica's foot nudged hers under the table, as if tapping out a question. "Angel escaped," Annabelle explained. "Like the slaves—right, Angel? She got emancipated."

"Emancipated minor," Angel corrected her. "The judge let me get free from my mom. She didn't give a shit anyway—too busy playing with her friends in Europe."

"But she's still a slave," Jamie put in.

Angel's face fell. "I moved in with Mouser and his brother."

"And his brother's lady, and his brother's kids, and his brother's dogs," Jamie added.

"Mouser's her boyfriend," Annabelle informed a wide-eyed Monica. "He's like, this insanely gorgeous surfer dude." She glanced back at Angel. "I can't believe you're still together."

"Yeah. I take care of his brother's rugrats and help with the housework, and they let me live there," Angel spoke with a conspicuous lack of enthusiasm.

"She's like that Cinderella chick," Jamie said. "Ariceli treats her like dogshit and Bad Bobby lets her. In fact, he kicks her ass if Ariceli tells him to. It pretty much sucks."

Angel ignored her. "It's not all that bad. I get to hang out sometimes, like now, for instance. Anyhow, what happened at Sorensen? They had a good thing going. Why'd they shut it down?"

Annabelle and Monica exchanged an uneasy glance. Annabelle still had a hard time talking about the horrors she had experienced in those last weeks before the school closed. She avoided a direct answer. "Ms. Sorensen's step kids took it over and closed it. I go to regular school now, with Monica. Hey, you won't believe this—I found out my father isn't really my father and my real father's a stuntman."

Angel's eyebrows shot up. "No shit?"

"I know, huh?"

"So, when do I get to meet Real Dad?"

"He's working on a movie in Canada all summer. I'm staying at Monica's aunt Claudia's."

"Well, I wanna meet the stuntman." Angel scraped back her chair and peeled off her sweatshirt, exposing the tattoo on her shoulder. "Keep my seat warm, sistas; gotta hit the little girl's room."

"Sweet tat," Annabelle said, watching her disappear at the back of the restaurant.

Jamie tugged her own shirt down, displaying some serious ink. A stark white skull with a red rose tangled in a mane of black hair. "We both got sugar skulls."

Annabelle stared with admiration at the mix of glam and horror. The tip of the nose formed a black triangle, the skull's eyes heavily outlined with charcoal and decorated with green petals. Black stitches sealed the lips. "That is *so* awesome," she exclaimed.

"It comes from some Mexican celebration," Jamie added. "The Day of the Dead, or something."

"*Dia de los Muertos,*" Monica said, looking abashed when the other two girls stared at her as if she'd said something dirty. "It's the day after Halloween. We studied it in Spanish class. People bring food and stuff to the cemetery to honor their dead relatives."

"That'd be so cool; a picnic on a grave." Annabelle's mind was already spinning with the possibilities.

But Monica wasn't having any of that. "Don't even think about it. We're *not* going to any cemeteries for a picnic."

Angel returned from the restroom and dropped into her chair. Her dilated pupils and glassy stare told Annabelle she'd taken a hit of something. Once, she would have asked to share, but she could feel something changing in her. Getting high didn't hold the appeal it used to.

"What'd I miss?" Angel asked with a big sloppy smile.

"Your old BFF is jealous of our tats," Jamie said.

"Does it hurt to get it done?" Monica asked.

Jamie gave a jeering laugh. "You didn't hear us crying. I guess it kinda feels like a bee sting. You gonna get one?"

"*I* want one," Annabelle broke in. "Where'd you get it done?"

"No parlor is gonna ink you," Angel said with certainty. "You're underage. They'd get busted and lose their license."

"*You're* underage."

"But the guy who did ours is a special friend. He knows we're not gonna rat him out."

"Would he do one for me? Yours are so awesome."

Jamie and Angel exchanged a look, then Angel giggled. "Viper? He might, but you'd have to fuck him, and he's an old dude. He's at least 40."

Annabelle wrinkled her nose. "Hells no, I don't want it *that* much."

"Maybe Crash'd do it," said Angel.

"Who's that?"

"He's just another old tattoo dude, but he doesn't got his own studio like Viper, so he don't have to worry about a license."

"He's a really good artist, though." Angel's lips pursed. "I might be able to talk him into it. He likes me."

"You better hope Viper doesn't find out you're hangin' with Crash," Jamie said.

Annabelle intercepted the warning look Jamie threw at her friend, but Angel brushed it off. "Who's gonna tell him? Anyhow, he's the one who sent me over there. He *wants* those guys to like me."

"Shut up, Angel. Viper doesn't need his business spread all over town."

Angel pursed her lips in a sulk, but she didn't argue.

Annabelle's curiosity nudged her. She wanted to ask Angel what she meant—who were the guys this Viper person wanted to like her? But she kept the question to herself. No point inciting any more friction.

Monica filled the tense silence. "You can't get a tattoo, Annabelle. Aunty C won't—"

"She doesn't need to know," Annabelle interrupted, shutting her down. She turned to Angel, all business. "So, you think this Crash guy will do it for me? Would you mind if I got one like yours? It's so cute."

"I wouldn't exactly call a skull with makeup cute," Monica protested. "And you should wait 'til your father gets back."

"Like he's gonna say yeah? I'm so sure." Annabelle shook her head. "Anyway, don't be such a wuss."

"She gonna rat you out?" Jamie asked, nodding toward Monica.

"Of course not," Monica indignantly declared. "I don't snitch, but she's gonna get in trouble. I don't think it's a good idea."

"Well, I do." Annabelle got out her cell phone. "Ask him, Angel. I'm gonna do it."

three

Sunday

"What are you so antsy about, Annabelle?" Claudia asked. "Do you think it's going to make the phone ring if you keep looking at it?"

"I'm waiting for a call."

"I guessed that much. Anyone interesting?"

"I ran into this girl I used to go to school with at Sorensen. We're gonna get together and talk about the bad old days."

"Anyone I know?"

"Nope."

"What's her name?"

"Angel."

"Angel what?"

"I don't remember her last name. It's really Angela, but she didn't like it, so we called her Angel."

"Where did you run into her?"

Annabelle made an exasperated noise. "Why are you asking me all these questions? Don't you trust me?"

"Of course I trust you. Do I have a reason not to?"

The answer came rapid fire. "No."

"Okay. But I have one more question. Do you need a ride?"

Annabelle looked abashed. "No, thanks. She's going to call me when she gets to Tyler's. I'll walk down and meet her."

Tyler's was the neighborhood coffeehouse about a half-mile away, down a steep hill.

"I'd be glad to drop you there. I'm going to the grocery store."

Annabelle's cheeks flushed a sudden bright pink. "You *don't* trust me!" She jumped up and flounced out of the kitchen, her words trailing behind her.

The slam of her bedroom door made Claudia wince. It had been some time since she'd seen this side of Annabelle. She pondered it, trying to figure out what was going on. The girl had been in an odd mood since her trip to the mall with Monica on Friday. That furtive behavior was hiding something, for sure.

She sighed. Three steps forward, two steps back. It felt like they were doing a dance. But it was to be expected. After everything Annabelle had endured last year, including being kidnapped and witnessing the brutal murder of someone she cared about, it would have been strange if she didn't continue to have bad days. And nights, though thank God, several weeks had passed without her waking up screaming.

Zebediah Gold, Claudia's old friend and Annabelle's therapist, confirmed the girl was suffering from PTSD—post-traumatic stress disorder. Maybe meeting up with Angel, who belonged to that old life and memories of the Sorensen Academy, had triggered a return of the nightmares.

After she had done her grocery shopping, Claudia resolved to put in a call to Zebediah and make an appointment for Annabelle.

four

Sunday afternoon traffic rushed past the corner of Jefferson and Pershing, where Angel had arranged for her friend Crash to pick them up. Annabelle craned her neck, looking for the white van Angel said he would be driving. "Are you *sure* he's coming?"

"Don't be scared, AnnaB, I told ya it's not gonna hurt too bad."

Annabelle glared at her. "I'm not *scared*. I just don't want Claudia to start looking for me when I told her we'd be at Tyler's."

"What's the big deal? She's not your mom."

"She's letting me stay at her house, and I don't need her telling my dad I messed up. Again."

"Screw her anyway," Angel said rudely. "I'm sticking my neck out for you, so don't go wimping out on me."

"I am not wimping out."

"Well, just make sure you don't. He's doing me a big favor."

"What*ever*."

Crash was already ten minutes late. Seeing how Angel was dressed in another baby hooker outfit, Annabelle was hoping nobody driving by would mistake them for pickups. She was getting tired of waiting. "Hey, what's up with that snake dude you and Jamie were talking about the other day?"

Angel scrunched up her nose as if not understanding. "What snake dude?" Then her face cleared and she laughed. "You mean *Viper?* He lets us hang at his place cause Bobby works there. There's always cool biker dudes. They like having young chicks around. Hella better than those little gangbangers you and me used to run with before Sorensen."

"Where's his place?"

"Dragon House? It's on Lincoln over near Rose in Venice."

"Cool name."

"Yeah. The guys buy us beer, and the other day, Viper's bodyguard, Big Carl, even rolled me a blunt."

Annabelle had never tried one herself, but she knew Angel was talking about a hollowed-out cigar filled with weed. "Did you like it?"

"Not so much, but I didn't want them laughing at me, so I faked like I did. You oughta come over there sometime."

"Yeah, maybe."

A year ago, Annabelle would have taken Angel up on her offer without a second's hesitation. But something in her had changed. Getting high with a bunch of bikers didn't sound half as much fun as it once would have. Maybe Monica had rubbed off on her. Or maybe she was starting to grow up. She liked that idea and decided that's what it was.

"What's Viper like?" Annabelle asked.

"Believe it or not, he's kinda hot for an old dude. And he lets us do stuff for him."

"Stuff, like what?"

"Oh, you know, deliveries and shit, when his other girls aren't around."

Annabelle knew what that meant—drugs. Knowing better than to pursue it, she changed the subject. "How come the other day Jamie said not to let him know you were hanging with Crash?"

Angel leaned in close and lowered her voice as if someone on that empty street corner might overhear what she was about to say. "I shouldn't tell you this, so don't spread it around, okay?"

"You know I don't have a big mouth."

"That's true. You were always cool about not telling shit." She looked around, making double sure there was no one within earshot. "Okay, this guy, Travis, opened a new tattoo studio down the street from Viper's place. It's called Under My Skin. Viper's mondo pissed about it because Travis used to work for him. So, he told me to go over there and hit on Travis and get him to fuck me."

"Why would he do that?"

Angel looked at her as if she were stupid. "Well, obviously because I'm underage and Travis'd get in trouble if I told on him. He'd go to jail for statutory rape."

"So, you mean Viper was setting him up?"

"Yeah."

"That's pretty nasty."

Angel shrugged. "Well, at least Travis isn't bad looking. Of course, he's around twenty-five or something."

"But what about your boyfriend? Doesn't he care?"

"Mouser isn't gonna argue with Viper, trust me."

"And is Travis going for it?"

"Well..." Angel looked away, avoiding Annabelle's questioning eyes. "Travis is nice to me. Nicer than Mouser, actually. I don't want to get him in trouble, so I told Viper he's not interested, but he keeps making me go back over there."

"What's Crash got to do with it?"

"He's been helping Travis get his place going. He used to have his own shop, but he retired or something like that."

"Well, I wish he'd hurry his butt up. Is he going to do my tat at Travis's place?"

"No, stupid. I told you Travis'd get in trouble and lose his license. Crash wouldn't—" Suddenly, Angel stepped to the edge of the sidewalk and began wildly waving her arms above her head. "There he is."

An old white cargo van that had seen happier days maneuvered its way to the curb. Someone had written 'CLEAN ME' in the thick coating of reddish dust on the side.

The driver leaned his elbow on the open window frame. He pushed his shades up on his forehead and squinted out at them. Annabelle guessed he was at least her father's age. With his ragged beard and moustache, and greasy-looking brown hair streaked with grey pulled into a ponytail, he didn't look any cleaner than his vehicle. He jerked his head toward the rear of the van, "Go get in back. I don't want no one seeing you."

The girls walked to the rear of the van. Angel pulled open one of the doors and stepped aside to let Annabelle go first. Annabelle climbed inside. A Harley with gleaming red fenders ate up half the cargo bay. She crawled in as far as she could, leaving room for Angel, and plopped onto a pile of moving blankets next to the bike. The blankets were probably a hundred years old and smelled funky. They looked about as clean as the van and its owner. Praying there was nothing creepy crawling in them, she turned back to see Angel was still standing in the street.

"Have fun." Angel started to close the door.

Annabelle jumped up and hit her head against the roof. "Hey, what are you doing?"

"Ariceli will have a shit fit if she gets home and I didn't start dinner."

The door slammed shut, leaving Annabelle alone in the dark cargo bay.

She started crawling toward the doors, but the van suddenly pulled away from the curb, knocking her onto her rear.

A metal grill separated the driver from the cargo bay. With the Harley in the way, she couldn't get close enough to touch it, but Annabelle could see the top of Crash's head rising above the headrest. Beyond that, she could see through the windshield when he turned right onto Jefferson and started driving toward the city of Inglewood. Her heart was thumping hard enough to crack her ribs.

"Where are we going?" she yelled.

He yelled back without even turning his head. "Don't worry about it."

Why would Angel do this to her? She had acted like they were going together to get her tattoo. Annabelle's stomach churned, remembering what Jamie had said about how she would have to have sex with Viper to get a sugar skull. Is that what Crash expected? After all the stupid shit Angel had gotten her into before, including the painful and humiliating experience of being used by the gangstas they hung out with, she should have known better than to trust her so-called friend.

Would it scare Crash if she told him that Claudia's boyfriend was a cop and she was staying with them? Annabelle and Jovanic were still far from being best buds, but they had been getting along better lately. She didn't dislike him anymore, anyway, and he treated her okay, even when Claudia wasn't around. At this moment, she needed desperately to believe that Joel would go after Crash if he raped her.

They passed the Ballona Wetlands, then the immense Playa Vista condo complex. Then they were driving under the 405 bridge and Crash turned onto a street that took them into an industrial area. Annabelle thought about the iPhone in her pocket. Should she call Claudia? No. She didn't want Claudia to know what an idiot she was getting into a strange man's van. Claudia would be disappointed in her, and she couldn't bear that.

If he kills me, she'll be really *upset.*

She would never have gotten in the van if she'd known Angel planned to ditch her. Annabelle took out her phone and debated for a long moment. In the end, she couldn't bring herself to confess to what she now realized was a pretty dumb move.

She scanned the cargo bay, looking for something that might serve as a weapon. From her experiences last year, she knew she wouldn't hesitate to use one if it came down to it.

Scrabbling under the pile of blankets, she found a screwdriver and a crescent wrench. Their gangbanger homies had taught her and Angel some of the tools they used, so the girls could hand off the right ones when they were working on their rides. The screwdriver was a smallish Phillips head that wouldn't be of much use unless she could jab him in the eye with it. The wrench was about a foot long and heavy in her hand. Wielding it made her feel slightly less vulnerable.

They had been driving for less than ten minutes when the van came to a stop and Crash got out. Annabelle positioned herself near the door in a crouch, holding onto the handle with one hand, the wrench in the other. She could hear the metallic sounds of a gate rolling open, then Crash climbed back into the driver seat and drove a few feet, turned a corner, then shut off the ignition and got out again.

She tried the handle, but it didn't budge. When Crash opened the door, she was waiting for him. Quick as a snake strike, he grabbed her upraised wrist and squeezed until she was forced to let go of her weapon and it clattered to the ground.

"What the hell you doin', ya skinny little shit?"

He bent down and picked up the wrench, sounding more amused than angry, and tossed it inside the van.

Annabelle stuck out her chin in defiance. "Where the hell are we?"

They were in some kind of a small yard. Beyond him, through the open door, she could see several cars in various states of decay. Across a chain-link fence was a one-story block-walled building painted a cheerful blue-green and cream color that seemed totally out of place in the drab neighborhood. A hand-painted sign on the wall read Deacon's Machine Shop.

Crash grinned at her, and for the first time she saw that his top front teeth were missing. He caught her looking. "Crystal meth. Don't do it if you want to keep your choppers."

"Where are we?" she asked again, promising herself that she would never, ever experiment with methamphetamine if that's what it led to.

"Welcome to my tattoo parlor. Nobody's gonna bother us here."

He was right about that. The neighborhood was deserted. Sunday afternoon, the workers who populated the industrial buildings during the week were home watching football, eating pizza, and drinking beer. He grinned at her through the big gap in his mouth.

"This place belongs to a buddy of mine. He ain't gonna mind if we park here for a while, so just sit yourself back down. Angel said you wanted a sugar skull like hers."

"Wait—you mean, you're gonna do it here, in the van?"

"That's right. It's plenty private. Believe me, I've inked folks in places way less fancy than this. You can lie on the blankets, be comfortable."

"Those blankets are gross."

"Aw, don't be so prissy. They're okay."

"Well, what's it gonna cost? Angel didn't tell me."

"How about a BJ and a pack of smokes?"

"How about *not*."

He showed her his toothless grin again and she guessed he was just joking about the blow job. Maybe he wasn't so bad after all.

"How much ya got, Skinny?"

Annabelle stuck her fist into her pocket and fished out three twenty-dollar bills. "Is this enough?"

He took the bills and crammed them into the pocket of his surfer shorts. "Been saving up your allowance?"

"As a matter of fact." The defiant attitude she had worked for months to overcome slipped right back in before she could stop it.

Crash pushed a big canvas bag across the van floor and waved his hands at her, gesturing at her to move back. Keeping a watchful eye on him, Annabelle scooted aside as he clambered up into the van with her.

"What's in the bag?" she asked.

"Gonna tattoo, need equipment."

Crash sat back on his heels and while he was occupied with removing small bottles of ink, a tube of Vaseline, and the tattoo machine, Annabelle slipped her cell phone out of her pocket and turned aside so he wouldn't see what she was doing. She had decided to text Monica so *someone* would know what had happened to her if she ended up in a jam.

A heavy hand on her arm made her jump. Annabelle gave a little scream and turned to look straight into Crash's scowl. "Hold on there, Skinny. What are you up to?"

"I'm just texting my friend. We—we're supposed to meet up later."

"Yeah? Well, you don't need to be doing that right now. Gimme the phone. I hate those things. I'll hang onto it until we're done."

"No! I'll put it back in my pocket. I'm not giving it to you."

"Yes, you are."

Crash snatched the phone from her hand and slid it across the floor behind the Harley where she couldn't reach it, then returned to arranging his equipment on a tray. She could tell he was watching her from the corner of his eye.

She was still contemplating how to get to her phone before he caught her when he reached back into his bag and took out a half-empty bottle of tequila. Annabelle gaped at him. "Hey, you're not putting needles on me when you're wasted!"

He unscrewed the cap and extended the bottle. "I'm not gonna be wasted, you are."

"What? No way. I'm not drinking that shit."

"If you want me to lay this ink on you, you are. I don't need no squirrely little kid squirming all over the place. It'll help you relax."

"I'm not a little kid. I'm almost sixteen."

"Then drink the damn tequila and let's get on with it or I'll just drop ya back where I found ya."

Annabelle took the bottle and sniffed. She seriously wanted the sugar skull and it wouldn't be the first time she'd drunk tequila, but she had promised Claudia she wouldn't do it again until she was legal age.

Promises were made to be broken.

Carefully wiping the lip of the bottle on her T-shirt to rub away any germs lurking there, she took a healthy slug. The alcohol rushed down her throat, setting her chest on fire and leaving her spluttering for air. She handed back the bottle, trying to salvage her dignity.

Crash took the bottle, and shoved it back in the bag, ignoring her discomfort. "Where you want the tat?"

"Someplace no one can see it, so I don't get in trouble."

"Pull your pants down and lie on your back."

"*What?*"

Taking a work light from the bag, he hung it on a hook on the wall. The cargo area lit up like a full moon. "You heard me, gal. I can't do it through your pants. You don't want it seen, it goes on the bikini line. So, drop 'em."

Annabelle stared at him in dismay. She hadn't thought this far ahead and it was pretty clear to her that Crash was reading her misgivings and finding them amusing. Resigning herself, she slowly laid back on the yucky blanket and unzipped her Levi's. She lifted her butt a little and wriggled the denim down an inch or so.

Before she realized what he was doing, Crash grabbed the waistband and yanked it down, exposing her blue and white striped cotton panties. When he started to put his hand on the elastic, she caught him in time and pushed it away.

"Don't!"

"How'm I supposed to…"

Annabelle pushed the elastic waistband below her belly button and held it there with both hands. "Do it like that, or I'm outta here." She wasn't sure how she would follow through on that threat, but Crash just grinned his toothless grin.

"Okay, Skinny. You da boss."

The tequila was working fast. She was already feeling a little light-headed. Cutting her eyes to the left, she could see him pulling on a pair of latex gloves. At least he was going to be sanitary about it.

Crash uncapped a bottle of green soap and soaked a paper towel with it. He began washing her abdomen near her hip in strong, sure strokes. "Why you wanna ink up this pretty young skin?"

Annabelle flinched as the cold liquid touched her flesh. The small smile she saw on his veal-colored lips totally creeped her out, like he was getting off on her embarrassment. "I—I guess—I—it just seemed cool and I liked Angel's—"

"And you want one just like those two chicks got—the same sugar skull?"

"Yeah. They said it was okay with them if I copied it."

"You sure? Better if I draw something special, just for you."

"No, I want one just like theirs. Are you going to do it or not?"

Crash held up a piece of tissue paper about four by four and showed it to her. On it was the sketch of a sugar skull that looked to her like a match for the ones Jamie and Angel had on their shoulders. "This is what you want?"

"That's what I want."

Annabelle didn't understand the sudden look of bitter hatred that crossed Crash's features. It was in his voice, too. "Inkslingers don't like it when someone copies their shit."

She tried to shrug off the uneasy feeling she was getting by giving him a pert response. "Well, you already drew it, so I guess that means you're gonna do it, right?"

"You sure about this, Skinny?"

"Stop calling me that."

"It ain't gonna wash off, you know. It's permanent."

"I know it's permanent. Why are you trying to talk me out of it?"

"What about your folks?"

"You don't have to worry about that."

"Okay, then, if you're sure." Crash separated the tissue from the piece of carbon paper to which it was attached and set it aside. He began to rub some kind of lotion on her. Even though the latex gloves kept his fingers from being in direct contact with her skin, Annabelle found the intimacy of the act repellant.

"You just lie back and relax."

"How long's it gonna take?"

"Maybe an hour."

With a warning to keep still, he placed the tissue paper on her with care and smoothed it out. She closed her eyes so she wouldn't have to look at the gap where his front teeth used to be, or smell his breath. When he pulled the paper away and told her to look, she stretched her head and looked down at the outline he had made next to her hip bone.

"That looks good," Annabelle said, and Crash got to work.

Jamie was right, the needles did feel like a bee sting. But it wasn't so bad that she couldn't take it. She stared up at the ceiling of the van while Crash leaned over her, his attention fixed on his work as he laid down the ink in small, tight circular motions. His clothing smelled musty, as if it had not been washed in a while.

Annabelle tried to focus on what he was doing. Tatting and wiping, laying on Vaseline, tatting and wiping some more. The drone of the tattoo machine was like bees, too. Hypnotizing. Her limbs relaxed and she started to feel pretty good, just buzzed enough.

five

Monday Evening

Kernels were still exploding as Claudia pulled the bloated Jiffy Pop pan off the stove. There was something soothing about standing there, shaking the aluminum pan back and forth, taking care the corn didn't burn before the foil expanded just the right amount. Just like back in the day, when she and her brother Pete used to fight over who got to be in charge of making the popcorn.

A cloud of hot steam rose as she ripped open the foil. She dumped the puffed yellow kernels into a bowl and drizzled melted butter over the top and carried it, and a pile of napkins, to the girls.

At the kitchen door Claudia stopped and listened. Something had changed since she'd left Monica and Annabelle giggling over Henry Cavill's skintight blue costume in the *Superman: Man of Steel* video they were watching. Their voices were lowered, as if they didn't want to be heard, but the inflections were clipped, sharp. Were they *arguing?* That was a first for these two, who had been joined like Siamese twins since their first meeting.

The words "get infected" caught Claudia's attention as she pushed through the swinging door into the living room. Monica, who had spoken them, abruptly stopped talking when she saw her aunt, her upturned face stricken.

Claudia raised a brow. "Superman's butt not so cute after all?"

Annabelle aimed the remote at the TV with a scowl and paused the movie. "That's so funny, I forgot to laugh." She got up off the floor to take the popcorn bowl.

"What's wrong?" Claudia asked, noticing that she winced as she climbed to her feet.

"Nothing!"

Avoiding her aunt's gaze, Monica reached for the napkins in silence. Questioning them together was not likely to produce a straight answer. Eyeing them both with suspicion, Claudia told them she would be working upstairs in her office.

"What are you working on, Aunt Claudia?" Monica asked, looking relieved at the change of topic.

"It's an insurance fraud case. I have to figure out whether some signatures were written at the same time or at different times."

"How can you do that?"

Annabelle, forgetting her pique, looked interested, too. "Do you look for different ink colors?"

"Different inks could be a clue, but there's more to it. Some doctors have their patients sign their name on a sign-in sheet every time they come in for treatment, then the insurance pays for those visits. In *this* case, they got people off the street and paid them a small fee to come to the office and sign their name about thirty times on the sign-in sheet. Then the doctor's front office person added different dates and filed a claim with the insurance company. In other words, they get paid for all those visits the 'patient' didn't have."

"Are you working for the insurance company?" Annabelle asked.

"Yes; this kind of thing is a huge problem for insurance companies. They want to get their money back—millions of dollars. I've worked on several cases."

"But how can you *tell* the patients didn't have all those office visits?" Monica wanted to know.

"Excellent question, and if you really want to know, come upstairs and I'll show you."

Claudia sat at her desk, the two girls behind her on either side.

Monica pointed at a three-inch high stack of papers. "Wow, are those all the sign-in sheets?"

"They are. I have several hundred to examine." She picked up the top sheet. "What do you see?"

"It looks like when I get in trouble at school," Annabelle snickered. "When the teacher makes you write a hundred times, 'I will not chew gum in class,' or something stupid like that."

"Yeah," Monica added. "You get bored with it and you write the first word all the way down the paper, then the second word, and..."

"Exactly." Claudia took some lined paper from a desk drawer. "Here, take a piece of notebook paper and sign your name twenty times, one to a line. See what happens."

The girls did as instructed. When they had finished, they looked at their sheets, then stared at each other. "It looks like that sign-in sheet," Monica said.

Claudia nodded. "When you sign all at the same time, it creates a pattern down the page. It's called synchronous writing, which means it was done all at once, or in groups of several signatures. See how the signatures move toward the right side of the paper as they go down the page? That's called margin drift. If you signed your name at different times, that pattern wouldn't appear—there would be a lot more variation in the writing. I can take a ruler and draw lines to show the pattern on the page. That's what I'll be demonstrating to the jury when I testify."

"That's awesome," Annabelle said. "Can you always tell when something was written, or just sign-in sheets?"

"Sometimes I get cases where the client wants to know if diary entries were written at different times. For example, in one case a home nurse was suing his employer. He claimed he wasn't paid for all the hours he'd worked. He produced a diary he said he'd kept with a record of the dates and times he'd supposedly visited patients over four years. If it were true, the employer would have to pay him for all that time. But the diary had patterns like these that showed he had made the entries in groups, not at different times."

"So, did you bust him?" Annabelle asked.

"I didn't have to. When his attorney told him that a handwriting examiner was ready to testify, the guy broke down and admitted he'd faked the records to get more money."

"How can people be so dishonest?" Predictably, it was Monica who asked the question.

"Are you kidding?" Annabelle's cynicism was well beyond her years. "*Most* people are just liars and fakes."

Claudia raised a quizzical brow. "You've had some horrible experiences, Annabelle, but that doesn't mean the whole world is bad. Wouldn't you say that most of the people you know personally these days are pretty decent?"

Annabelle put a finger to her chin and looked skyward. "Let's see—there's you and Monica, Joel, my father. You guys are okay. Everyone else pretty much sucks."

Claudia grinned. "Well, I'm glad to be counted among the privileged."

"Don't let it go to your head," Annabelle giggled, but Claudia had noticed something odd about the way she was standing.

"Are you in pain, kiddo? You look—"

Annabelle's face darkened and just that fast, the scowl was back. "I'm fine, okay?" She turned to Monica. "The popcorn's gonna be cold. Do you want to watch the rest of the movie, or what?"

When the girls had gone back downstairs, Claudia turned to her case, baffled by Annabelle's behavior. Over recent weeks she had seemed happy, attending summer school and even doing homework without too much complaining. But her old sullen behavior had returned with a vengeance. Thinking it over, Claudia realized it had started up again after Annabelle had come into contact with her old school friend—what was her name? Angel.

Yesterday, upon her return from Tyler's, Annabelle had gone straight up to her room, complaining that she didn't feel good, and hadn't reappeared until this morning. Could she have lied about meeting her friend? Had she been meeting a boy?

Claudia's stomach dropped. Monica had said something about an infection. Oh God, could Annabelle have an STD? As far as she knew, the girl wasn't interested in any particular boys, and hadn't been sexually active. *As far as she knew.*

Feeling like a failure as a surrogate mom, Claudia asked herself whether it would have made a difference if Annabelle had been her natural child. Would a birth mother have some kind of sixth sense that would tell her if Annabelle was having sex? She quickly dismissed that idea. If that had been the case, Claudia's own mother would have known that their next door neighbor had molested her, starting when she was ten.

Annabelle's father was due back from Canada soon. What if she had to tell him that his daughter had a sexually transmitted disease; that she had failed in her promise to keep the girl safe?

Claudia pored over her insurance case until her neck was stiff. She got up and did a few stretches, then carried a stack of fresh towels to the upstairs guest bathroom, which Annabelle used when she stayed over. A small pile of clothes lay on the floor next to the tub. She picked up the clothes with a sigh of annoyance—she really should make the girl come and do it herself—and took them to the laundry hamper. As she shook out the T-shirt and undies, a small stain caught her eye.

She went onto the landing and leaned over the banister. "Annabelle, would you come up here, please."

"Right now? The movie's almost over."

"Pause it. I need to see you."

Even from the second floor, Claudia could hear the longsuffering sigh and grumbling. Then the clomping of reluctant feet on the stairs.

"What'd I do now?"

"That's what I'd like you to tell me."

"Huh?"

Claudia held up the T-shirt and blue-and-white striped cotton panties. "What's with the blood?"

Annabelle snatched the items from her hand. "Eww, gross. What are you doing, snooping in my stuff?"

"If you hadn't left them on the floor, I wouldn't have picked them up and seen that there's blood on them. Now stop deflecting the question and tell me *why* there's blood."

"I—I cut myself."

"Doing what?"

"Uh, shaving?"

"Annabelle, I'm not joking. I'm responsible for you while your father is away and I expect the truth. Now tell me what you've been doing. Were you really with that girl you told me about yesterday?"

"Yes!"

"The whole time?"

"Why are you being such a bitch?"

Claudia took a deep breath and silently counted to five. "Where were you yesterday afternoon, Annabelle? Answer me now."

Without a word Annabelle spun around and ran into her room, slamming the door shut behind her.

Monica was curled up on the sofa, staring at the TV screen, where Superman was frozen mid-fight with General Zod. Judging from the wary expression on her face, she had heard the exchange upstairs.

"Does she have a boyfriend?" Claudia asked bluntly.

"No."

"Could she have one without you knowing?"

"How? We're best friends."

As if that explained the world. And Claudia supposed it did. "You wouldn't lie to me, would you?"

"Of course not. Even if I tried, it wouldn't come out right."

Claudia had to admit the truth in her statement. Even as a small child, Monica had never been able to tell a successful lie. The moment the words left her mouth her fair skin would splotch bright red and give her away. She gave her niece a hard look.

"Fine, but whatever's going on, *please* use your head and don't let Annabelle talk you into something that will get you in trouble—or get *me* in trouble with your dad."

And having dropped that load of guilt on her niece, Claudia went back upstairs and knocked on Annabelle's bedroom door.

"*What?*" The girl's muffled voice came back terse.

Claudia turned the knob and entered. "We need to talk."

Annabelle was sitting on her bed with her head bowed. "Why do we have to talk? You know I always mess everything up. Just leave me alone."

Claudia sat down beside her. "I need you to tell me why you were bleeding. I'm not going to get mad or yell. Just—tell me."

"I don't want to."

"Did you get into a fight? Is that what happened?"

"No!"

"Honey, you looked like you were in pain when you got up off the floor, and there's blood on your clothes. Can't you see that I have to know what's going on?"

"Monica tried to stop me. And just so you know, she wasn't even there."

"Okay, thanks for telling me that. Monica wasn't where?"

Annabelle slid off the bed with unmistakable reluctance and unzipped her Levis. She grabbed the hem of her T-shirt and yanked at it. With the other hand, she pushed the waistband down a few inches, quick to cover it back up.

Claudia clamped her lips shut, but she couldn't stop her eyebrows rising into her hairline. The fresh tattoo was red and slightly swollen.

"This is where you went yesterday?"

Annabelle turned a mutinous face to her. "Nobody said I couldn't."

"That's supposed to be an excuse?"

Her shrug was less than convincing.

"Where did you get it done?" Claudia asked. "You can be sure they know it's illegal for them to tattoo anyone younger than 18 without adult permission."

"My friend's friend did it."

"Where? What's the name of the tattoo parlor?"

What Claudia didn't say was, she intended to ask Joel to arrest the owner. She knew he would be as incensed as she was, and furious at Annabelle's latest escapade. *Oh hell, what will her* father *say?* A little voice whispered that at least it wasn't an STD.

"There's no *parlor,* okay?"

"Then, where, goddammit? Somebody's house? You need to tell me where you went, and I mean now."

Annabelle heaved a big sigh, making like she was bored with the subject. "His van."

"*His what?* You got a tattoo in somebody's *van?* Who is this guy?"

Annabelle glared at her, triumph gleaming in her eyes. "You said you wouldn't yell. I knew I shouldn't tell you."

"Oh my God, Annabelle, give me a break. You have no idea how much I'm not yelling right now. Do you realize that's *permanent?*"

"Of course I do."

"I want this person's name and phone number. Give it to me, please."

"Can't."

"This is not a joke. Give it to me now."

"I don't *have* it. Angel talked to him for me."

"Then give me Angel's number."

"I don't have it either."

"Yes, you do. She called you yesterday, so it's in your phone."

A dull red flush spread over Annabelle's pale cheeks. "I don't have my phone. I left it in the van." She scowled at Claudia's incredulity. "I didn't *mean* to. I was in a hurry to leave, and I forgot it wasn't in my pocket."

Claudia released a long breath and shook her head. "I can't believe this. I thought everything was going well—you've worked hard and got your grades up. Then the minute you meet up with this Angel, everything goes to hell. What were you *thinking?*"

"Angel and Jamie had matching ones on their shoulders and they looked really bad. So, I wanted one, too."

"When you say 'bad,' I'm guessing that means 'good?'"

"Yeah. Crash made mine just like theirs."

"Crash? That's the guy's name?"

Annabelle nodded. "The artist."

"Who else was with you besides *Crash* and Angel?"

Annabelle hesitated. "Um, I thought she was going, but after he got there, she left."

"Let me get this straight. You were alone in a van with a stranger and you let him stick needles into you? Good God, Annabelle."

Annabelle's gaze was pointed at the floor. "Why's it such a big deal, anyway? Nothing happened, I didn't get hurt. The tat doesn't even show."

"Let me see it again," Claudia said with another sigh of frustration.

Despite the inflammation around and under the ink, the artistry was obvious in the delicate lines of the skull's face, the swirly decorations around the eyes and mouth. Claudia's mouth twitched in disapproval.

"Well, he did a good job, anyway. What did this—*jerk* charge to deface your fifteen-year-old body with a painted skull?"

"Ummm, sixty."

"Where'd the money come from?"

"I saved most of my allowance my dad's been sending me."

"And you've lost your cell phone?"

"It's not *lost,* it's in Crash's van. He didn't want me texting while he was doing the work, and I—I forgot to get it when he was done. I was in a hurry. I didn't want to be late getting back."

A memory flashed of Annabelle's unsteady gait when she had returned home the day before. "What did this Crash guy give you—drugs, alcohol?"

"Well—"

Under the heat of her glare, Annabelle was becoming increasingly fidgety. A vein throbbed in Claudia's neck and her lips bunched with suppressed fury. "What did he give you?"

"Just a shot of tequila."

"Just a—no wonder you forgot your phone. No wonder you were sick."

"He reeked of weed, but I didn't even smoke."

"Is that supposed to make it better? You know I'm gonna have to tell Joel about this. And when your father comes back—"

"Fine!" Annabelle shot back. "Go ahead and tell everyone how I disappointed you! That's what I do. I *always* do the wrong thing. I *always* screw everything up."

And with that, uncharacteristically, Annabelle burst into tears.

six

Claudia was assuring Annabelle that, tattoo or not, she still loved her when Joel arrived home. She heard him in the service porch, heard the metallic clank of the washing machine lid closing. That indicated he had been at a particularly stinky crime scene. He would have left his suit in the garage, then discarded the rest of his soiled clothing in the washer and donned the clean robe hanging in the porch for occasions like these. It wouldn't do to have him traipsing through the house in his underwear while Annabelle was staying with them.

Claudia left her lying on her bed, face to the wall, and went downstairs to meet him. Her brother had already collected his daughter. In a tacit agreement with Monica, nothing was said about Annabelle's absence, except that she was upstairs in her room. The measured look Pete gave Claudia over Monica's welcoming hug, told her he'd caught on that something was wrong. It was a big relief when he had the good sense to refrain from asking about it.

The acrid odor of smoke clung to Jovanic's skin.

"I know," he said when Claudia wrinkled her nose. "I need to hit the shower."

"Where've you been? Somewhere nasty, for sure."

"Tattoo parlor in Venice. Somebody firebombed it."

Her insides did a little flip. "A tattoo parlor? *You* got a callout?"

"Yeah. Couple of Molotov cocktails through the front window. It started spreading to the store next door; took LAFD a while to knock down the fire."

"Someone didn't make it out."

It wasn't a question. There was only one reason the homicide unit would have been called to a scene that would be worked by the fire department.

"They've had several break-ins recently, so they'd beefed up security. Windows in back were barred; metal door had a deadbolt and the key was in the lock. They found the victim near the door while they were looking for the flashpoint. Probably got disoriented in the smoke."

Claudia shuddered, hoping death had come quickly for that poor victim.

"With all the fuel it spread fast," Jovanic continued as they mounted the staircase. "Everything went up—couches, posters on the walls, magazines. They think he died from smoke inhalation, which I guess is marginally better than being burned to death."

"Was it the owner?"

"No positive ID so far. We waited for some employees to show up this morning, but nada. The people on the block said the shop was just open pretty recently and he didn't have anyone else working for him yet. We couldn't get anything on ownership."

"What was his name?"

"Travis Navarette. We're looking for next of kin."

A little ribbon of relief threaded through Claudia's pity for the fire victim.

Not Crash.

The firebombing had nothing to do with Annabelle. She knew it had been an unreasonable fear, but experience had taught her that when it came to Annabelle, anything was possible. "Was it a gang thing?" she asked.

"More like an extortion thing. We're pretty sure we know the asshole who ordered it. Been looking at him for years. He runs his own shop and skims 40% from the competition. They don't pay up, he burns them out."

"And he just gets away with it?"

"Getting the evidence is the problem. He scares any potential witnesses shitless. But it's different this time."

"Because of the homicide?"

"Yeah."

"Well, I hope you nail him." Claudia gave him a little push toward the staircase. "Leave your robe in the bathroom. I'll wash everything in the morning."

"Thanks, babe." Jovanic gave a yawn big enough to show his molars, didn't bother covering it. "God, I'm starving. Have we got anything quick and easy?"

She took in the shadows staining the skin under drooping eyelids; the day's growth of grizzled stubble on his chin. "You look dead on your feet, Columbo. If you think you can stay awake long enough, I'll heat some pizza and dig out a couple of beers."

He yawned again, wider. "What a woman. No wonder I adore you."

Claudia grinned. "Pepperoni and extra cheese coming up. Go take your shower. I'll turn on the TV in the living room."

They had reached the foot of the staircase. Jovanic jerked his chin upwards. "What's up with the kid?"

"She's in the doghouse. Ironically enough, she came home with a tattoo. As you can imagine, I wasn't thrilled."

"Ah, shit. Where the hell'd she get a tattoo?"

"Back of some guy's van. We can talk about it later."

He rolled his eyes skyward. "Unfuckingbelievable. Just when we thought all was quiet on the home front."

Claudia joined Jovanic at the TV for the eleven o'clock news. Channel 2 made a brief mention of the firebombing, panning across the blackened storefront on Lincoln Boulevard in Venice.

Jovanic made short work of his dinner, then his head lolled back against the couch cushions and in seconds he was snoring. He didn't stir when Claudia took a half-eaten slice of pizza from his fingers and carried his plate out to the kitchen. She disposed of the remains and loaded the dishwasher, then covered him with a light throw and went upstairs. He would nap for at least an hour or two before he would wake long enough to trudge up to bed.

Settling back at her desk, Claudia picked up where she had left off earlier in her stack of sign-in sheets. Using a six-inch metal ruler and pen, she examined one sheet at a time. Where she could tell the signatures had been written in groupings, she drew a straight red line from the first in the group to the last, creating a visual image for the judge and jury. The work absorbed her, and she was deep into it when more than an hour later, her cell phone rang and startled her.

She had no love for the ringtone—a Lady Gaga song called *Poker Face*—but Claudia had allowed Annabelle to choose the one she wanted to represent her phone number. Then it struck her: *Annabelle's phone is in the tattoo artist's van.*

Claudia dove for her phone. "Hello?"

She had expected a man's voice—Crash, the tattoo artist—but it was a young female, speaking almost in a whisper: "Who's this?"

"You called me," Claudia said. "Who's this?"

"Angel. Lemme talk to Annabelle."

"It's after midnight. She's asleep."

"I gotta talk to her."

"Are you okay? Why are you whispering?"

"I don't want my boyfriend to hear. Just wake her up, okay? It's important."

"Sorry, I'm not waking her up. She has school in the morning. Don't you?"

There was a long silence. Then the tremulous whisper. "I'm in big trouble. Shit. What am I gonna do?"

"What kind of trouble? Is there something *I* can help you with?"

"He's gonna hurt me."

"Who is?"

"Oh shit, I screwed up big-time."

Claudia's heart skipped. The girl sounded genuinely frightened. "Angel, tell me where you are; I'll call the police."

"*No,* I'd be screwed even worse."

"Who's threatening you?"

"Forget it. I need to talk to Annabelle."

"Angel, let me help you. I'll—"

"Fuckit. Tell her she can get her phone back at the coffee place right after school."

"Wait, Angel—" But it was too late, the girl had clicked off.

"You should've woken me up." Annabelle snatched a box of cereal off the shelf, spilling granola onto the countertop in her haste. "She needed to talk to me."

"What were you going to do for her after midnight? If it was an emergency, you couldn't help her, and believe me, I would've called the police if I'd known where she was. I tried calling back, but it went right to your voicemail. She must have turned the phone off."

Annabelle let out a deep, exasperated sigh and dug in the dishwasher for a clean bowl. "Jeeeez, Claudia, you're just like a mom."

The comment was intended as an insult, but Claudia, congratulating herself that she had done the right thing in not waking Annabelle, took secret pleasure in it. Still, she couldn't help being worried about Angel and hoped she was all right. Who was she afraid of? Crash?

Claudia poured herself a mug of Starbucks breakfast blend and took a carton of cream from the fridge. She sat down and poured a generous dollop into her mug, then added sugar. "Tyler's is the coffee place Angel meant, right? Where you met her the other day? Assuming you were telling the truth about that."

"Of course I was telling the truth." Annabelle plopped into her chair, her show of righteous indignation ironic given her recent deception.

Claudia let it slide. "At least you'll get your phone back. How's the tattoo today?"

"Itchy."

"Well, don't scratch it."

Annabelle leaned low over her cereal bowl and scooped a spoonful of granola. "Duh. I slap it. Crash told me to treat it like a cut. He said to put moisturizer on it."

"I guess as long as you're going to get an illegal tattoo, it's smart to listen to the guy's advice. But what you did is still unacceptable." Claudia leveled a stern gaze at her. "And I still can't believe you let some stranger tattoo you in the back of a van."

seven

Tuesday morning

Even before he entered the rear door of Kitchens-4-U, the odor of soggy charred wood and chemicals clogged Jovanic's nostrils. The store next door to Under My Skin had suffered significant smoke and water damage in the fire department's efforts to knock down the blaze.

Two men stood near the boarded-up front windows, their backs toward Jovanic. They turned as he came in. He observed a camera strap attached to a professional-looking piece of equipment hanging around the neck of one man. The other, who he assumed was the owner, was instructing the photographer on where to shoot, no doubt for the insurance claim he would be making.

"Reza Madani?" Jovanic called out, weaving his way across the space through stainless steel kitchens, country kitchens, Cape Cod kitchens, and a few other styles he wouldn't be able to identify on a test. By the time he was halfway across the floor he was regretting that he hadn't brought a HEPA mask to filter the overpowering stench that seeped through the common wall between the storefronts.

The man he had ID'd as Madani glanced over at him. "Yes? What is it?"

Jovanic displayed his badge wallet. "Detective Jovanic. We spoke on the phone earlier."

Madani, a slight man in a short-sleeved shirt and jeans, was unimpressed. "You can see I'm a little busy now."

"I won't take much of your time, sir. Just a few questions to help with the investigation."

The owner gave an exaggerated sigh to make sure the detective knew just how busy he was, then turned back to the photographer.

"Make sure you get it all. I pay a big insurance, now I get my money back. Don't leave anything out. I'm watching you." He turned back to Jovanic, who caught the photographer's eye roll. "Come into my office. It's smell better."

The small office was located at the rear of the building close to the door through which Jovanic had just entered. Unadorned concrete block walls, a cheap Formica-topped desk littered with paperwork. Security bars covered the windows like the ones that had turned Travis Navarette's tattoo parlor into a deathtrap.

Madani squeezed behind his desk and plopped into his chair, gesturing at the barred window behind Jovanic. "What you supposed to do? No bars and let the criminals rip you off whenever they want, or get burned alive?"

Jovanic seated himself in one of two plastic chairs and handed the man his business card. "Did you know Travis Navarette?"

"That his name? Next door? He was my neighbor for couple months. That's how much I know him."

"Ever have any conversations with him?"

Reza Madani gave him a skeptical look. "This is Venice, Detective. Who has conversations? He's not a customer, I got no need to sit around, chatting."

This was not a promising start. Jovanic tried again. "When was the last time you saw him?"

"I don't keep no log."

"Best guess."

Madani pushed back in his chair, crossed one leg over the other and stared at his sandaled foot. "Far as I know, he was there in the place when I left yesterday at seven. I saw his motorcycle."

"But you didn't see him?"

"No."

"Was anyone else over there?"

"How do I know that? I just saw his bike—one of those pocket rockets. I don't peep inside the back door to check on him."

"Do you remember whether any cars were in the lot?"

"Just mine. But people park out front or on the side. There's street parking. They can go in from the front. I don't watch. How do I know who goes in and out?"

"What kind of neighbor was he?"

"Seem like an okay kid, never bother me. Just one time I go over there and ask him to turn the music down—Grunge, I think they call it. Loud. Ugly. He apologize and turn it down right away. I was surprised. The way he look, I figure I was gonna have some problems with him."

"The way he looked?"

"You know—head shaved bald, except for stupid little rug on top. Long, ratty beard halfway down to his belt. If my son look like that I disown him. That guy wore a lot of necklaces—what do they call that? Tribal jewelry? Big piercing on his ears. They think that look good? Every time I see him he's wearing a necklace with black and white skulls. Tattoos all over his arms. So I thought he might be trouble."

"But he was cooperative with you about the music?"

"Right away, he turns it down."

"Are you aware of any problems he might have had with any of the other neighbors, or anyone else?"

"How would I know? That was only time I talk to him."

Jovanic gave a brief smile. "No rolling out the welcome mat for the new neighbor?"

Madani spread out his hands. "Detective, don't think I'm an unfriendly guy, but I got enough friends. I keep my nose out of his business, I expect him to keep out of mine." He paused. "Look like *somebody* didn't like him. Now, I gotta get these insurance papers done. Sorry I got nothing to help you."

"One more question, Mr. Madani. It's important. Did you ever notice anyone particular hanging around the shop? Since Mr. Navarette didn't have any employees, we're looking for any acquaintances or clients that we can talk to."

The owner, who had risen, ready to dismiss him, paused. "Maybe you try the girl."

"The girl?"

"Pretty little thing, but all covered in makeup, dress up like a tart. Young—a teenager, I think. She's there almost every day the last couple weeks."

"Would you happen to have a name?"

"Maybe I do. Or maybe just a nickname he call her."

Jovanic waited.

"I was on the way out to my car. This was a couple days ago. The guy—Travis, you said? He was standing at the back door and they were sort of arguing. I hear him say, 'Come on, Angel, you can't do this no more.'"

Jovanic made a quick note in his notebook. "Did you hear anything else?"

"Seemed like he was telling her not to come back, and she was crying that she was gonna be in trouble."

"You saw she was crying, or you got that impression?"

Reza Madani wiped his fingers down his cheeks. "All that make-up—that black stuff on her eyes—it was running down her face. She was a mess, getting hysterical. Then he saw me looking, he pulled her inside and slammed the door. That's all I know."

The information might be significant. Why hadn't Madani offered it sooner? "How did she get here?" Jovanic asked. "Did she park in back?"

"I never see a car or anything else. Maybe she walk."

"So, other than this girl who he referred to as Angel, did you notice anyone over there regularly? See him arguing with anyone else?"

"Like I told you, I got my own business to look after."

Seeing that he wasn't going to get any further, Jovanic rose. "Thank you, Mr. Madani. You've got my card if you think of anything. Call any time, day or night."

"Fine, fine." Madani walked him to the door. For the first time in their short visit, Jovanic heard something like compassion. "I hope you get the bastards who did this. He seem like an okay kid."

eight

Under My Skin was located on the corner of the block. Huey Hardcastle, one of the detectives on Jovanic's four-person homicide team, had already canvassed the other stores within the perimeter that was set up on the previous day by patrol officers. Nobody knew anything, nobody saw anyone.

According to Jovanic's conversation with the LAFD Battalion Chief, a 9-1-1 call had been logged at 1:57 a.m. Monday morning. First-in engine company arrived on scene at 2:01 and found the tattoo shop fully involved. With all the furniture and papers that had been in the storefront it had gotten really hot, really fast. Then, in the Chief's words, the whole thing went to hell in a handbasket and the fire started spreading to the kitchen design store next door, turning it into a three-alarm blaze.

The victim, Travis Navarette, was found within a few feet of the back door. The key was in the lock, but likely disoriented by the heavy smoke and flames, he had apparently succumbed to smoke inhalation.

Jovanic shuddered; a terrifying and horrific death. Navarette had escaped the flames, had come so close to getting out.

Driving an unmarked department vehicle, he made a left onto Courtleigh Drive and drove along the street, turning at the bottom of the cul-de-sac so that his vehicle pointed toward the open end of the block. A quick double-check of his pocket notebook gave him the address he was looking for. He had not gotten into the habit of using his iPhone for notes and doubted he ever would. Technology had its place, but he preferred to rely on his own handwriting, a habit that had earned Claudia's approval.

Paul Warner, the 9-1-1 caller who had reported the fire, lived in Mar Vista, a few miles from the ruined tattoo parlor. Jovanic pulled to the curb behind an old stake bed truck parked in front of a modest fourplex a few houses down the street from his destination. He crossed the sidewalk to the one-story building and made his way past a threadbare lawn. Warner's unit was the second door along the path.

Jovanic could hear the sound of Whoopie Goldberg's voice on *The View* through the door. The sound was muted when he knocked and the door opened, framing a heavyset middle-aged man.

"You the detective?" The man opened the door wider when Jovanic confirmed that he was. "C'mon in. I'm Paul." He stuck out his hand and after they shook, stepped back from the door, inviting Jovanic to enter the small, neat living room. "Something to drink, man? Coffee, water?"

"No thanks, I'm good."

"Okay, have a seat. There's not a whole lot to tell."

Jovanic sat with his back to the TV, ignoring Whoopie, who, as he seated himself on one end of the sofa, was gesticulating at a thin blonde woman at the table. Warner took the other end and picked up a coffee mug from the end table.

"I heard on the TV this morning someone died in that fire."

"How'd you happen to be in the neighborhood Sunday night?" Jovanic asked.

"Sundays I play sax at Smooth Sam's—it's a jazz club in Santa Monica."

"I've been there."

"Is it the awesome burgers, or you like jazz?"

Jovanic smiled, creating a connection between them. "Good food, good music. Can't ask for more than that."

Warner nodded approvingly. "So, anyway, I stayed for a while after the show, jammin' with the guys. Left around 1:30. I took Lincoln home."

Jovanic waited while he paused, and gave him some space to gather his thoughts.

"There wasn't a whole lot of traffic—Sunday night—actually, Monday morning, I guess. So, I'd just crossed over Venice and I saw this kinda orangey-red glow in the sky about a block away on my right. Then I saw smoke. When I got closer and saw the flames, I grabbed my phone and called 9-1-1."

"Did you notice anyone outside the building? Any vehicles or people? Anyone watching the fire?"

"Naw, man, I cruised by kinda slow while I made the call, but I didn't see anyone. I almost didn't call it in. I thought somebody else would. *Did* anyone?"

"No."

"What the hell's wrong with people? I couldn't have been the only person who drove by, even that time of night." He shook his head as if perplexed. "They said on the news it was arson. There was a shitload of flames in the front of the store, like it started there. Molotov cocktails or something, right?"

"Something like that. Is there anything else you can remember that might be helpful? Anything that seemed unusual or out of place? Anything at all?"

"Sorry, dude, I didn't wait for the fire trucks. I made the call and buzzed on home."

Jovanic gave him a business card, went through the "call me if you think of anything" routine and took his leave.

His stomach rumbling, he stopped at a mini mall on Venice Blvd, and grabbed an apple fritter and a coffee. Taking a small table at the rear of the deserted donut shop, he reviewed the list he had made at his desk before starting out that morning.

His partner, Randy Coleman, was running a background on Travis Navarette, looking for next of kin and acquaintances of the victim, anything that would provide evidence leading to his killer and the motive. Although they had a pretty good idea of who was behind the arson—Navarette's competitor—he would also background Paul Warner. You never knew; sometimes a firebug got off on reporting their own dirty work.

Jovanic was in the men's room, washing the glaze off his fingers, when his phone buzzed in his pocket. The ringer was turned off, but Coleman's number came up on the screen.

"Yeah, Randy, what've you got?"

"Nothing on next of kin so far."

"Okay, keep looking. And make sure you get a background on the owner of the store next door. Name's Reza Madani. He's not too broken up about filing a claim with his insurance company. Check his financials."

"Will do, JJ."

Coleman knew Jovanic hated being called JJ. He must be pissed at being stuck on the desk. Jovanic ignored it. "What are Scott and Hardcastle up to?" RJ (Rebecca) Scott was the fourth member of the team.

"Scott called in sick; said she was puking."

Half the personnel in the office were out with a virulent flu, so this was not surprising news. Coleman continued, lowering his voice confidentially. "As for Officer Half-Ass? Playing solitaire on his phone."

A fizz of anger made Jovanic grind his teeth. Hardcastle was getting lazier by the day. He would have to be dealt with, but now was not the right moment. "What's the other thing you've got?"

"The uniform you left on Under My Skin just called in. Client showed up for an appointment, hadn't heard about the fire. You wanna talk to him?"

Jovanic tried to bite back his annoyance, but it leaked into his tone. "Of course I want to talk to him, Randy. What do you think?"

"Okay. You ready? Here's the number."

The tattoo customer's name was Jack Solis in West Hollywood. According to Coleman, Solis was pretty shaken up by the news.

"Did they keep him there?" Jovanic asked.

"Nope. You're gonna have to catch up with him in WEHO."

"Great. That just about makes my day." Jovanic clicked off and after getting a refill on his coffee, plugged the Genessee Avenue address into Google Maps.

Tuesday noon, traffic felt like moving through sludge. By the time Jovanic reached West Hollywood it was close to 1:00 and he was glad for the apple fritter he'd eaten.

The area in which Jack Solis lived was, for L.A., considered lower-end real estate, which meant houses went for around three-quarters of a million bucks. Small homes built around the turn of the last century, mixed with newer apartment buildings. It was one of the latter that housed Solis. According to the parking signs, Tuesday was trash day and there was no parking on that side of the street during the morning.

Lucky for Jovanic, the pickup had already been made. He maneuvered around the empty wheelie bins lining the street and parked, then took the flight of stairs that ran outside the building to the second floor. He hadn't called ahead, preferring to catch Solis off guard.

The upstairs landing was surrounded by a tall wooden lattice, overgrown with crimson Bougainvillea, leaving barely enough room for Jovanic's six-two frame on the porch. A heavy-duty security screen which secured the front door was locked. Before he could ring the doorbell, what sounded like a small dog began barking inside the apartment. He pressed the bell and stepped down onto the top stair, leaving some room.

Inside, a woman yelled in an East Coast accent, "Rocco. Rocco, knock it off." The dog took no notice and continued to yap loudly as the front door opened. The iron mesh screen made it impossible to see inside, but the barking came from up high, and the dog, in its owner's arms, tried to lunge for the screen.

Jovanic held up his badge wallet. "Detective Joel Jovanic with LAPD. I'm looking for Jack Solis."

"That's me."

"You're *Jack?*"

"Short for Jacqueline. This about Trav?"

"Yes, I'd like to talk with you for a few minutes. Could I come in?"

There was the metallic click of the lock and she pushed open the door. The dog, a teacup Yorkie, squirmed in her grasp, struggling to free itself. Jacqueline Solis raised her voice over the continuing racket. "Rocco! Stop it. Come in, Detective. Let me put him in the bathroom."

"Feisty little guy," Jovanic remarked as Solis returned, followed by the sound of yips and miniature claws scratching at the bathroom door.

"He weighs all of four pounds, but he's got the heart of a Pit Bull." She gestured Jovanic toward a table next to the kitchenette. "Come, sit. Let's go over here."

Solis was almost as tall as Jovanic, with a muscular build and a diamond stud piercing her nose. Black bangs framed ironed-straight fuchsia-colored shoulder-length hair. A black spaghetti strap T-shirt displayed a tattooed water lily on her right shoulder and barbed wire ink around her left bicep. The tail of a blue dolphin peeped out from the bottom of her cutoffs. West Hollywood. With those broad shoulders, he briefly wondered if she was a drag performer.

"I understand you had an appointment yesterday with Travis Navarette," Jovanic began.

Solis's liner-rimmed eyes filled with tears, which she dabbed with a fingertip. "Oh, my God, I can't believe he's dead. Is this really happening?"

"How well did you know Travis, Ms. Solis?"

She let out a long breath. "Not all that well, but still. He did some work on me." She pointed at the dolphin on her thigh. "He was covering up someone else's shitty work." Her voice cracked. "How could anyone *do* that to him?"

"Any idea who might have had a beef with him?"

"Hell no. Travis hadda be the sweetest dude on the planet. He would never hurt *anyone.* Why would someone kill him?"

"That's what we're trying to find out. How did you meet him? Were you referred by someone?"

"Yeah, a guy I know knew him from when he was working up the street at Dragon House 'til he went out on his own."

"Travis worked at Dragon House?"

"Yeah, that's where he started out."

"What's this guy's name, your friend who works over there?"

"Big Carl. I don't know his last name."

"Do you know any of Travis's other clients or friends?"

"Not really. A few people came by while he was working on me, but I don't know any of them."

"Anyone you saw more than once?"

"Sometimes there was this girl, but she wasn't a customer. She just hung out. Like a tat groupie, you know?"

"Was she Travis's girlfriend?"

Jacqueline Solis pulled a skeptical face. "A wannabe more like it. Little ho kept gettin' in his face, trying to turn him on, even while he was working. She was *über* obvious about it."

"I guess that'd be pretty flattering for a young guy like Travis."

She thought about it, then shook her head again. "Trav treated her nice, like he did everyone. He wasn't interested in fucking that little piece of jailbait ass." Solis snapped to attention. "Hey, you don't think *she* did it, do you?"

"Right now, we're just gathering information. Do you have any reason to think she might have some involvement in Travis's death, Ms. Solis?"

"It's just, she seemed kind of desperate to get his attention. Maybe she set the fire and didn't know he was inside. Maybe she didn't mean to kill him." Her face hardened. "This is *so* fucked up."

"Yeah, it is," Jovanic agreed. "Do you happen to know this girl's name?"

"Uh, Angie, Angela; something like that."

"Any idea how old? High school? Out of school?"

"Teenybopper," Jack Solis said with certainty. "She talks like a kid. I'd swear she's no older than sixteen, if that. She's got a few miles on her, though. She could maybe pass for eighteen."

"Can you think of anything else that might help us locate her?"

"You should check with Big Carl at Dragon House."

"I'll do that." Jovanic rose and held out his hand. "I'm very sorry for the loss of your friend."

nine

Claudia was wrapping up her report on the insurance case when she heard the back door slam, signaling Annabelle's arrival home from school. "I'm in the office," she called out.

Annabelle's footfalls pounded on the staircase. "Okay, be right there."

For someone who was four-ten and weighed maybe eighty-five pounds, she had a way of hitting the stairs like a herd of wild elephants. She had *sounded* reasonably cheerful, which was a relief. At least the dark moods that used to sometimes last for days at a time now seemed to clear up much faster.

Ten minutes later, having switched her school clothes for shorts and T-shirt, Annabelle sidled into the office. "Is it okay if I go to Tyler's and get my phone back from my friend?"

"No, it isn't okay. You're grounded, remember?"

Annabelle wrinkled her nose. "It was worth a try."

"Well, it didn't work. There are consequences to sneaking out and getting inked."

"But I *need* to get my phone."

"Of course. What's life without a phone?"

"You said Angel was going to bring it. You wouldn't want her to show up for nothing, would you?"

"Oh, you're going to lay a guilt trip on me, are you?" Claudia grinned. "Come on, let's go. I want to meet this Angel person."

A look of alarm crossed Annabelle's face. "You don't have to. I can walk down there."

"I know you can. And I still want to meet her."

"Seriously, you don't need to. Look, I'll come right back, I promise. I just want my phone."

"Is there some reason why I shouldn't meet her?"

Annabelle hesitated. "Well—noooooo, but, I just don't want you asking her a bunch of dumb questions and embarrassing me."

"You have absolutely nothing to worry about. I will sit silent and keep my lip zipped tight."

"Like that ever happened."

Claudia hiked a brow. "Are you saying I have a big mouth?"

"Well...not exactly, but..."

"Face it—if you want your phone, you're going to have to stand my company. But here's the good news—I'll pay for the drinks."

⁓ℓℓ⁓

There were two customers at Tyler's when Claudia and Annabelle walked in, both male. Annabelle grabbed a table near the front window so she could watch for her friend. Claudia went to the counter and ordered a green tea Frappuccino for herself and a chocolate smoothie for Annabelle.

A few minutes later she set their drinks on the table. "I tried calling your phone again this morning to make sure she was still coming, but she didn't pick up."

"She *said* right after school," Annabelle retorted. "At least, that's what you told me."

"I know." Claudia broke off, still wishing she could have persuaded Angel to confide in her when she'd phoned the night before. "Tell me about her. Were you close friends at the Sorensen Academy? How come I've never heard about her?"

"Noooo, not close. She's a year older than me, but we both hung out with the same people." Annabelle blushed. "Actually, we got arrested together the time I got sent to juvie. Our parents knew each other and they decided to put both of us in Sorensen."

"Ah." That was before Claudia had met Annabelle. Before the girl had attempted suicide.

"Angel got out of Sorensen before I did," Annabelle went on. "That was the last time I saw her 'til the other day. I mean, we're not exactly Insta friends or anything."

"What about her parents? Does she live with both of them?"

"Uh uh. Her mom is always going to Europe. I think she's an actress or something. Her father's kind of like mine—not my real father. Nick. Her father got married to someone else and then her stepmom had a kid, so he has his new family and they live in New York. He never calls Angel. So, anyway, since both her parents don't care about her, she went to court and filed some kind of papers to divorce them."

"She's an emancipated minor?"

"Yeah, that's it. The court said she could dump her parents if she could support herself. So now she lives with her boyfriend and his brother's family. She takes care of their kids."

"I wonder if it was her boyfriend she was afraid of."

"How would I know?" Annabelle shot an accusatory glance across the table before scooping whipped cream off the top of her smoothie and licking it from the spoon. "You didn't let her talk to me."

Claudia glanced at her watch. They had been at Tyler's for fifteen minutes and so far there was no sign of Angel or Annabelle's cell phone. There had been no opportunity to say anything to Joel about the late-night call from Angel, or to ask his opinion on what to do about Annabelle's tattoo. After dozing in the living room the night before, he had stumbled up to bed and fallen straight into a deep sleep. When Claudia awoke, he was long gone. She had learned to expect the long hours when there was a homicide investigation on his rotation.

They had shared a quick phone call mid-morning while he was driving to West Hollywood to interview a witness. This afternoon she knew she would not hear from him, as he would be continuing his part of the investigation into the background of the firebombing victim.

Claudia pulled her attention back to Annabelle, who was griping about having to prepare for an upcoming exam at school. "Why do I have to learn science, anyway? I'm not going to be a scientist."

"There's plenty of stuff you learn in school that you think you'll never use, but you might be surprised. You like baking, right? A cake recipe is a scientific formula," Claudia said. She couldn't explain the itchy feeling she had about Angel, but she wasn't going to project it onto Annabelle.

"Dissecting frogs isn't like baking cakes."

"Suck it up, kiddo. On some things we don't get a choice and that includes school. It's something you have to get through." Claudia paused, then changed the subject. "Where does Angel live?"

"I don't—"

Before she could finish her answer, Claudia's cell phone rang in her purse. *Poker Face.* Annabelle's ringtone. Angel.

"Let me talk to her please." Annabelle begged as Claudia dug the phone out of her purse.

Claudia held up a restraining hand and tapped the screen to engage the call. "Hello, Angel?"

There was a pause, then the same voice she had heard last night came on the line, normal now, not whispering. "Yeah, it's me. Is Annabelle there? Can I talk to her now?"

"Are you okay? We're at Tyler's. I thought you were coming to return her phone."

"I know. I got stuck with the kids. I can't leave right now."

"Why don't you give me the address. I'll drive Annabelle over and she can get the phone from you."

"No, it would just create a bunch of hassle for me. Could I please just talk to her? *Please?*"

On the other side of the table, Annabelle was bouncing in her seat, dying to get hold of the phone. Realizing she was not going to get anywhere with Angel, and relieved that she was okay, Claudia handed it over. Annabelle jammed the instrument to her ear and told the caller to wait, then jumped up and slipped through the front door.

Claudia watched her through the window, talking animatedly to her friend. Annabelle's face cycled through a whole series of expressions, none of them happy. Then, as if realizing she was being observed, she turned her body away so Claudia could no longer read her face. Still, her body language spoke volumes—she was not enjoying the conversation.

Returning to their table less than five minutes later, Annabelle plunked into her chair and returned Claudia's phone with mumbled thanks.

"That was quick. Did she tell you what happened last night?"

"She couldn't talk about it right then. She's gonna get a ride over to your house and drop my phone off later."

"Today?"

"Yeah, tonight. After Ariceli gets back and Angel can leave the kids."

"And Ariceli is—"

"Mouser's brother's chick."

"I take it Mouser is Angel's boyfriend?"

"Well, yeah."

"Who's giving her a ride?"

Annabelle gave the shrug. "Don't worry about it."

"Sorry, but I *am* worried about it. I don't like the feeling I'm getting about this whole situation. I don't like it that this girl left you with some strange guy in a grungy van. I don't like you hanging out with someone who's scared enough to call after midnight, looking for help. You've gone through enough of your own stuff."

"Omigod," Annabelle protested hotly. "I'm just supposed to ditch my friend?"

"I thought she wasn't such a close friend."

"What difference does it make? Anyway, she's still got my phone."

"Yes, there is that." Claudia groaned inwardly. Most of the time, she enjoyed Annabelle, but right now she was looking forward to the girl's father returning home and relieving her of the responsibility. She put on her firm voice. "When Angel shows up tonight, you are to bring her in and introduce her to me, got it?"

Annabelle's mumbled response could have been anything.

"I'm serious. Don't try to wiggle out of it."

"Are you going to ask her about Crash?"

"Take a guess."

"I *knew* you were going to embarrass me. And you still don't get why I don't want you to meet her?"

Annabelle's voice had risen an octave. A customer who had just entered turned a disapproving glare on them.

"Keep it down," Claudia cautioned. "We don't need a scene."

"I told you I won't do it again. Why can't you just let it go? Crash was nice to me. He didn't try to hook up with me or anything like that."

"That's supposed to make it okay, because he didn't rape you? It's not just the illegal tattoo, Annabelle. He also gave you alcohol. That's not acceptable. And this is non-negotiable. I want to meet Angel." Her silent thought continued: *And if "Crash" is the one who gives Angel a ride over, he'd better be prepared to face me.*

She got the one-shoulder dismissal. "Whatever."

It was no surprise that Angel was a no-show that evening and she didn't phone again. Annabelle, who ate dinner in virtual silence, went upstairs as soon as she had helped clean up the kitchen, and stayed in her room all evening, claiming to be studying for her science test. She didn't seem particularly upset at being stood up, which made Claudia wonder whether the girls had plotted something during their short conversation that she ought to know about.

Jovanic dragged in around nine and they had a repeat of the previous evening. He didn't want to talk about his case.

He and Claudia watched a mindless sitcom together while he ate the dinner she had put aside for him. He looked so exhausted that once again, she did not have the heart to burden him with her quandary about Annabelle. When they went to bed together at eleven, he was too tired for sex. Claudia, whose mind was still on the unreliable Angel and her situation, cuddled against his back and fell asleep early.

Jovanic was still on call that night and his cell phone woke them both at two thirty-three.

Another homicide. A kid. She could tell from his hesitation how much he dreaded what he was going to find.

Claudia was left with a heart beating too fast, feeling for the parents whose child needed the ministrations of a homicide detective in the middle of the night. She tossed around in the bed for a while, and when she couldn't get back to sleep, got up and slipped on her kimono.

As if drawn by an invisible thread, she padded barefoot across the shadowy landing to Annabelle's bedroom door. A strong urge to reassure herself that the girl was safe prompted her to turn the knob and enter.

Annabelle's bedroom was at the front of the house, facing the ocean. The window blinds were open, the way she always kept them, even at night, with the window ajar so she could listen to the waves at the bottom of the cliff and across the highway. She said the sound helped her sleep.

Claudia could hear the mellow shushing now as she tiptoed to the bed. She need not have bothered to silence her footsteps. As she came close, she took in the rumpled blanket, the bare pillow where there should have been a tangle of black hair, and her heart thumped harder.

Annabelle was gone.

ten

Early Wednesday morning

"Sir, you need to stop right there, this is a restricted area."

The young patrol officer moved toward Jovanic, one hand on his weapon, the other outstretched in a 'halt' gesture. Jovanic did not recognize the guy, but from his high-handed attitude, figured him for a rookie who was enjoying his job of controlling the handful of gawkers huddled in robes and jackets a little too much. Older cops in the department referred to officers like this guy as 'boots'—fresh out of boot camp.

The kid should have known that someone showing up in a suit at this hour was supposed to be there. He could have been an asshole about it, but Jovanic just moved his suit coat aside to show the badge clipped to his belt and identified himself. "Who's in charge?"

Through the semi-darkness he could see the rookie flush bright red as he recorded the detective's name on his crime scene log. Everyone who came in and out had to go on the log.

Jovanic strode past him, then past the black and white patrol car parked diagonally, blocking the alleyway in front of Harvey's Neighborhood Market.

Located on a small side street, the market was a mere fifty steps east of the sands of Venice Beach. Through the wide front windows, Jovanic could see that it was the kind of neighborhood store where local residents and tourists might stock up on booze, snacks, magazines, cat food; play a video game or two—like an independent 7-Eleven. Inside the store, a uniform stood over a man seated on a chair in an aisle. The man was leaning forward, elbows on knees, head in hands.

Continuing through the alley, Jovanic took note of the security-grill windows set in a red brick wall painted with cartoon characters and a friendly *Welcome to Harvey's, we love you.* A cheerful contrast to what was awaiting him at the rear of the building.

A second black and white blocked the small parking lot behind the store, and a third behind that one. Yellow crime scene tape had been anchored to the passenger side spotlight of the first unit and stretched across the lot, ending up wound around a drain spout attached to Harvey's back wall at the other side.

Jovanic approached with care, watching where he walked. A blue trash dumpster was jammed between the store's back wall and a telephone pole inside the taped perimeter. A six-foot chain link fence behind the market and the adjoining stores separated them from the parking lot and terminated at a gate that led onto the beach.

As he approached, the driver's door of the rear patrol car opened and a burly uniform exited. The security light gleamed off his shave dome. Sergeant Marvin Williams, six-five, the color of sable. A voice that boomed as though he were speaking through a megaphone, even when he was supposedly keeping it down. Jovanic had run into him at the tattoo parlor scene, too.

"Gotta stop meeting like this," Williams greeted him.

"Getting to be a bad habit. What've you got this time?"

"Caucasian female, fifteen to eighteen."

Jovanic nodded. This much he knew from the phone call that had brought him here. "So, what's it look like, Marv?"

"A bloody fucking mess, that's what. Somebody beat the shit out of her." The big cop jerked his head at the trash dumpster, whose lid was down. "Body's in there."

The security light was on the parking garage at the north end of the lot, leaving this end shadowy. Using the Maglite he had brought with him, Jovanic scanned the outside of the dumpster, then the ground around their feet and farther out, observing that the concrete and asphalt were surprisingly clean. As far as he could tell, there was no blood on or around the dumpster. He squatted on his heels and shone his light underneath. No blood on the ground, either.

The big question in his mind was, if a killer needed to get rid of a body, why take the trouble to bring it to a crowded residential neighborhood where it would certainly be found, and relatively quickly? Most killers would dump the body in the nearest ditch outside of town. There were thought to be hundreds of undiscovered corpses in the desert around Southern California.

Maybe someone wanted to send a message: *She's garbage.*

"Who found her?" he asked the sergeant.

"Store owner." Williams took a notepad from his pocket and checked it. "Khan Khosa. Brought out the trash when he was locking up and there she was. LaRue's sitting on him inside."

"Any wits?"

"Not so far. Got a couple guys knocking on doors across the alley."

"Okay, Sarge, thanks. My partner's on his way, if you want to go."

Williams nodded and strolled back to his unit. Where was Coleman, anyway? Randy had sounded groggy over the phone. He knew better than to drink while on his rotation. If he didn't show up soon, Jovanic was going to kick his ass all the way downtown and back. Then he mentally kicked his own ass for acting like a geezer, and moved on to the next task.

Once he had gained a sense of the crime scene it would be his job to call the coroner, and crime scene techs if he needed them. As the lead investigator, the crime scene belonged to him, but the body belonged to the coroner's office. Nothing could be done with it before the coroner's investigator arrived—no checking of pockets or rolling the body over and looking underneath.

Jovanic did a slow 360, taking in his surroundings with a meticulous eye, snapping pictures with his phone. Two stories of condos rose above the gated parking garage comprising the first floor of the building straight across the alley from Harvey's. Several windows from that building and adjacent ones had direct views onto the area behind the store. Despite the late hour, choosing such a populated area for the body dump showed brazenness. Had a resident chosen to look out of one of those windows at just the right moment, they might have witnessed it.

Lights showed behind several window blinds. People woken by the officers knocking on doors, no doubt. Jovanic could hear them in his head: "Sorry for the inconvenience, sir, but we've got a situation..."

Some of the residents would feel no concern over a homicide that was not directly connected to them. They were the ones who would complain about being disturbed in the middle of the night. Others would lock themselves back inside their homes with a macabre thrill that something as frightful as murder had come so close. The rest were the curious who made up the group now standing on the sidewalk being barked at by the rookie to stand back.

Pulling on a pair of latex gloves he had brought from his vehicle, Jovanic prepared to raise the dumpster lid. In his twenty-three years of being a police officer, fifteen of them as a homicide detective, he had never quite become hardened to the first sight of the havoc humans wreak on one another. He told himself that when he did, it would be time to quit the job.

Breathing through his mouth to avoid the stink of rotting food and God knew what else might be in the bin with the body, Jovanic propped open the dumpster lid with a stick he found leaning against it for the purpose.

It was always worse when they were young.

The victim—what had once been a real girl with a real future—now nothing more than an empty shell—lay on her right side a foot below the rim. She had been left on top of a pile of bulging trash bags. Some had been ripped open by scavengers, decaying waste spewing from them. Thanks to the cool nighttime temperature, the flies had not yet arrived. Still, the faint odor of death was already in his nostrils.

She was small and slender, roughly Annabelle's size and age. The unwelcome thought pushed its way through. Jovanic had never aspired to be a parent, but the past summer spent with Claudia and her young charge had awakened something in him, if not a desire for fatherhood, an awareness that he had never had before. He had learned to see past Annabelle's armored exterior to the defenseless child inside.

And now, this girl in the dumpster, who had been somebody's daughter, stared through him with vacant blue eyes under half-closed lids, and made him think of Annabelle.

Her left arm covered her head as if she were trying to protect herself. But Jovanic was certain that by the time she had arrived in the alley, even a tank could not have protected her.

Without touching anything, he ran the Maglite over the young victim's face, noting the tiny red dots of petechial hemorrhaging in what he could see of the sclera and the skin below the eyes. That pointed to probable strangulation. The corneas had already started to dry and cloud over, which told him she had been dead for at least two hours.

It would not be a stretch to assume that the trails of black mascara on the pallid flesh had run with tears before smudging into the bruises on her face. He pictured her crying, begging her assailant to stop hurting her. The smeared blood around the swollen mouth was still pretty fresh. Broken front teeth showed through parted lips. A deep gash on her cheek could have been made by a blow from a heavy ring. Whoever had done this to her had plenty of physical strength.

The left arm and hand also bore bruises. Broken fingernails—defensive wounds sustained while trying uselessly to fend off the killer's savage blows. The right arm was tucked under her, but Jovanic guessed it would reveal more bruises and abrasions.

He knew he shouldn't touch the body before the arrival of the coroner's investigator, but he was impatient for answers, impatient to find the killer and get justice for his victim. Pushing down a rush of anger he reached out a gloved finger and carefully lifted a strand of blonde hair off her neck. There were no ligature marks, but three long red impressions had spread out behind her ear, ending in deep scores. The scores were the fingernail marks of a killer who had used his bare hands to choke the life out of the girl. If they got to the body soon enough, the coroner might be able to lift prints from her skin. If so, and the prints were in one of the databases, the case might be solved fast and easy.

Who had killed her? A drug-crazed boyfriend? A drunken father or stepfather? A pimp? He didn't think a stranger had randomly chosen her off the street. It was unlikely that a stranger would have taken the time to place her in the dumpster.

Her clothing appeared to be of decent quality. The faded denim jeans, black tube top and tennis shoes on otherwise bare feet might not be what a hooker would wear on the street to draw attention, but despite her obvious youth, Jovanic's instincts told him she might be a working girl. If his instincts were correct, she would not be the youngest hooker he had encountered.

He took close-up photos of her face with his phone. Assuming they got a line on who she was, he would need them for initial identification. Having to show a photo of a dead child to her parents had to be the worst duty of his job.

There would be more evidence for the body to divulge, but that would wait for the autopsy. More urgent was the need to question the witness who had made the gruesome discovery. He removed the stick, closed the dumpster lid and started toward the front of the store.

The sudden sound of muffled music stopped him mid-stride.

eleven

Making a quick about-face, Jovanic ran back to the dumpster and raised the lid with a still-gloved hand. The sound emanated from deep inside the bin. A tantalizingly familiar cell phone ringtone that died as abruptly as it had started.

Goddammit.

The call had either gone to voicemail or the caller had given up and clicked off. He was forced to wait for the coroner's work to be done and the body removed before the phone could be retrieved.

Khan Khosa, a Pakistani immigrant, informed Jovanic that he had purchased Harvey's Neighborhood Market from Harvey himself two years earlier. A slender brown man in his forties, he was puffing hard on a Dunhill, the half-empty box beside an ashtray brimming with butts smoked down to the filter.

Jovanic was a reformed smoker who now favored toothpicks. Approaching the owner and Officer Ron LaRue, he was hit by a sudden desire to join Khosa in a smoke to deaden the scent of death lodged in his nose.

Instructing LaRue to wait outside and let him know when the crime scene people arrived, Jovanic pulled up a chair next to the shaken owner.

"Look at my hands." Khosa held them up so Jovanic could see. "I cannot stop them from trembling. It has already been more than two hours, but they will not stop."

"You had a big shock. Why don't you tell me what happened."

"All right." Khosa gulped a deep breath and let it out on a big sigh. "I had already locked the front door of the shop and finished sweeping in the back—it is very important to me to leave everything clean and tidy, inside and out before I go home..." He stopped abruptly.

"I noticed how well-maintained your store is out back," Jovanic encouraged him.

"Yes. I wash down the concrete nearly every night. This is a respectable neighborhood. Even though we have the drug rehabilitation clinic on the next block, they have never given any trouble. I cannot understand why someone would do such a terrible thing. To leave this young woman in *my* rubbish bin. Why me?"

Khosa pushed away a thick lock of coarse black hair off his forehead. "When I opened the top of the bin, there she was, staring straight at me." He gave a violent shudder. "I dropped the top, and to tell you all the truth, Detective, and I am sorry to have to say this, but I very nearly tossed my cookies."

Jovanic suppressed a smile at the euphemism. "About what time was this, Mr. Khosa?"

"I close the shop at eleven o'clock. Usually, it takes about an hour to do the clearing of everything up. Tonight, though, after I swept up behind the shop, I came back inside to do some paperwork on the computer. My wife does not like me to bring work home, but these accounts must be taken care of or there will be no shop. Do you have a wife, Detective?"

"No," Jovanic said truthfully, though lately he'd begun to think Claudia's commitment-phobia might finally be thawing.

Khan Khosa nodded sagely. "Ah, well, perhaps you are lucky. I adore my beautiful wife, but sometimes she can be, well, a little difficult. When we got married, ten years ago…"

Jovanic, who hadn't gotten enough sleep before being woken by the phone, felt himself zoning out at the ancient history. He let the man ramble for a moment before breaking in. "You were going to tell me what time you went out back."

The store owner slapped his forehead. "I am so sorry, Detective. Forgive me. It was one-fifty-seven."

"That's very specific, sir. How can you be so precise?"

"I looked at the clock on the computer before I switched it off. I wanted to see how late I had stayed, and how much explaining I would have to do to my wife. Even though it is a good neighborhood, she worries about me working late at night. And now, after tonight, she will be worrying even more."

"Did Officer LaRue give you a chance to call your wife and let her know you would be staying even later?"

"Oh, no, no, no. I sent her a text message. Believe me, Detective Jovanic, if I woke her up, my life would not be worth any more than that poor girl out there."

Jovanic gave a brief understanding smile. "Did you hear anything unusual at any time last night?"

"Cars pass by all of the time. A lot of people live around here. Youngsters come into the shop after school and try to steal from me. I always catch them. But I did not hear anyone at my rubbish bin, I assure you."

"Does anyone else besides you use the trash dumpster or the area behind the store?"

Khosa nodded. "Dumpster Dave."

"Dumpster Dave?"

"Yes. I did not think of him until this very moment. He is a homeless person, quite harmless I believe, but he looks in all the rubbish bins for items to recycle, sometimes late at night. I try to shoo him away, but I know he sometimes sleeps behind the fence in back. It hides him from the other street people."

Jovanic remembered the torn open trash bags under the body, possibly the work of Dumpster Dave. He would have his partner check around for the homeless guy and ask whether he had seen or heard anything.

Accepting that he was unlikely to get anything else of importance from the store owner at the moment, Jovanic asked Khan Khosa to write out a statement and released him. At least Khosa had been able to supply a loose time frame for the body dump: after eleven o'clock, the store's closing time, and before one-fifty-seven, when he took the trash out back.

Randy Coleman showed up at last, yawning, but looking perfect, as always. His suit could have been tailored right on him. Mid-thirties, Jovanic's partner was fit and good-looking, with wavy black hair that was the envy of men who were mourning their own balding pates.

While he waited for the coroner to arrive, Jovanic sent him to look for any sign of Dumpster Dave. Then he started his chrono—notes that detailed everything he had done—and a diagram of the crime scene.

The coroner's investigator made it to the scene at four twenty-five bearing a cardboard tray with two large Styrofoam cups in one hand and an equipment case in the other.

"Sorry it's plain wrap." She set her case on the ground and offered a cup to Jovanic. "Starbucks needs to open an all-night store in the 'hood.'"

The pre-dawn temperature had chilled the air and Jovanic was glad to accept the coffee with thanks. "Not to sound ungrateful, Shirl," he added. "But, no donuts?"

Shirley Lorraine grinned. "Bad for your cholesterol. I wouldn't want you ending up on one of our tables with fatty arteries because of me."

Ash blonde with a dusting of grey, Shirley was a hot forty-five who looked thirty-two. Several years earlier when they had first met, there was an attraction and they had dated casually. But the chemistry was not quite right and after a few months they came to a mutual agreement that they made better friends than lovers. The friendship had endured and even now, during those times when they were not working a crime scene together, they stayed in touch. Jovanic was grateful that Claudia was not the jealous type. She liked Shirley—even analyzed her handwriting for her. "Got a pretty nasty one for you," he said.

"Yeah? So what else is new?"

She wore a black Polo shirt and tactical pants, and carried a folded Tyvek "bunny suit," which she pulled on before they went to the scene.

Once she'd suited up, he led her behind the store to the dumpster. While she gloved up, he prepared her for what she was about to find. He propped open the lid with the stick, then hauled a plastic milk crate over from a stack near the back door of the market. Shirley was about five-six, but she needed the extra height to see into the dumpster.

"Jesus." She shook her head in disgust. "What the hell is wrong with people?"

"I'll take that as a rhetorical question." Jovanic knew her well enough not to offer his opinion about the victim. She would want to make her own assessment first.

Opening her bag, Shirley unfolded a heavy paper sheet and threw it over the lip of the dumpster, to preserve any possible fingerprints and to keep her protective clothing away from the grimy metal surface. Next, she removed a scalpel and a digital thermometer with a six-inch metal spike that looked like a meat thermometer.

She made a note of the ambient temperature and climbed up on the crate. Standing off to the side, Jovanic watched her run a practiced eye over the body the way he had watched her numerous times before. She was serious about her job, and for someone who spent most of her time with corpses, she was remarkably good-humored.

After completing her visual inspection of the body, Shirley leaned into the dumpster and peeled up the bottom of the victim's tube top. More bruised flesh. With her fingertips she felt her way along the bottom of the sternum. When she found the spot she was looking for, she incised a slit in the skin with the scalpel, then guided the thermometer through it into the liver.

When he was still new on the job, Jovanic used to cringe, watching an ME perform this task, but his presence at hundreds of homicides over the years had hardened him. The ME's unfortunate patient felt nothing at this further violation.

Shirley read the digital display aloud. "91.6. She's in rigor, but it's not full."

Jovanic was aware that body temperature drops by about 1.5 degrees per hour after death. Rigor mortis begins within ninety seconds, but does not become full for about twelve hours, after which it begins to release. As he had suspected, the coroner's investigator's findings confirmed his guess that the victim had been killed late in the evening before being transported to the alley.

Using a red pen, Shirley drew a circle around the slit she had made. It would tell the pathologist at autopsy that the incision was hers, and not a pre-mortem injury.

The cell phone in the dumpster rang twice while she was inspecting the body. The first time it startled her and she nearly fell off her milk crate. The second time she turned with a stern glare to Jovanic, who was hovering at her shoulder. "No, you can't have it until I'm done here."

He did his best to sound hurt. "I didn't say anything about wanting to get that phone *right now.*"

"Uh huh. But you were thinking it."

"It could help me find out who she is."

"I know. I'm nearly there."

When she was done, the investigator instructed her assistants to photograph and then remove the body from the dumpster.

They might have been window dressers working with a mannequin, Jovanic thought, watching the two assistants wrestle the corpse from the dumpster as rigor continued to stiffen the muscles. Shirley Lorraine was well aware that he was itching to get his hands on the phone, but she refused to be rushed.

The assistants placed the body on a plastic sheet on the ground and as she continued her careful inspection, Jovanic was forced to wait until she gave the word. She checked the dead girl's pockets. Finding them empty, she rolled the body onto its left side. A hank of white blonde hair fell aside, exposing a tattoo on one thin shoulder.

There were a lot of tattoos around the Venice area, but given the arson case he was already working, the coincidence nagged at him. He could photograph and email it right now to the gang division. They would compare the glamorous sugar skull design to a catalogue they maintained of tattoos worn by gang members and their associates. If this particular sugar skull was among them, it would give him a place to start in his interviews.

Shirley pointed to the purplish discolored area of skin that showed between the tube top and Levi's. "See how the livor mortis is pronounced on the side she was lying on? That's where the blood pooled post mortem. She was relocated here soon after she was killed."

The sun was straining to push through the marine layer as dawn broke. People were already starting to leave their homes, heading to work and school, griping about access being blocked by crime scene personnel.

Shirley Lorraine directed her helpers to get the victim into a body bag, away from the prying stares of the lookie-loos in the windows of the apartment building across the alley.

"Can you do a blue check?" Jovanic was referring to a technology the department had started to use. With a device the size of a cell phone, an investigator could send a picture of the victim's fingerprints to check against the law enforcement database. The Blue Check didn't always work, but if it did, and the victim was in the system for any reason, he could have a positive identification within moments.

"Yeah, sure." Shirley instructed one of her techs to take the prints from the corpse's left and right index fingers. He held the screen against each in turn and sent it in. A few seconds later the results came back. "She's got a sealed juvenile record," the investigator reported. "Name's Angela Eliana Tedesco, AKA Angel. Wow, think her family is Italian, or what?"

Jovanic's attention snapped fully onto the tech. "Did you say '*Angel*'?"

twelve

The tech turned his screen to show Jovanic a photo of a younger version of the victim. He read the information, hardly daring to conclude what was staring him in the face.

"Holy shit."

Shirley, who was already packing up her case, glanced up at him. "What?"

"You hear about that tattoo parlor arson Sunday night? I'm looking for a teenager called Angel. A witness told me she's been spending time there. Fits this girl's description, too."

The main difference between the photo and the corpse was her hair, which on-screen was so black that it had to be a chemically induced color. Her sullen expression in the photo reminded him again of Annabelle when they had first met. The kid had been a real piece of work before Claudia started helping her. She still had plenty of problems.

"Do you believe in coincidences?" Shirley asked.

"Not one this big." There was no question in Jovanic's mind that the two cases were connected. "Can you have the CSIs fume her wrists and ankles?"

"You're thinking there might be latents?"

"It's a long shot, but you never know."

"Okay, tell Maria what you need."

Jovanic went to the tech, who was standing by the SID van, waiting for the ME's summons, and explained what he wanted. She clambered into the back of the vehicle, calling to the other assistant, a wiry Filipino trainee named Roberto Castillo, to help her. Castillo stood at the door to the cargo bay while Maria handed out a cardboard box and a coffee maker.

"Better make it quick," Castillo muttered, heading over to the body. "The media assholes are coming."

He was right. The increasing whirring of the news copter overhead spurred Jovanic to hurry. He didn't want telephoto lenses transmitting pictures of Angela Tedesco's battered body to their studios before her family could be notified. Besides, with a victim this young, there would be a lot of extra pressure from the brass to solve the case.

Carrying a bottle of water, a small container of superglue, and a heavy orange extension cord, Maria jumped down and followed her trainee. One end of the extension cord was attached to the 110 plug system in the van to provide electricity for the coffee maker, which would heat the water they needed under the hood to create humidity.

While Jovanic watched them set up the temporary fume hood, he called Huey Hardcastle at home and told him to come to the scene. The detective had done his best to get out of doing any real work for long enough. He had run out of excuses.

The coffeemaker would take a good ten minutes to heat the water under the box, and taking latent prints from skin was iffy at best. The greatest chance of success was when the corpse was freshest. Jovanic kicked himself for not thinking of it before the CSI techs had removed Tedesco from the dumpster.

When Hardcastle arrived, he pointed out Maria Abadias. "When Maria is done fuming the vic, she's going to put another sheet on the ground. There's a phone in the dumpster. I need you to suit up and get it."

"What the fuck? Why me?"

"Why not you, Huey?" Jovanic could feel his ire building. "It's your turn to do the scut work. So unless you've got a note from mommy saying you can't get your shoes dirty, get the fuck in the dumpster. When you find that phone, I want it right away. Same goes for a purse or anything else that looks like it might belong to the vic. You can hand the trash bags out to Maria and then we'll sort through everything on the sheets."

As he walked away, Jovanic was pretty sure Hardcastle called him an asshole under his breath. He grinned to himself. He might be an asshole, but he was the asshole in charge.

It took about thirty minutes before Hardcastle unearthed the phone, and it was ringing again when Jovanic grabbed it out of his hand. The first thing he noticed was its pink case, just like Annabelle's. He turned it over and saw Claudia's image on the screen, and almost dropped the phone. Then it hit him why the ringtone sounded so familiar.

He didn't know the song title, but sometimes when he and Annabelle were home alone together, Claudia had phoned her.

This was the tune that played on Annabelle's cell phone.

Annabelle's phone in the pink case.

His heart raced. He slid his finger across the screen to connect the call. "Claudia?"

His question was met with stunned silence. "Claudia?"

He heard her sharp intake of breath. "What—*Joel?*"

"Where's Annabelle? I need you to tell me, *right now.*" He knew the urgency in his voice would terrify her, but it couldn't be helped.

"But—how did you get her phone?"

"*Listen* to me, Claudia. Go and check her room."

Her next words stopped him cold. "I've already checked it. She's not in the house. Joel, what's going on? Where are you?" He could almost hear the penny drop when she got it. "Oh my god...*Annabelle?*"

"No; it's not her."

A moment of silence. Then, "Oh, hell, it's Angel, isn't it?"

Jovanic's attention snagged on one thing. "You *know* Angel?"

"She's the girl who helped Annabelle get the tattoo I told you about. Annabelle left her phone behind in the guy's van. Angel was supposed to bring it over to her tonight, but she didn't show. Oh, please don't tell me she's your victim."

thirteen

Joel's silence was the answer Claudia feared. All of a sudden her anger at Annabelle's nighttime vanishing act hardened into a glacial mass of fear. Angel was dead and she'd still had Annabelle's phone. So, where was Annabelle?

"I'm going to get dressed and look for her." Claudia headed for her bedroom, pulling open dresser drawers, grabbing T-shirt, jeans, underwear.

"Go where?" Joel asked. "Where are you going to look?"

"Anywhere. I can't just sit here."

"What kind of car was Angel driving?"

"She doesn't have a car. She was supposed to get a ride over here." A dozen scenarios ran through Claudia's head, none of them relieving her anxiety. "Annabelle talked to her on the phone yesterday afternoon. They must have made arrangements to pick her up after we went to bed. What the hell were they planning? Where is she?"

She heard him take a deep breath. When he spoke, his voice was level, but knowing him inside and out the way she did, her intuition told her that underneath the calm he felt a foreboding that mirrored her own.

"Who was supposed to drive her?" he asked.

"I have no idea. Maybe it was her boyfriend, or that guy Crash, or—"

"Crash? Who's that?"

"That's the tattoo artist who did Annabelle's work. We never got a chance to talk about it. He—"

"Wait," Jovanic interrupted. "You're going to have to make a formal statement. Meet me at the station and you can tell me everything then."

"But what about Annabelle?"

"You don't know what kind of car she's in or who she's with."

"If she's with Crash, he has a white van, but she didn't tell me the make."

"And you don't know if that's who Angel was with."

"That's who had Annabelle's phone."

"Okay, I'm gonna run the name and see if anything comes up under that moniker. But you do know how many white vans there are driving around West L.A., right? Do you have a description of this guy?"

Claudia felt a sudden wave of despair, realizing how little she did know. "Annabelle just referred to him as an 'old dude.' That could be anyone over twenty-two. I was so angry when she told me he gave her tequila, and then she was crying about being a disappointment to me. I didn't think about asking for a description." She zipped up her jeans and slipped into a pair of Sketchers. The crunch of Joel's footsteps on gravel echoed through the phone.

He spoke quietly, as if he didn't want others to hear. "Don't beat yourself up, babe. We'll find her. Right now, I gotta turn the scene over to Randy, then I'll meet you at the station. Forty-five minutes, okay?"

"I guess. See you there."

Claudia clicked off and dragged a sweatshirt over her head. Pacific Division police station where Joel worked was less than four miles from her home in Playa de la Reina. Forty-five minutes would give her time to drive the neighborhood. Whatever good it might do. She grabbed her keys from the kitchen counter and ran down the back stairs, backed her classic 1985 Jaguar out of the garage.

Oh, Annabelle, what have you gotten yourself into this time?

At six-thirty a.m. the roads were relatively empty, but on the way down the hill, though she knew the chances of her spotting Crash's white van in the neighborhood were close to nil, Claudia found herself looking from side to side as if she were following a tennis match.

For an instant, her hopes rose as she drove past Tyler's and saw a girl who, from behind, resembled Annabelle. But as Claudia slowed, about to call out to her, the girl turned and it was the face of a stranger looking back at her.

Joel was waiting for her at the station. He took her to the squad room, which was still empty at that time of the morning, and put his arms around her. "It's gonna be okay. He rested his cheek against her hair. "This isn't the first time Annabelle's given us a scare."

Through her fear, Claudia heard his use of "us" and felt a wave of love and gratitude that he was in her life. He had been at her side throughout the many trials she had shared with Annabelle—through kidnapping, murder, and more. Starting at age six, when she'd survived the automobile accident that killed her mother, Annabelle had experienced more trauma in her young life than anyone should have to.

Claudia realized she was trembling all over. Joel gave her a final squeeze, then released her and went to fetch her a chair. She clenched her hands, willing herself not to panic. She had been through too much with Annabelle to lose her now.

"We have to call her father."

Perched on the edge of his desk, Jovanic shook his head. "Not yet. We don't have anything to tell him."

"Except that Annabelle is missing and the girl who was coming to see her has been murdered." Claudia looked up at him. "What happened to her? Angel, I mean. How did she die?"

"You don't wanna know."

"Please don't patronize me, Joel. I *have* to know."

He gave her a long, considering look before giving his answer. "She was beaten and strangled. We'll know whether there was sexual assault after the autopsy."

Claudia sensed that he was leaving out the more horrific details. As if what he had said wasn't horrific enough. "Have you talked to Angel's boyfriend yet, Mouser?"

Joel's left eyebrow hiked in that certain way she found so sexy. "You seem to have a lot more information than we do. Start from the beginning and tell me everything you know about Angel."

What she knew about the girl was little enough, but by the time she was finished, Claudia could see she had provided some valuable facts he could run with.

"'Mouser' could be a gang name. 'Crash,' too. I'll put them into the system, see if anything pops up." With an apologetic glance, he leaned down and withdrew a form from his desk drawer and pushed it across to her. "I need you to write out your statement."

Claudia gave him a sardonic look. "Why? Are you going to have my handwriting analyzed?"

She finished writing down everything she could think of and left the station. Joel had names to run that he hoped would lead to interviews, and she wanted to get back to prowling the streets. The connection between

Angel and Travis Navarette, the tattoo shop victim, which Jovanic had just told her about, made her queasy.

She checked her cell phone every five minutes to make sure she had no missed calls or texts. The hour was still early, but as she cruised the streets of Venice she phoned her friend Zebediah Gold. Annabelle had not required regular therapy for a while now, but maybe he had heard from her.

Zebediah had not.

"Put it in perspective, darling," he suggested in a gentle tone. "This is pretty typical Annabelle behavior."

"It used to be, but she hasn't done anything like this in a long time."

"Didn't you tell me the other day that she secretly got a tattoo?"

"That's because of Angel's influence."

"Annabelle isn't all that easily influenced. She's pretty strong-minded. She must have wanted the tattoo before Angel set it up for her. Look, sweetie, it's fine to be concerned, but at this point, I don't think you need to be alarmed."

"That's easy for you to say, but a girl's been murdered!" Claudia could not remember ever being angry with Zebediah in their long relationship, but she could feel the heat rising in her now. Her cheeks, even the tips of her ears burned with it. Before he could respond, she ended the call and nearly in tears, called her closest friend.

"Jesus," Kelly Brennan breathed. "That kid is a shit magnet. Some people are like that, you know? No matter how good they try to be, trouble follows like a little dark cloud over their shoulder."

"Thanks so much, Kel, that's what I wanted to hear."

"Well, in Annabelle's case I'd say she's got a pretty damn good guardian angel. Look at all the crap she's lived through, and yet, she's been doing okay since you've been playing mommy substitute. In my practice, I see kids dealing with one-tenth her problems go right off the rails."

Kelly was a family law attorney. Much of her work was contracted by the public defender's office, which sometimes brought her in contact with the seamier side of society. "What is it you're afraid of, Claud?" she asked. "Say it out loud."

Claudia took a deep breath and plunged in. "I'm afraid this guy Crash picked up the girls and killed Angel. That either he's got Annabelle stashed somewhere, or..." She broke off. Giving voice to her deepest fears was too much like making them a reality.

"What would his motive be?" Kelly asked, sounding like the defense attorney she once was.

"People who deliberately kill children don't need a motive. They're just evil."

"You're right about that. But think about it. This Crash guy had her alone in his van with him for what, an hour or more? He got her drunk. She was in his control. If he planned to hurt her—or worse—why wouldn't he have done it then?"

"Who knows? Why would he—or someone—strangle a kid like Angel? Why would Annabelle disappear on the same night Angel's killed? And why the hell would she sneak out like that?"

"Listen, Claudia, it's natural for you to feel a little betrayed. You've given her a home and treated her like family. The thing is, she's *acting* like family—the only kind she's ever known—a dysfunctional one. She was doing the same thing long before you knew her, wasn't she—running off at night?"

"You're thinking of when she tried to kill herself. That's not what's happened here."

"No, that's not what I was thinking."

"What, then?"

"She knew Angel from her days at Sorensen—they were in juvie together."

"Yeah, so?"

"They were in juvie together because they got caught hanging with gangbangers boosting cars. Right?"

"Right."

"Not to be obvious, but she's reconnected with Angel, who is now, well, deceased. Maybe Angel put her back in contact with those gangbangers. Maybe that's where Joel should start looking."

"Much as I hate to admit it, you may have a good point. But bottom line, this is the second time Annabelle has gone missing and someone turned up dead. The first time it was by the grace of God that she escaped. So to tell the truth, Kelly, your scenario doesn't make me feel any better."

"Want me to come over and wait with you?"

"No, thanks, I'm gonna drive around some more. It's better than sitting in the house."

"Okay. Call me if anything changes."

Claudia promised she would, but after the call disconnected, she flipped her indicator and made a right onto Jefferson, giving in to the realization of how fruitless it was to drive aimlessly around a city as vast as Los Angeles—even this small part of it. Needle in a haystack didn't begin to describe the problem.

The dashboard clock showed twenty-seven past eight. On a normal day, Annabelle would be grumbling about having to go to school. Claudia drove past the Ballona Wetlands in a fog of anxiety. The tiny main drag of Playa de la Reina came up fast, with Tyler's on her left. She made the turn there and drove up the hill and onto her street.

A few yards from her house, something caught her attention. A car door opening—an old navy blue Honda Civic that could have benefitted from a paint job.

A teenage girl she did not recognize stepped out and stretched. Something made Claudia put her foot on the brake. As she slowed to look, the passenger door of the parked car opened and Annabelle exited.

fourteen

Oblivious to Claudia's presence, the two girls started walking up the block toward the house. She passed them and parked the Jag in the driveway, not bothering to put it in the garage. She climbed out and leaned against the car, waiting for them.

Annabelle kept shaking her head no at the girl walking with her, who apparently was saying something she did not like. As they neared the house she glanced up and her eyes connected with Claudia's. Her shoulders sagged with resignation and she slouched past without speaking.

"Annabelle?"

Annabelle stopped at the foot of the staircase and half-turned, her chin thrust out the way it did when she knew she was in the wrong and intended to brazen it out. "*What?*"

"Where were you all night?"

"Right *there*." She flipped a thumb at her friend's car down the street. "I was in Jamie's car the whole time. Can we go in the house now?" Without waiting for an answer, she started up the stairs.

Claudia turned to the other girl, relief tangled up with anger and frustration. And the knowledge that she was going to have to tell them about Angel. "You're Jamie?"

The girl nodded, eyes darting from Claudia to Annabelle, who had reached the front door, then back again.

Jamie was taller than Annabelle by almost a head, and looked significantly older. Too thin, with bony wrists emerging from the sleeves of the hoodie she hugged around her, dark, pained eyes stood out against the unhealthy pastiness of her skin, like an Animé cartoon.

Wondering when she had last eaten a decent meal, Claudia extended a hand to indicate that Jamie should follow her friend up the staircase. "Let's go inside."

"...so we decided not to do anything in case we made it worse."

The two girls were seated in the breakfast nook with mugs of hot chocolate, eating scrambled eggs and toast as if this were their last meal. Jamie hunched over her plate, shoveling food into her mouth in a way that made Claudia think of a prison inmate at chow.

The food seemed to revive Annabelle and brought a little color to her face. She explained that their plan had been for Jamie to pick up Angel and bring her over to Claudia's house to return the cell phone and hang out for a while. But upon Jamie's arrival at the place in Mar Vista where Angel was staying, Angel's boyfriend Mouser had come to the door and said she wasn't there, that Big Carl had picked her up earlier.

Claudia took her coffee cup to the sink and rinsed it out. "*Who* is Big Carl and why would Angel go with him if she was waiting for Jamie?"

"He's Viper's muscle."

"And who is Viper?"

At the same time Jamie, who had remained silent until now, shot a warning look at Annabelle. "Just a guy."

Yeah, right. Every guy needs his own personal muscle.

What had these girls gotten themselves involved with? Claudia focused her gaze on Jamie. "Tell me, why does Viper need Big Carl for protection?"

"Claudia," Annabelle broke in with exaggerated patience, as if Claudia were a child. "I thought you wanted to know what happened last night, not ask a bunch of lame questions."

Claudia regarded her through narrowed eyes. "Fine, but we're not finished with the lame questions. Why did this Viper person send Big Carl to get Angel?"

"Mouser said that Viper was majorly pissed about something, and Angel was gonna have to pay."

"Shut the fuck up." Jamie hissed.

Annabelle blushed scarlet and ducked her head, busying herself with sweeping toast crumbs off the wooden tabletop into her hand. "Sorry."

Claudia ignored the outburst. "Any idea what upset Viper?"

"How should I know? Mouser told me to beat it, so I came and got her," Jamie jerked her head in Annabelle's direction. "Then we went back over to his place and waited outside for a long time, but Angel never showed up."

"So, we came back here," Annabelle added, carrying her plate to the sink. "We sat outside for just about forever, waiting for Angel to call Jamie. It was freezing, but I guess we fell asleep."

"Yeah," Jamie added. "That's all we know."

Jamie was lying about something. Claudia could feel it. She aimed to find out what was going on in the way she knew best. Taking a pad and pen from the counter she slid them in front of Jamie. "Write down Angel's phone number and address and yours, please."

"Why?"

"Because I asked you to."

Jamie's flat black stare radiated a feral suspicion. "What are you going to do with it?"

"She's gonna analyze your handwriting," Annabelle told her with an impudent grin. "Aren't you?"

Claudia did a Groucho Marx bounce of her eyebrows. "You never know."

"But I don't like to write."

"Do you know how?"

"Well, yeah, of course."

"Okay, write it then. Also, what about Angel's parents? Do you have their contact information?"

Jamie picked up the pen and stared at it with revulsion, as if it were a poisonous snake. "Her old man lives in New York. Her mom is in Italy or someplace in Europe. Why?"

"Just write everything that happened last night."

Annabelle sat back down and stirred her hot chocolate with a defeated groan. "I guess I'm in trouble again?"

"We'll talk about that later," Claudia said. "You pretty much scared me to bits, disappearing like that."

"How'd you know I was gone?"

"Joel got a callout and I couldn't get back to sleep, so I looked in on you." She caught Annabelle's half-smile and smiled back at her. "Took about five years off my life when I saw you weren't there."

The heart-shaped face filled with contrition. "I'm sorry, Claudia, I really am; I promise. When I talked to Angel—you know, on your phone when we were at Tyler's? She told me to meet her outside at ten last night, but when I went out it was just Jamie, and, well, I was just down the street in her car; I didn't know we were going anywhere. And you and Joel already went to bed, so I didn't want to wake you up."

"That's not a good excuse, you know that, right?"

"I guess, but—"

"You've got people who care about what happens to you. Please always remember that."

Annabelle looked down at her hands. It was going to take a long time for her to accept that she was truly loved. How on earth was she going to break the news that Angel was dead?

She would have to call Joel soon, too. He would want to interview Jamie in case she had anything valuable to contribute. She hated seeing Annabelle subjected to questioning, too.

From the corner of her eye, she noted that Jamie had covered about a half-page with just a few lines. "You can also write down anything you know about Viper."

Jamie looked up from the pad, where she seemed to be taking great pains with her writing, holding the pen awkwardly between her second and third fingers. "I don't know anything. We just hang out at his place."

"What place is that?"

"Dragon House."

"Let me guess; it's a tattoo parlor?"

"Well, yeah."

"Is that where Crash works, too?"

"Claudia!" Annabelle exclaimed, telegraphing a clear message that told Claudia Annabelle's tattoo had been arranged between her and Angel alone, and she did not want Jamie to know about it.

Jamie flashed her a quick look through narrowed eyes. "How do you know Crash?"

Claudia let the question go. "How old are you, Jamie?"

"I'll be eighteen in November."

"You like to hang out with younger girls?"

"Hell, no. Viper told me to keep an eye on Angel bec—" Abruptly, Jamie cut herself off and threw down the pen. She shoved the pad to the center of the table.

"Because why?"

"When Viper says do something, you don't ask questions."

"What happens when you ask questions?"

Jamie shifted uneasily in her seat. "What is this, like, the fifth degree or something?" She picked up the last bit of toast on her plate and shoved it in her mouth, chewing madly.

"No, it's not the *third* degree, but I'm responsible for Annabelle while her father's out of town, and she was with you, so I'd like to know a little background. What happens when you don't do what Viper says?"

"Nothing. He gets mad."

"I get that. But what happens when he gets mad. What does he do?"

"He—he gets real quiet."

"And?"

Jamie hesitated and Claudia could almost see the lie forming in her mouth. "Nothing. He doesn't do nothing."

Claudia noted Annabelle's expression of disbelief, though she refrained from contradicting the older girl. "What do you like about hanging out at the tattoo studio?" she asked Jamie, to put her off her guard. When the girl's eyes brightened, she knew the ploy had worked.

"It's fun. There's always hot dudes there, and they like me. They take me out on their bikes and shit, er, I mean, stuff. Viper gives me money and I, uh, do, uh stuff to—for—him."

Claudia wasn't about to ask her what kind of stuff. With every answer Jamie gave, the realization was growing that Joel would need to interview her. And with that growing realization came the horrifying understanding that these two girls might be in possession of critical information about the homicide. It was time for her to butt out and let the police take over.

Leaving them at the table, she ran up to her office. Joel didn't answer his phone. She left him a voicemail about the developing situation, then returned to the kitchen to check out Jamie's handwriting.

The ink trail confirmed her hunch. The handwriting was excessively large, the letter forms as circular as little open mouths waiting to be fed. Claw-like shapes in the e's and a's, extra strokes stabbing into the loops of o's. Jamie had more miles on her than a Mack truck and less common sense than a goldfish. One thing was sure: she had not yet made friends with the truth.

It was obvious to Claudia that the girl had been abused early in life in a variety of ways that had interfered with the development of a healthy ego—she hadn't a shred of doubt about that. Jamie was already emerging as a full-blown narcissist who would put her own needs ahead of anyone else's. Definitely not an appropriate companion for Annabelle, who was still struggling to overcome the results of her own victimization.

She laid the paper on the table and looked at Annabelle with serious eyes. "There's something I have to tell you."

"Something happened to Angel," Annabelle spoke without inflection, but the apprehension was there in the tautness of her mouth, the rigidity of her shoulders.

Claudia reached out and took the small, icy hands in hers. Sometimes she thought the girl was psychic. "Yes, something happened."

"She's dead."

"Yes, sweetheart, I'm so sorry."

"It's my fault. I'm a jinx." There was a quiver in Annabelle's voice, though she tried to control it. "People I care about always get killed."

Claudia sat down next to her on the bench and slipped her arm around the stiff shoulders. "Annabelle, listen to me. You are *not* a jinx. This has nothing to do with you. Whatever happened to Angel, the only person responsible is the one who did it." She had worked for so long to break through the walls behind which Annabelle hid that she was surprised when she felt the slim body relax into her and she started talking.

"She was supposed to get this guy, Travis, to hook up with her so—"

Jamie jumped up from the table, her eyes smoldering. "Shut the fuck up, you moron!" She stabbed her finger at Annabelle, her shout as jarring as a gunshot.

"Sit down, Jamie." Claudia hardened her tone enough to get the girl's attention. "What's your problem?"

"She's talking shit. She doesn't know nothing about it."

"Well, if *you* know something, you'd better tell me, right now."

"I'm not telling you *anything.*"

Annabelle's face had drained of color. "Angel's dead," she cried. "Don't you get it?"

"Well, you'd better shut up, or you'll be dead, too."

"I don't *care*, Jamie!" Annabelle looked up at Claudia. "Angel was supposed to get Travis in trouble because she's underage, but she liked him and she wouldn't do it."

"You stupid little c—"

"Be *quiet*, Jamie." Claudia said sharply.

Travis. The name rang a bell. Then she remembered, Travis was the name of the firebombing victim who had been killed at his tattoo shop. The dots connected. It struck her afresh how close Annabelle had been, both to that crime and Angel's murder. Why hadn't Joel called back yet? She needed to get Jamie out of her house.

"Tell me about Travis, Annabelle. Did Angel say why Viper wanted to get him in trouble with the police?"

"You're so stupid," Jamie hissed. "You don't know—"

"Viper was mad because Travis wouldn't give him money from his tattoo studio. Viper found out that Angel didn't do what he said—" Two tears splashed onto her Levi's.

Claudia reached out to her, but Annabelle jerked away. Apparently, there was a limit to the walls she was willing to break down, and they had reached it.

fifteen

Joel finally called.

Once she had brought him up to speed, he asked her to bring the girls to the station.

Claudia's heart sank. "Do I have to bring Annabelle?"

"Yes. Someone else will have to interview her, not me."

"She's pretty traumatized. I doubt she'll talk to a stranger."

"You should have brought them in right away."

The hint of a rebuke put her on the defensive. "They were hungry and cold."

"Which makes it more likely they would have told the truth."

"Well, it's done now. Anyway, she can't change her story. She's given it in front of two witnesses."

"Sure," Jovanic said drily. "People never change their stories."

"Okay, I know. You've seen it all." Claudia yawned. "I'm so relieved Annabelle is safe. Now all I want is to crawl back into bed."

"But that's not what you're gonna do, right? You're gonna get right back in the car and deliver that little package to me, aren't you?"

"Of course, my darling. You are my Viper. I am but your errand girl."

"What?"

"See you in a few."

At Pacific Division Police Station, Jamie Parker stared at Jovanic across the table in an interview room, refusing to answer his questions. Even when he showed her the photos he had taken of Angel in the dumpster, she showed no discernible reaction. An Oscar-worthy imitation of a stone.

When Claudia brought her in, she told Jovanic that the only way she'd been able to persuade Jamie to come with her was by convincing her that she could be prosecuted as an accessory to Angel's murder, and that it was in her best interests to go to the police before they came looking for her. True or not, the threat had been enough to scare the surly young woman into reluctantly agreeing. But it wasn't enough to persuade her to part with any information.

Jovanic left Jamie alone to stew for an hour or so while he ran a background on her.

This was not her first time in an interview room. Her juvenile record included arrests for drugs and prostitution starting at thirteen, and a long string of foster and group homes. Too bad there were no outstanding warrants he could use to scare her into talking.

When he returned, she looked up with a bored face. "You got a Coke? And I need to pee."

"How about giving me some answers first?"

"I told you already, I'm not gonna narc on anyone. Even if I had anything to say, which I don't."

Jovanic perched on the corner of the table. "Why would you want to cover for someone who killed your friend?"

Jamie shook her head with a chilling expression of disdain. "That little ho is *not* my friend. Anyway, if you knew who did her, you wouldn't have to keep me stuck in this shithole the whole fuckin' day."

"If she wasn't your friend, what was she?" Jovanic tipped his chin at her off-the-shoulder shirt, which gave him an eyeful of the sugar skull tattoo. "You've got the same tat as Angel. Did Viper do them for both of you?"

She made a noise in the back of her throat as if bored with the whole conversation. "Hey, dude, you gonna let me go to the john, or you want me to let loose right here?"

Jovanic had no doubt she would make good on her threat. The only available female detective was RJ Scott, whose eyes were still bloodshot and droopy from her bout with the flu. He stood as far from her as he could without being obvious and asked her to escort Jamie to the restroom.

Afterwards, Scott took a run at the girl herself. Having no better luck, she stepped out into the hallway with Jovanic, shaking her head in disgust.

"That girl is as tough as a cockroach. Either she's not talking because she's scared of this Viper dude, which she doesn't seem to be, or maybe she's got the hots for him. We're lucky your girlfriend got as much as she did from the chick. Maybe enough to bring him in for a one-on-one."

As tired as he was, and more than a little frustrated, Jovanic had to admit that Claudia had obtained more information in the few handwritten lines Jamie provided her than he had managed in the two hours he had spent with the girl.

"Viper's been on our radar for a while," he told Scott. "See if there's anyone at his studio we can lean on. We're not gonna bring him in until we've got something that'll stick."

Scott left to make some calls and Jovanic went to his desk and phoned Claudia.

"I'm going to have to release her, but I hate to just let her go. At her age, DPS won't take her, but I'm concerned about her safety. According to what she told you, Angel ended up dead in the trash when she got Viper's bad side."

"Annabelle asked if Jamie could stay with us," Claudia said wryly.

"No fucking way. I can't be staying in the same house as a witness." He heard the snarl as the words came out and felt like kicking himself. Claudia was not the enemy. He felt even worse when she didn't snap back at him.

"Don't get your panties in a bunch, honey. I told her it was out of the question. I don't want her near Annabelle, anyway. There's something wrong in that girl's head."

"Sorry, babe. I'm just wound up."

"Probably need some lunch, too."

"Yes, Mom."

"Okay, that did it. You can figure out Miss Jamie by yourself. I'm hanging up now."

"No, wait. I'm sorry."

"That's two 'sorrys' in thirty seconds."

"Believe me, I do *not* think of you as my mom."

"You're sure about that?"

"I couldn't be more sure. The things I think about doing with you..." Jovanic broke off as Randy Coleman appeared in the doorway and approached his desk. "Let's finish that conversation tonight. Can you come and take Jamie back to her car?"

"Sure. Be there in ten minutes." A thought struck her. "I wonder if Kelly would take her for a day or two. At least until you arrest Viper."

"Talk about the blind leading the blind."

"Kelly's an attorney, not a criminal."

"There's a difference?"

"Jeeez, Columbo, I guess I fell right into that one."

He caught the grin in her voice as she said goodbye and clicked off.

"I don't need a babysitter," Jamie snapped.

"Trust me, you do." Kelly Brennan opened the passenger door of her shiny red Mustang convertible and stood back for her to get in.

"Last time someone said 'trust me,' it meant 'fuck you.'"

"Okay, but I don't. Get in the car, please."

They were standing in front of the Pacific Division Police Station, having just left the building and met up with Claudia and Annabelle on the sidewalk.

"Just take me to my car, okay? I need to go—"

"Sorry, Viper's going to be a little busy today," Kelly said, not unkindly. "How about some lunch? You hungry?"

"I'm dying for a smoke," Jamie said. "Got one?"

Ignoring the request, Kelly turned to Claudia. "How about it? Lunch? I'm thinking Cowboys."

"Do you feel like eating something?" Claudia asked Annabelle, resting a gentle hand on her shoulder. Annabelle just shook her head. She hadn't spoken since Claudia had insisted that she go with her to meet Kelly at the police station. Now, staring at the sidewalk, she seemed lost in her own world.

Watching Kelly climb into the Mustang, Claudia wondered whether she had done the right thing, asking such a big favor. Her friend had agreed almost too eagerly to take on the challenge of hosting Jamie for a day or two, but Claudia had the feeling that she didn't fully understand what she had agreed to.

<h1 style="text-align:center">sixteen</h1>

Back at his desk, Jovanic wolfed the Double Double and fries he'd grabbed at the In-n-Out on Washington, and washed them down with Diet Coke. He was starting his second murder book of the week and the lack of sleep was catching up with him.

The three-ring binder he had opened on Monday for Travis Navarette, the arson victim, was joined by a new one for Angela Eliana Tedesco, AKA "Angel." The two cases had to be related, no question about it. But each required its own unique murder book that would soon be filled with witness statements, descriptions of the crime scene and the evidence, a listing of all officers and others who had been at the scene, investigative reports. The medical examiner's findings at autopsy would be added later.

By the end of the investigation, the murder book would provide a complete history of what had transpired in the case. Assuming enough evidence had been gathered to charge a suspect, when the case went to court, all the t's would be crossed and the i's dotted. That was the goal, anyway.

Jovanic reviewed his list of witnesses to be interviewed. Dumpster Dave, whom Khan Khosa had mentioned, was at the top of the list. They were still at the scene when Randy Coleman located the homeless man asleep on a thin pile of burlap sacks behind Le Petit Bakery, a small bistro café a few yards west of Harvey's Market.

Jovanic could smell Dumpster Dave from six feet away. Like many street people who rarely got to shower, the man wore a filthy knit cap pulled down low over his eyebrows and an overcoat crusty enough to stand up on its own. Life on the street added a lot of years to a face. He could have been anywhere from thirty to seventy.

Dumpster Dave was less than pleased to be rousted by the cops, even ones who were not ordering him to move his makeshift bed at six o'clock in the morning. He hauled himself unsteadily to his feet. "What the hell do you assholes want?"

"What's your name, sir?" Jovanic asked.

"I haven't done anything wrong." His pitch was raspy but not old.

"We just need to ask you a couple of questions; it'd be nice to have your name."

"David," the man said grudgingly. "David Robinson."

"Thank you, Mr. Robinson."

"You around here most nights?" Coleman inquired.

Dumpster Dave looked up at him with a sneer that revealed broken upper teeth on one side of his mouth, vacant gums on the other. "Nossir, most o' the time I'm stayin' over at the Ritz Carlton, but last night I thought I'd camp out and look at the stars."

"Listen, wiseass," Coleman said, bringing out the tough guy. "Just answer the question. Did you hear anything unusual last night?"

Jovanic put up a restraining hand. "Hold up, Detective. Mr. Robinson isn't suspected of a crime. We're looking for his help." He pulled a twenty-dollar bill from his pocket and let the homeless man see it.

Dumpster Dave leaned over for a moment, hands on his knees, and hacked up a nasty wad of phlegm. It landed on the sidewalk an inch from Coleman's polished Oxfords.

"Hey!" The younger detective jumped back, his face furious, then he lunged toward the homeless man. Jovanic grabbed his arm and jerked him away. "We heard you sometimes crash behind the market," he said to Robinson. "Why'd you move down here last night?"

When the man straightened up, Jovanic noted a crude spiderweb tattoo across his Adam's apple, the spider hidden under the collar of his overcoat. A prison badge of honor for a kill.

Dumpster Dave reached for the cash, scowled when Jovanic held it back. "What d'you care where I sleep? I mind my own business, don't bother no one. Don't know nothin'."

"That's not a good answer." Jovanic moved to stuff the money back in his pocket.

The scowl deepened. "What th' fuck? That raghead down the store was late gettin' out. If I'd took my usual spot, asshole woulda hosed me down like he done before."

"So, getting back to my question, *sir*," Coleman said tightly. "Did you hear or see anything out of the ordinary?"

Coleman was getting on Jovanic's last nerve. He made a mental note to give the junior detective a verbal ass kicking after they'd left the homeless man. It was time he learned that it didn't cost anything to be courteous. Sometimes, just the act of being nice to people produced valuable information they would have otherwise kept to themselves.

Dumpster Dave scratched at the scraggly white beard outlining his chin. It was easy to see the wheels turning as he calculated how much he might be able to scam out of the two cops. He hunched his head down into his coat like a tortoise. "I got the cancer, man. I'm gonna be worm food by the end of the year. Can't you do a brother some good?"

The dullness of his rheumy eyes, the sunken cheeks, the sallow skin corroborated his tale about his illness. Jovanic peeled off another twenty and held out the two bills, this time let him take them. "Just tell us what you know, Dave. That's all we want."

"God bless you," the man mumbled. He hurried to stash the money somewhere deep inside his coat and crossed his arms over his chest as if the two detectives might try to wrestle it back. "I *mighta* heard somethin', but I don't wear no watch, so I don't know what time it was and I know you're gonna ask me that."

"What did you hear, sir?" Jovanic repeated.

"Like I said before, the raghead didn't come out like usual. I know it was pretty late. So I'm checkin' the recycle bin for cans, you know, while I'm waitin'?" He pointed vaguely in the direction of Harvey's Market, where a few feet from the body dump, a smaller bin was designated for recyclables.

"Go on."

"One o' those big mutha SUVs comes crawling down the alley real slow, no lights on. I figure somethin's up and I git down behind the wall."

Jovanic reckoned he was referring to the concrete wall at the rear of the businesses adjoining Harvey's, which separated the businesses from the parking lot in back.

"I duck way down so they can't see me. They stopped behind Harvey's. First it was quiet, then I heard a kinda grunt, then the dumpster lid banged down like it was dropped. One of 'em cussed, kinda quiet, but pissed, know what I mean?"

Jovanic assured him that he understood, and waited for him to continue his story.

"A few seconds later I hear three doors shut. One, two, three."

"Three car doors?" Coleman put in. "You sure it was three?"

Dave glared at him. "Maybe I sleep in the street, muthafucker, but I can count to three. I went to college—"

"Okay," Jovanic broke in. "You heard three doors shut on the SUV. Tell me about the people in the vehicle. What'd they look like?"

Dumpster Dave smooshed his lips together and glared at the two detectives as if he couldn't believe they would ask him such a dumb question. "Fuck if I know, man. I stayed down behind my wall till they was long gone. I don't need to be up in nobody's bidness. Leavin' shit in a dumpster in the middle the night sez it's *risky* bidness." He showed the detectives a lopsided grin. "So, what happened, officers? Somebody dump a body in there?"

The two detectives glanced at each other. "Thanks for your help, Mr. Robinson." Jovanic handed him his card. "If you remember anything else, give us a call."

Claudia tried to concentrate on the probate case on her desk. Her client claimed that his parents had signed a will in his favor, cutting his sister out of the sizeable estate. The sister was challenging the authenticity of the will. The client had retained Claudia in the hope that she would write a report that would benefit him.

Little more than a cursory glance at the documents and her gut said her client was lying to her. The signatures on the will had not been written by either of the parents. She took her time to do a full examination, evaluating all the documents and confirming her opinion.

There had been an attempt to simulate the two signatures, but it was a poor attempt. Simulating someone else's signature rarely resulted in a successful copy. The shakiness along the line of ink was often the first giveaway. Most cases of tremor resulted from one of two causes: illness, or trying to simulate a handwriting that was not natural to the writer. In this case, Claudia knew it was not the former because she had asked the client whether either of his parents had suffered an illness. The answer was no; they were both in good health when they died in the crash of a private plane. Between the poor-quality simulation and the tremor, it was clear the client was lying, and that pissed her off.

She had already been paid a retainer. Even when she couldn't provide the answer that a client was hoping for, her contract made it clear that regardless of her opinion—whether it supported the client or not—she had earned the fee. She gazed at the enlarged signatures on her computer monitors. The alleged signatures of the parents filled one screen, the authentic ones for comparison on the other.

If the client had been smart enough to hire a lawyer to retain her as a consultant rather than a designated expert witness, her opinion would have remained protected. As it was, if the case went to court, her findings could be used against him. If he had any brains at all, the client would not want her to write a report.

Reluctantly, she picked up the phone and punched in his number.

The client soon realized he had picked the wrong expert to lie to. Claudia hung up from the brief call and put the files aside. She leaned back in her chair, pondering how she could help Annabelle through yet another loss.

The short ride home from the police station had been made in silence and once they got home, Annabelle had gone straight to her room and shut the door. Moments later, a metal album blasted through the walls. Normally, she would ask her to turn the music down, but today was different. Angel was dead.

Joel had said that neither of the victim's parents had been located, so as yet, her name was not being released to the media.

Once more, Claudia went back over her two brief conversations with Angel, torturing herself over whether there was anything she could have done that might have saved the girl's young life. Finally, letting out a sigh filled with regret and sadness, she got up, crossed to the sliding glass door and stepped out onto the deck.

Like Annabelle's room along the hall, Claudia's office faced the ocean. The sun had peeped out after the clouds burned off around three o'clock, leaving clear skies. Beyond the flat rooftops that lay close to the beach far below her, the water was pale blue and calm, no waves for the surfers to ride today. From her vantage point she could see Jamie's old Honda parked crookedly at the curb fifty yards down the street. Although she had her doubts, she hoped that by now Kelly and Jamie might be doing some quality female bonding. From what little Joel had told her of their interview, Jamie was one tough nut to crack.

If anyone could break through that hard shell of defiance, Kelly was the one.

Suddenly, Claudia realized that the music had stopped. At the same moment she heard the front door close, quietly, surreptitiously. If she had been at her desk, she would have missed it. Leaning over the deck railing, she called to the girl hurrying down the wooden staircase. "Annabelle, where are you going?"

Annabelle swung around and looked up, her expression mulish. "Why are you spying on me?"

"You know the rule—if you're going out, you tell me where you're going."

"For a walk, okay? I can't fucking breathe." And with that, Annabelle took off running.

seventeen

The next name on Jovanic's witness list was Angel's boyfriend Mouser.

Randy Coleman navigated the department Dodge Charger through the narrow streets of Venice, looking for the address Claudia had given him. "What kind of bullshit name is Mouser?" Coleman grumbled, steering the car with his knee while attempting to open a packet of Juicy Fruit gum.

"Give me that before you run us off the road." Jovanic snatched the pack from his partner. He unwrapped a stick of gum and handed it back, stuffing the balled-up wrapper into the cup holder. "I don't like going in blind. Did you at least run the tattoo parlor where the brother works?"

Coleman nodded. "I checked the lease. The owner of Dragon House is Alvin Lester Rousch, AKA Viper."

"Almost as bad as Mouser."

"No lie. Alvin Lester? His parents must have hated him to hang that name on him."

"Could be worse."

"Yeah? Like—?"

"How about Adolph? Or Willard, like the rat."

Coleman, who was ten years younger than Jovanic, laughed. "You gotta be as old as dirt to remember that movie. Anyway, Willard was the boy."

"That's right, the rat was Ben." Jovanic grinned. "Yeah, I'm old. But I'm your senior officer, so show a little more respect."

Coleman took a left off Palms onto Elmwood, which was a short block of a dozen or so homes on each side—a mélange of ages and styles, kempt integrated with neglect. As Coleman slowed, Jovanic started counting down house numbers.

The residence they were looking for, where Mouser lived with his brother's family, was set back from the street by a patchy front lawn that needed re-seeding. The small ranch style 1930s model was flanked by a remodeled two-story casa with a red tile roof and another Depression-era house in rundown condition.

Jovanic didn't say so out loud, but the white trimmed shutters against dove-grey stucco walls reminded him of the wimples the nuns wore with their habits at the convent school he had attended in early childhood, back in Chicago. A lifetime ago.

A neon yellow late model Camaro sat outside the single car garage, looking far too flashy for the little house. "Nice ride if you painted it a decent color," Coleman remarked as they cruised slowly past. "Looks like a goddamn banana."

Before exiting the Charger, Jovanic called in the license plate. The Camaro was registered to Robert Lewis Morgan, Jr., residing at this address. Morgan, presumably, was Mouser's brother. They also learned that Robert Morgan had a minor arrest record for misdemeanor battery—maybe street or bar fights—and drug use. He had not been in any trouble over the past three years. If Mouser was home and drove his own vehicle, it was not in the driveway, nor at the curb in front of the house.

Leaving their vehicle parked down the street, the two detectives walked back, watching their step. The roots of old growth trees planted at least forty years earlier had buckled the sidewalks into an ankle-busting obstacle course.

"Hope the little bastard's home," Coleman said.

Jovanic jabbed a warning finger at him. "Keep it chill, Randy. Try to establish rapport. We don't jack him up unless we have to."

The front door of Robert Morgan's residence stood wide open. As they advanced up the front walk, raised voices reached them from deep inside the house, one high-pitched, female, the other deep, male.

The detectives exchanged a quick glance and a nod. Jovanic removed the toothpick he'd been chewing and dropped it into his pocket. Shadowing his eyes with his hand, he peered through the screen into the tiny living room. From what he could see, it was unoccupied. After unsnapping his holster, he rapped on the door frame, then stood back, hand lightly resting on his weapon in case the argument inside escalated. Coleman stepped to one side in the same position, mirroring his actions.

The female voice got a whole lot louder, spewing a barrage of angry-sounding Spanish. Jovanic knocked harder against the metal frame and called out in a loud voice, "Hello?"

For a moment the voices went silent. Then the man yelled, "What?"

Jovanic knocked again, saying nothing.

A man entered the room, shirtless and barefoot, wearing jeans. Around five-ten, late twenties, dark hair shaved close to his skull. Wooden tribal gauge earrings made huge holes in his earlobes. A match for the DMV photo they had viewed on Coleman's mobile phone. Under tattoos that extended from shoulder to wrist, well-defined muscles said he pumped iron pretty hard. A fire-breathing dragon curled around one arm, a skull's red eyes glowered from the other.

"Robert Morgan?" Jovanic asked.

"Who wants to know?"

"I'm Joel and this is Randy. We're detectives with LAPD."

Morgan pushed the screen door halfway open and stood in the frame, scratching the sprig of hair on his trim belly. He glared at them with suspicion. "*Joel and Randy?*' Don't sound like any cops I ever met."

"It's just a friendly visit. Is Mouser here?"

"What do you want with Mouser?" Morgan glared at them, narrow-eyed. "What's he done?"

"Nothing that we know of. We'd like to talk to him about his girlfriend, Angel." Jovanic noted the immediate shift in the younger man's expression.

"He's not here."

"Where is he?"

"Gone surfing, then he'll hang with his buddies. Won't be back till late."

"Okay, we can come back. But as long as we're here, maybe we could ask you a few questions. Would you mind if we came in?"

Shaking his head, Morgan started to pull the screen door closed. "I'm kinda busy—" As if to back him up, a baby began to howl from somewhere at the rear of the house, followed by a woman shouting, "Get back here, Bobby, you need to help me."

Morgan twisted his head toward and yelled, "Shut up!" He turned back to the men on his porch. "Mouser's a good kid. You stay away from him."

Coleman stepped up. "If he hasn't done anything, what are you worried about?"

"I know how you assholes are. He doesn't *have* to do anything. You'll find something to pin on him."

"Sounds like you've been through the system, Robert," Coleman said. "That's a pretty good size chip on your shoulder."

"You just leave us the fuck alone."

"We don't want to hassle you," Jovanic said. "Your brother's not in any trouble with us."

"Then why are you here?"

Jovanic, sensing that Morgan's belligerence had deflated, modulated his manner, hoping to get something useful before they were forced to leave. At this point, they didn't have anything they could use to take him to the station. "We're just looking for some information. Maybe you could tell me what you were doing around one o'clock this morning."

After a moment's hesitation, Morgan went for nonchalance. "I was in bed with my old lady, bangin' her brains out."

"Yeah? You weren't out driving around Venice?"

"Why would I, when I got a sweet piece of ass keeping my bed warm?"

"Robert." The woman's rising pitch had the whine of a dentist's drill. "I *tole* you I need—"

Jovanic, who was several inches taller than Morgan, could see over his shoulder when she appeared in the kitchen doorway. Five-two if she stood on tiptoes, she had the clear skin and prettiness of youth. With hands balled on hips, she marched over and pushed in front of Morgan. The glare she turned on Jovanic and Coleman had the ferocity of a two-hundred-pound gorilla.

"The fuck is going on?" she challenged them.

Morgan flicked a glance down at her. "Cops."

"No shit, Sherlock. Like I can't see that?" She twitched the glossy black hair over her shoulder and cocked her chin at the detectives. "What you want?"

"What's your name, ma'am?" Randy Coleman asked.

She gave a shriek of laughter. "*Ma'am?* Are you fucking kidding me? *Seriously?*"

"Shut up, Ari." The lack of force with which Robert Morgan spoke confirmed who was in charge of this household. "Her name's Ariceli Lopez."

"*You* shut the fuck up, Bobby. I can talk for myself."

Ariceli Lopez was wearing a pair of skimpy cutoffs with a wife beater T-shirt emblazoned across ample breasts with the words "If I had balls, they'd be bigger than yours." Jovanic had an uneasy feeling that the statement was true.

"They're asking about Mouser," Robert Morgan told her, with a look that relayed a private message.

"It'd be easier if we stepped inside," Jovanic said, not giving Lopez space to respond. He kept a grasp on the edge of the screen door, holding it open. "Unless you don't care if your neighbors know your business."

Morgan hesitated, then pushed the screen door wider and stepped back, pulling the suddenly acquiescent Lopez with him. "Hurry it up, okay? I gotta be to work by five."

They caravanned through the living room, which was dominated by a playpen and an assortment of toys littering the floor, and into the kitchen. Robert Morgan shoved a highchair back from the old-fashioned metal-trimmed table. The men took a seat, Ariceli Lopez leaned against the sink, her arms folded in belligerence.

Jovanic sat back in his chair, careful to keep his arms off the pink speckled Formica tabletop, which was coated with grape jelly and smeared baby food. Coleman wasn't quick enough and got jelly on his perfectly pressed coat sleeve. Lopez, looking amused, watched him rub at it, but didn't offer him anything to clean it. His flushed neck said he was too embarrassed to ask.

"What kind of work do you do, Mr. Morgan?" Jovanic asked conversationally once they got settled.

Robert Morgan crossed his arms and leaned back in his chair, tilting the front legs off the floor. "Inkslinger."

"You work at a studio?"

"Dragon House."

"That the place over on Venice?"

"Yeah."

"That's a nice piece you've got." Jovanic nodded at his arm, where a skull peered out of skillfully inked torn flesh. "Done at your studio?"

Morgan, trying not to look pleased at the compliment, nodded. "My boss did it. He's fucking amazing."

"And he would be—?"

"Name's Viper."

"You're right, he does great work. I've been thinking about getting some work done myself. Maybe I'll stop by."

"Yeah, you do that."

"Viper won't ink a cop," Ariceli interjected. She picked up a pack of cigarettes from the counter and lit up, expertly blowing smoke upward from the corner of her mouth. "He hates cops."

Jovanic showed her a thin smile. "But we're so lovable."

She snorted scorn. He turned back to Robert Morgan. "I expect you heard, one of your competitors up the street had an unfortunate fire the other night."

Morgan dropped his chair back up onto all four legs. His eyes tightened to slits. "*That's* why you're here?"

"No. But as long as we're talking about it, did you know the guy who died?"

"Travis? Yeah, I knew him. Used to work for us. We taught that little fucktard everything he knew, then he stole our clients and opened his own studio." Morgan seemed to remember who he was talking to and hurried to add, "But that don't mean we torched his shit, if that's what you're thinking."

"We're not thinking anything, Robert. Remember, we're just gathering information. So, how long have you worked for Viper?"

Morgan closed his eyes, his brow furrowed as he counted back in his head, then opened them again. "Around eleven years."

"You must have started right out of high school."

"Yeah."

"Does Mouser work there, too?"

"I told you, leave my little brother out of this. He surfs and he goes to school. That's all."

"What's he studying?"

Morgan sat up a little straighter and Jovanic could see the pride in his younger sibling. "He's gonna be a architect. Gonna make somethin' out of himself."

Jovanic glanced over at Ariceli, who was still standing at the sink, her full ripe lips pursed. The pungent aroma of her cigarette smoke curled into his nose and he allowed himself the luxury of enjoying it. For the past couple years since quitting, he had satisfied his oral need with toothpicks. Not much of a substitute.

"How long have Mouser and Angel been dating?" he asked Ariceli, drawing her into the conversation.

Considering him through eyelids lowered to half mast, she shrugged. "A long time."

"How long is that?"

"I dunno, maybe a couple years."

"And they both live here with you?"

"She didn't live here all that long."

"Okay, how long has she lived with you?"

"A few months. She helped with the kids."

Jovanic noted the young woman's use of the past tense. It confirmed what he suspected: these people knew that Angel would not be helping with the kids any longer.

"Where *is* Angel?" Jovanic asked.

"She didn't come back last night," Ariceli countered.

"Is that unusual?"

"Uh, I guess."

"Any idea where she might be?"

"Nope."

"Are you worried about her?"

Ariceli tossed her head. "Who has time to worry? I been too busy running after the kids by myself all day."

"When did you last see her?" Coleman asked.

Now it was his turn to get the evil eye turned on him. "Why?" Ariceli snapped. "What's up anyway? She get herself in trouble?"

"How about you just answer the question, Ms. Lopez, and we'll get out of your hair?" Coleman snapped back.

Seeing another teachable moment for the younger detective, Jovanic discreetly kicked his partner under the table. Being the hard ass worked better when dealing with extreme situations, like "Drop the gun or I'll shoot you." He had learned the hard way over the years that it was a greater strength to find a way to defuse a witness's anger and turn him or her into someone willing to cooperate.

From the bedroom, the baby started screaming again. Ariceli turned to Morgan. "Bobby, go see what's going on. Sounds like little Bobby's poking the baby's eye out or something."

Without a word, Robert Morgan slid off his chair and disappeared from the room. The bedroom door slammed behind him. There was a yelp from an older child, and a moment later the baby quieted. Ariceli leered at Jovanic from under her lashes and blew him a kiss. "You know, you're kinda hot in a grandpa kinda way. Are you the good cop or the bad cop?"

Wincing—he wasn't *that* old—Jovanic smiled back at her. "We take turns. So, while it's my turn to be the good cop, why don't you tell me when you last saw Angel."

"I'd rather play bad cop with you. I be the bad girl, you can cuff me." She pointed at Coleman. "It'd be different if babyface wasn't here, huh, sweetie?"

When Jovanic failed to respond, she showed him the pink tip of her tongue. "Aw, you're no fun. Angel left outta here last night around nine."

"Did she leave by herself, or did someone pick her up? Or maybe Bobby took her somewhere?"

Ariceli began to look a little uneasy. "Why are you asking all these questions?"

"Is there some reason you don't want to tell us?" Jovanic added a small show of force. "Maybe we should take this conversation to the station."

"Hey, I didn't do nothing wrong. You can't make me go to the police station. I know my rights."

She was right, but that didn't mean he couldn't bluff.

"Since you seem to be the last person here who saw Angel, you're a material witness. So, yes, we *could* make you go to the station." He softened his tone. "But you've got the kids and Bobby needs to get to work. Come on, Ariceli, we're not interested in making things hard on you, so why don't you just tell us, who took Angel last night?"

She stubbed out her cigarette in the sink and ran water over the butt. "If I tell you that, will you leave us the hell alone?"

"Try me."

She showed Jovanic a pout and hesitated. The silence drew out until at length, she made up her mind. "Big Carl from the studio came and got her."

"What about Bobby? Did he go with them?"

"No; he was here, he was right here with me all night." She glanced to the left, and Jovanic got the impression she was lying.

"We'll need you to write out a statement—what you've just told us."

"What the hell? You said—"

"If you'd rather come to the station, you can come in tomorrow. Do you need a ride?"

"No, I don't fucking need a ride. Fine, I'll write it, but you better be getting' the hell out of here two seconds after I'm done."

eighteen

Annabelle ran until she was out of breath. She ran so fast as she rounded the downward curve of the street that she tripped and before she was able to catch herself, went down on one knee. Before anyone could witness her embarrassment, she jumped to her feet, throwing a furtive glance around to confirm that no one had seen her fall.

Examining the grazed skin on her kneecap and the blood dribbling down her bare shin, Annabelle told herself she was lucky not to have landed on her face and split her lip or broken a tooth. It would have been a good excuse to cry, but she still couldn't do it. The tears were squeezing against her eyeballs so hard it felt like they were going to pop out of her head. But she had practiced not allowing herself to cry for so long that even when she had a good reason—and Annabelle thought your friend getting murdered was a pretty good reason—the tears had dried up and refused to cooperate.

Her therapist, Dr. Gold, had explained that she had something called post-traumatic stress. It was like when soldiers went to war and had to see and do terrible things. When they got home, they sometimes experienced flashbacks and thought they were still fighting in the war. Dr. Gold had worked with her for a few months because she kept getting really pissed off that she'd had no control over what had happened to her and the person she had witnessed getting murdered. Another murder of someone she'd cared about.

Sometimes it seemed like it all happened a really long time ago, like when her mother died. But other times it was as if it had only just happened. She hadn't slept at all last night. Angel's face kept floating in front of her eyes, even when she closed them. That helpless feeling billowed over her again and made her want to punch something.

Tyler's Coffee House was at least another half-mile down the hill. Annabelle limped as fast as she could, feeling like crap for being so bitchy and yelling at Claudia. She knew Claudia was right. Ever since she'd met up with Angel, it felt like she had lost all the ground she had gained. If she could let herself admit it, getting the sugar skull tattoo had been a way to hang on to that part of her she'd sworn to leave behind.

The rebel in her hadn't wanted to totally give up the old Annabelle, even though that girl had gotten her into some serious shit. Still, she must have changed *some* because when Crash offered her the shot of tequila, she had actually considered refusing it and telling him to just take her back home.

Annabelle pulled open Tyler's front door and went straight to the restroom at the back of the café. Luckily it was unoccupied. The bleeding had already stopped, but her knee burned like someone held a lit match to it. She wet a paper towel in the sink and dabbed at the scrape, then washed the sticky trickle of blood off her leg and dropped the stained towel into the overflowing trash bin.

Stepping back into the crowded coffee house, her anxious gaze darted over the line of customers at the counter and the people seated against the side window plugged into their tablets and phones. The person she had come to meet had not yet arrived. She could have gone at a slower pace and saved herself the road rash.

Taking her place at the end of the line, Annabelle pulled her phone out of her pocket. The touch of the slick pink plastic case made her shiver.

She imagined Angel holding it, calling her the night Claudia had refused to wake her. Annabelle was convinced she had jinxed her friend. For punishment, she pinched her arm hard, using her fingernails for extra bite. The pain made her feel a little better and took her mind off her knee.

Aside from the time and date, her phone's screen remained blank. No new messages or texts. Joel had gotten it back for her from the coroner's investigator. Annabelle had heard Claudia tease him about the investigator being his old girlfriend, and that's how come he had gotten the phone back for her so fast. She didn't care why or how he had gotten it. Being without her phone had been excruciating, but now that she had it back, it felt like it wasn't hers anymore. Waiting for the barista to make her drink, she mused on whether she could talk her dad into replacing it with a new one.

She had just picked up her Vanilla Spice Latté when the front door opened and a young dude entered. Annabelle caught her breath. Dark golden tan, white-blonde hair falling over his forehead, dark glasses. He wore a sun-faded T-shirt, knee-length Hawaiian print surfer shorts and sandals. The quintessential Surfer Boy. He caught her eye across the café and she gave him a small wave. He nodded acknowledgment and threaded his way between the tables toward her.

Monroe Simon Morgan, AKA Mouser, said, "Let's grab a seat in back."

Fearing that there was a special place reserved in hell for girls whose hearts fluttered over their dead friend's boyfriend, Annabelle got her drink and followed him. She couldn't help it, he was *that* hot.

Luck was with them. Mouser snagged them a vacant spot against the wall. The painted surfboard mounted behind the black leather loveseat seemed an appropriate touch.

When he had called Annabelle, urgently asking to meet with her, she'd invited him to Claudia's, but he went all cloak and dagger, insisting on meeting away from the house. Since she didn't have wheels, the best she could come up with was Tyler's.

He had warned her not to tell anyone where she was going, which was why she had tried to sneak out without Claudia knowing. She vowed to be extra nice when she got back home, and make up for being such a bitch.

Annabelle took a sip of her drink and set it on the low table in front of the loveseat, not knowing how to get the conversation started. "Sorry about Angel," she mumbled.

"She shouldn't have dissed Viper." Mouser's low voice trembled.

Up close, when he removed his shades, Annabelle could see that his eyes were red-rimmed. She hoped it was because it meant he had cared about Angel and not that he'd been blazing a bowl. "Jamie said it was because of that guy—the one who got killed in that fire."

His face darkened. "Jamie. That skank. It's *her* fault Angel's dead."

"What are you talking about?"

"She's jealous of Angel. She ratted her out to Viper. My brother said so."

"He told you that?"

"Naw, I heard him telling his lady. My room is right next to theirs and the walls are like plastic wrap. I can hear him and Ariceli breathing."

"Wait. You think Angel is dead—because of something *Jamie* said?" Annabelle felt a guilty thrill of relief as she mentally shifted the blame from herself over to Jamie.

"She's the one who told Viper that Angel wasn't doing what he told her to."

"So, he *killed* her?"

Mouser fidgeted uncomfortably. "Could you keep it down?"

"You're saying he kills people?" Annabelle stage whispered.

"All I'm saying is, when Viper tells you to do something, you better friggin' do it."

"What—what did he do to her?" Claudia had been so freaked about it, she had refused to give Annabelle the details.

"My brother wouldn't tell me what happened, but like I said, I heard him through the wall. He kept saying it made him sick and he didn't want any part of it. That's *crazy.*"

"Why's it crazy?"

"'Cause, dude, Viper's like, his idol. You'd think he was Bobby's dad."

"Don't you have a dad?"

"Yeah, but he's a lifer. I go see him once in a while, but he doesn't like me seeing him in lockup. Bobby never goes. He hates the dude."

Annabelle tried to bring him back on track. "So, now Bobby totally doesn't like Viper anymore because of Angel?"

"I dunno. Just, he was, like, really upset."

"The cops talked to Jamie. They made her go to the police station."

Mouser stared at her. "If Viper hears that, she's toast."

"She didn't tell them anything. But after the cops let her go, she went to stay with this lady lawyer. I don't see how Viper can find that out."

"Viper *always* finds out."

"I'm pretty sure she didn't tell them anything. Anyway, how's he gonna find out, unless you tell him?"

"I *oughta* tell him—payback for ratting out Angel."

"You can't do that."

"Why not?"

"Because if he kills her, it would be your fault."

"I don't give a shit what happens to her. She deserves it."

After that gloomy pronouncement, Mouser fell silent and chewed on his lower lip until Annabelle began to feel uncomfortable. Then he said,

"Angel told me how she met up with you on the boardwalk. She was real happy about seeing you again."

Mouser swiped a hand across his face. Apparently, *he* didn't have any trouble releasing his tears. He leaned down and grabbed the napkin under Annabelle's drink, blew his nose on it. "This is totally fucked up. She was my chick for years, you know?"

"Yeah, it sucks." Angel must have already had Annabelle's phone in her pocket, ready to return to her. "You've gotta tell the cops what you just told me."

"Angel told me you live with a cop. That's why I wanted to talk to you."

"I'm staying at his girlfriend's house for the summer and he lives with her."

"Close enough. You tell him. Just leave my name out of it."

"No way. You have to tell him yourself."

Mouser stared at her in horror. "Dude, are you psycho? There's no way I can talk to the cops myself."

"You *have* to. When you tell someone something and then they tell someone else what you said, they can't use it to arrest the dude. It's called 'hearsay.' I heard Joel talking about it."

"Who's Joel?"

"The cop who lives with my friend. He's a homicide detective. He could make Viper pay for what he did."

Mouser shook his head with some force. "I'm not telling them jack shit. I don't need Viper sending Big Carl after me or Bobby."

"Then why are you even bothering to say anything?"

Mouser hesitated for a long moment, looking as though he was still trying to work out the answer for himself. "Bobby was saying Viper got all coked up and raging last night. He got Angel over there and beat her down like a fucking *dog*." He stared at his hands, which were twisting the napkin into a ragged mess.

"What about your brother and Big Carl? Why didn't they stop him?"

Mouser ignored Annabelle's question. "I guess he fucked her up more than he meant to and she bit the big one. He told Bobby and Carl to ditch her in some trashcan down at the beach."

Annabelle stared at him, aghast. "A *trashcan?* Are you serious?"

Claudia had withheld that piece of information from her. Did she think she was a child? Didn't she deserve to know the truth? The omission made her burn with rage. "You can't fucking let him get away with that."

"I don't *want* him to get away with it, but I can't go to the cops. What if he hurt my brother, or the kids?"

"Okay," Annabelle said, though she was doubtful Mouser's plan would work. "I'll tell Joel for you. But I don't think it'll do any good. He's gonna want to talk to you if you really know anything. Or maybe you're just guessing about it?"

"It's pretty obvious, isn't it?" Mouser's voice had started to rise. He lowered it again to a hiss. "Even if I didn't hear what Bobby told Ariceli, everyone down at the studio knows Viper was pissed at Angel. Big Carl comes to get her. The next day she's dead. What else do they need?"

"I think that's what they call circum—um—circumstantial evidence," Annabelle said, proud of herself for pulling the legal term out of the air. "They have to get something that proves Viper did it. *Bobby* should talk to Joel if he saw it happen."

Mouser withered her with a look that told her he thought she was a stupid dork. "You think Bobby wants to get fucked up or killed? Or his family? You don't get who this guy is, do you?"

She got it, crystal clear. But she couldn't very well tell him she had faced a killer before. He would never believe her. "Who else knows?" she asked. "Someone who might not be scared to talk about it?"

Mouser considered her question, nodding, and Annabelle thought she had redeemed herself a little. "You know, there's this guy been hanging around the studio. He's a writer, says he's writing an article about 'the world of tattoo' or some shit. He's been there for days and he's always asking questions. I mean, nobody's gonna tell him anything important, but you never know. Tell the cop to talk to him."

"You don't care if Viper goes after this guy?"

He looked at her with an expression of bafflement. "Why should I care? I don't even know him. He's just some reporter asshole."

"What's his name?"

"Shane. Just don't say I told you anything." Mouser glanced around, his eyes darting from one patron to the next, as if there might be a spy for Viper in the coffee house. He lowered his voice another notch. "If you tell them anything about me, I'll say you're lying."

Annabelle lifted her chin, less impressed with him after their conversation. "That sounds kind of chickenshit," she said with spirit. "Angel was your girlfriend, but you let him pass her around to his friends. How could you do that?" Her voice wobbled. "She was barely sixteen."

Mouser jumped up off the love seat, putting Annabelle's latté in danger of spilling. He glared down at her. "Just forget I ever called you, okay?"

nineteen

"...thirty-seven year-old mother of two was shot at close range in her Cheviot Hills home. There was no sign of forced entry, and police believe the victim may have known her attacker. The woman's body was discovered by her teenaged children when they arrived home from school..."

Claudia pointed the remote at the small flat screen TV on the kitchen counter and muted the news. With Angel's death and Travis Navarette's, she had heard enough about murder to last a year. Besides, it was past five and she needed to think about dinner.

She was rinsing a package of chicken breasts in the sink when the back door opened. She turned, surprised when it was Joel who entered, not Annabelle, whom she had been expecting.

"You're home early." She smiled with pleasure. When he was working a fresh homicide, it was rare that he came home at a decent hour.

His fatigue-shadowed eyes flicked to the TV, where police crime scene tape fluttered around an upscale house. "What's that?"

"Poor kids found their mom shot to death. No suspects. Cheviot Hills—not the kind of neighborhood where those things happen."

"There's no such thing anymore." Joel laid his briefcase on the breakfast table and snapped it open. Cheviot Hills was outside of Pacific Division's coverage area, and he had two homicides of his own on his hands. "I have some handwriting for you to look at." He took out some sheets of notebook paper. "It's a statement. I just need to know whether you think the person who wrote it is telling the truth."

Claudia wiped her hands on a dish towel and slid into the breakfast nook. "Are you home for the night?" She accepted the two pages he handed her and laid them side by side on the table, glancing through them, getting a first impression of the handwriting.

"Yeah. Randy's going to the station for a while. He wanted to bring the murder books up to date and write some reports before they get away from him. Nothing else we can do until tomorrow." Jovanic pointed to the papers in front of Claudia. "So?"

"Just so I'm clear, you don't want a personality profile? You just want to know whether she's lying—assuming this is a 'she'?"

Jovanic was still wearing his suit coat, but had loosened his tie. His shirt was open at the neck, tempting her to unbutton the rest of it and slip her hands inside. She kept her thoughts to herself as he cracked open a beer and dropped into the seat across from her.

"I already know everything I need to know about her personality. She's a nasty little piece of work who likes to run the show."

Setting aside her desire to lead him up to the bedroom, Claudia focused on the handwriting "I can see that. I would expect her to be diagnosed with Narcissistic Personality Disorder. As far as honesty goes, I can tell you right now, she doesn't begin to know the meaning of the word, let alone apply it to herself."

Jovanic told her then that upon leaving the Morgan house he had requested a criminal background check onAriceli Lopez. She was twenty-two, older than she looked. She had a sealed juvenile record and had been arrested twice for shoplifting when she was eighteen, twice more for domestic abuse over the ensuing year. Lopez had spent a week in the

Twin Towers Women's County Jail when she was unable to make bail. That sounded interesting.

From her handwriting, Claudia had already concluded that she was the type who would habitually attract the wrong sort of man into her life. It wouldn't surprise her to hear that the writer had been on the receiving end of the domestic abuse and then turned on her attacker. She would not be the first young woman Claudia knew of who had been jailed under those circumstances. Then again, maybe Ariceli was just an abuser herself. Her handwriting suggested that either or both could be true.

Getting up, Claudia riffled through the junk drawer for a hand magnifier and took it to the table. She held it over the lined paper Ariceli had torn out of a spiral-bound notebook and took a closer look at the ink line—the ductus—which often provided important clues that could not be seen with the naked eye.

The writing was printed rather than cursive—fewer and fewer public schools had taught cursive handwriting over the past years. Ariceli had probably been in one of those classes that did not bother with penmanship training.

The printing was large and rounded, the words crowded close together. Some letters butted up against each other with hook-like forms intruding into many of the vowel letters—forms that were often found in the handwritings of habitual liars. Claudia continued to pore over the statement, not reading the words, but letting her eyes relax and absorb the patterns created by the writing and the spaces between words and lines.

Coming to an area with extra-large spaces between words, she stopped and read what it said:

So Angel was   fine   when she left out of here. I don't know anything about what happened to her after that.

The slant of the words "I don't know anything" changed from upright to leaning to the left. Both the additional spaces and the altered slant told Claudia that something was amiss with the emotion behind those sentences. The left slant in a writing that was generally upright indicated that the writer wasn't being truthful in what she wrote.

While Joel changed his clothes, Claudia took the sample into her office and made a photocopy. She placed the original in a special acid-free mylar sleeve to preserve it. Using a yellow highlighter on the copy, she marked the parts of the statement she believed to be false.

Looking more relaxed in shorts and a T-shirt, Joel came up behind her. Her body molded itself into the circle of his arms. They tightened around her, making her feel safe and loved.

Claudia wanted to soak up every second of this unexpected interlude. But he had two homicides to solve. So, after a lingering kiss, they returned to the kitchen together and took their places at the breakfast nook.

She pointed out the words she had highlighted on the copy of Ariceli Lopez' statement. "See how the word 'fine' is isolated from the words around it? She had to stop and think about it before she wrote it and before she went on to the next words. If it was true, and she knew Angel was 'fine' when she left the house, she could have continued writing without the pause that created the extra spaces.

"And if the next part were true, where she writes, 'I don't know what happened to her after that,' the slant would have continued in the same direction. Again, it's because she had to pause and think of the lie that she was about to write. The slant changed to an unnatural one for her because her brain didn't want to tell the lie."

"So, that might mean either Big Carl roughed her up before he took her, or she wasn't fine because she knew something bad was going to happen and she was scared, maybe resisted going with him."

"Scared, and with good reason."

"Too bad we couldn't get anything out of the Parker girl," Joel said. "By the way, how's the kid doing?"

"She was pretty upset after we got home from the station. She went for a walk." Claudia glanced at the clock and saw that more than an hour had passed since Annabelle left. "She should have been back by now. I'll give her a call. Since you were nice enough to get her phone back, she just might answer."

Jovanic let loose a tired sigh. "I don't remember being such a pain in the ass when I was her age."

Claudia grinned. "I wonder if your mom would remember it the same way."

"Probably not."

"This situation with Angel has brought back everything that happened last year at the Sorensen Academy. She started having PTSD episodes again."

Jovanic opened his mouth to reply, then stopped, his ear cocked toward the back door. Footsteps sounded on the back stairs. The door opened and Annabelle entered. When she saw them at the table she came to an abrupt halt.

"Oh, cool, you're here," she said to Joel.

Claudia and Joel glanced at each other in surprise. He and Annabelle had arrived at an uneasy truce some time ago, but it wasn't often she volunteered to speak to him. Cops were not on her A-list, even the one who lived with the person she loved most, next to her father.

"Why are you limping?" Claudia asked, then she spotted the abrasion. "What happened to your knee?"

"I tripped. No biggie."

"It looks like a pretty nasty scrape. Go and put some ointment and a band-aid on it."

"I will, but I have to talk to Joel first."

"Have a seat," Jovanic said. "What's up?"

While Annabelle grabbed a soda from the fridge, Claudia folded the statement they had been discussing and returned it to its folder, hiding it from the girl's curious stare. She slid over to make room and Annabelle settled herself in the breakfast nook beside her.

"I met up with Angel's boyfriend, Mouser, at Tyler's," she began, by way of explanation. Beginning with Mouser's assertion that Jamie's betrayal was the reason for Angel's death, Annabelle launched into an account of her encounter with Mouser. She related everything she could remember about the conversation he had overhead between his brother and Ariceli Lopez.

"I told him *you* had to talk to Bobby," she finished up, taking a long drink of soda before looking over at Jovanic. "Because you can't use hearsay—right?"

Jovanic looked impressed. "You got it, kiddo. Is there anything else, or is that everything?"

"That's pretty much it. Are you gonna go talk to Shane, the writer guy?"

"I'll be talking to everyone."

"I bet they won't talk to you. They're all scared of that Viper dude."

"Thanks, Annabelle. You did a great detective job. I'll take it from here."

Annabelle pouted. "So, I did good, but now you want me to butt out?"

"Well, I might put it a little more elegantly, but the fact is, I don't want you anywhere near any of these people. Claudia and I want to keep you safe."

"That's for sure," Claudia chimed in. "Your job is to be fifteen years old, not some kind of avenger."

"But Angel was my friend. I could help—"

Jovanic interrupted, "Listen to me, Annabelle. Next time Mouser calls you, I want you to tell him you can't meet him. With somebody like Viper involved, it's just too dangerous. I don't want you getting hurt again."

"Mouser's not gonna call me again. He's way pissed."

"Well, in case he does, just let me know. I'll handle it."

"Fine."

The offhand way Annabelle said it made Claudia nervous. It was unlike her to give up without an argument. She was not convinced that the message was getting through to the girl. "Annabelle, you have to trust us on this," she said.

"Why? Because Angel ended up all dead in the garbage?"

Claudia couldn't hold back her shocked gasp. She could see from Jovanic's face that Annabelle's words had taken him aback, too. "How did you—"

"Mouser told me that, too. Why didn't *you* tell me?"

Jovanic fixed her with a stern glare. "Listen up, Annabelle, and listen good. That's not something we're releasing to the news. It's important that you don't repeat it to anyone. Do you understand me?"

"I don't repeat stuff when I'm not supposed to. I'm not a gossip girl."

"I know you're not. I'm just saying, this is something we need to keep under wraps. Don't even tell Monica."

"Duh. As if."

Claudia covered the girl's hand with her own. "Annabelle, I didn't want you to know about that. The fact that she was killed is enough. You don't have to hear all the details."

"Yes, I do! Otherwise, I just keep imagining what that crazy ass dude did to her, and that's even worse."

"Haven't you been exposed to enough violence?"

Jovanic glanced over at Claudia, but he spoke to Annabelle. "She was strangled."

"Joel," Claudia protested.

"How?"

"With his bare hands."

The color drained from Annabelle's face. She had to be remembering the strangulation murder she had witnessed. Claudia wished Jovanic had kept that from her. What good could it do?

Annabelle was silent for a long moment. She swallowed hard. "Mouser heard his brother say Viper kicked the shit—I mean the crap—out of her. Is it true?"

"Yes, it's true."

She stood up. "Thanks for telling me. I'm gonna go band-aid my knee."

twenty

Thursday morning

The homicide team met for breakfast at The Firehouse on Rose, a cop-friendly restaurant where they knew the waitresses wouldn't spit in their coffee. They'd been coming there so long, they had their own booth along the wall, near the back.

Without bothering to peruse the menu, RJ Scott ordered her usual breakfast BLT. Health-conscious Randy Coleman wanted the Bodybuilder—egg whites, oatmeal, and a buffalo patty. Rationalizing that he needed to fortify himself for the long day ahead, Jovanic ordered a breakfast burrito with the works, and Huey Hardcastle, sour-faced, asked for a tofu scramble.

"My wife would freak if I ate that," Hardcastle groused about Jovanic's order as the waitress left them. "She's always nagging about my cholesterol."

"What, she's got a nanny cam hidden in your lapel?" Scott wisecracked. "You need mommy to order for you?"

Coleman scowled at him. "Hey, Baby Huey, maybe if you got your ass to the gym once in a while, your wife wouldn't have to worry about those extra pounds you've been piling on."

"Yeah, Huey. A few pushups, pump a little iron—" Jovanic didn't smile when he said it. Lately, Hardcastle had been finding excuses to do as little work as possible. Something was going on with him. He had his suspicions, and he would have to get to the bottom of it when he had time to breathe again. That was the down side of being lead detective.

"Forget I said anything," Hardcastle muttered, burying his face in his coffee mug.

Jovanic had been up since before dawn. He counted himself lucky to have snagged four hours of sleep after a scorching session of lovemaking, which he had to admit was worth the lack of zzzzs. Long before Claudia woke, he had dragged himself out of bed and gone to the station to go over the two murder books and make plans for the day's activities.

Their conversation meandered desultorily while they waited for the food to arrive. RJ Scott's family was planning a big barbecue for her parents' 50th anniversary. Hardcastle made a point that his department vehicle needed to be serviced—it had to be done on a strict schedule for insurance purposes. Jovanic made himself a private note to follow up and make sure it wasn't just another excuse for him flaking.

The waitress brought out their food. Coleman's cooled while he took a phone call. The mother of one of his cold cases called him every few months, demanding to know whether any progress had been made in finding her son's killer. There had not, but he grabbed an empty booth where he could speak with her in private.

Once Coleman rejoined them, Jovanic called the meeting to order. "Listen up, guys. You are not gonna believe what I got last night."

"We don't need to hear about your sex life," Hardcastle cracked.

Jovanic shot him an acid look that made the other detective shut up and shove a forkful of scrambled egg white into his mouth. "Turns out our 'angel in the dumpster's' boyfriend spilled his guts to our young houseguest. Some good stuff."

That caught their attention. He brought them up to date on what Annabelle had told him and Claudia. "I talked to the ME this morning," he added. "They were able to get a partial print off the body at the scene. They're going to try again at the morgue, but I don't want to wait to see if that works."

Jovanic had been on the phone early with a request for the post mortem on both Travis Navarette and Angela Tedesco to take place at the same time—first thing tomorrow morning. As long as nothing more urgent came in, the medical examiner had promised to accommodate him.

First, though, he planned to re-interview Robert Morgan and talk to the other guy both Annabelle and Jack Solis had told him about—Big Carl. If he had a snowball's chance of getting anything from him, it meant tackling Carl away from Viper's tattoo parlor.

Jovanic gave RJ Scott her assignment for the day: "You and Randy follow up on the Travis Navarette case. See if LAFD has anything new yet. Collect whatever evidence you can find. I'll go back and talk to Jacqueline Solis, get a description of this Big Carl character."

Hardcastle, chewing on a piece of wheat toast, no butter, wanted to know what he was doing.

"I want you to sit on Dragon House, see who comes and goes. I'll call you when I get a description of Big Carl. If he goes out for lunch or whatever, get his license plate and follow him. Call it in and get an address. He's Viper's muscle. He's gotta have a record. Once we know what we've got on him, we can find his weak spot and squeeze his balls."

Jovanic rubbed the heels of his hands over his eyes. He should have remembered to stick some Visine in his pocket to wash out the grit. The few hours of shuteye he'd gotten was not enough to make up for the deprivation of the last few nights.

"This journalist—Shane something—we need to locate him; see if he's got any intel. Huey, see what you can dig up. You can do it while you're surveilling the tattoo parlor."

"Who's he write for?"

Jovanic stared him down. "That's *your* assignment, Huey. Find out who he is, who he writes for, where he stays. 'Shane' isn't all that common a name." He turned to Scott. "Any luck locating Navarette's next of kin yet?"

She pushed away her empty plate and shook her head. "Nothing so far. Maybe he didn't have anyone. I'll keep digging. If there's someone, I'll find them."

"We know Angel and Travis were connected, and we know why—Viper wanted to set up Travis for underage sex. We need something that ties him to the arson and the homicide. Randy, you talk to the fire investigator. Why'd they torch the place? Was it because of what Bobby Morgan told us—that Travis was the competition after Viper trained him, and Viper wanted revenge? Or was the Molotov Cocktail a cover-up for something else?"

"You know he did it to send a message to the other parlors," Coleman said. "'Don't fuck with Viper's business.'"

"We've never been able to make anything stick to that asshole before," Hardcastle said. "He always alibis out."

"Nobody died before," Jovanic said. "The stakes are higher now. Somebody's going to screw up, and when they do, we'll be there."

"The autopsies are tomorrow morning?" Coleman confirmed. "Think the ME can tell whether the vic died in the fire, or was already dead?"

"I'm not looking forward to that post," Hardcastle said. "Crispy critters gross me out."

"Just don't eat breakfast first," RJ needled him. "Less cookies to toss."

"Okay kids, knock it off." Jovanic mopped up the last of the ketchup on his plate with O'Brien potatoes. "Anything else before we split up?"

The other three detectives shook their heads and Jovanic grabbed the bill. "This one's on me."

Jacqueline Solis was on her way out the door when Jovanic reached the staircase to her apartment. Her initial look of alarm at the large man ascending the stairs changed to one of recognition.

"Hey, Detective. What's up?"

As Jovanic neared her, he could hear the frantic barking of Rocco, the little Yorkie, inside. He came up the steps, forcing Solis to move backwards onto her small balcony. "I'll just take a moment of your time. When we spoke yesterday, you mentioned a friend of yours, Big Carl, who works at Dragon House."

"What about him?"

"What can you tell me about him? What does he look like?"

"Well, he's big, obviously, but not tall."

"How big would you say? Compared to me?"

Solis stepped back and sized him up. "You're tall, but Carl is just *huge*. I'd say he's about 5'8", but he's wide—not fat, just wiiiide. Time he came over here I was afraid he wouldn't fit through the door." She laughed. "Well, that's a slight exaggeration, but he comes by his nickname honestly. He's the size of a bus."

"So, maybe 250-300 pounds?"

"Yeah, somewhere in there."

Jovanic smiled and nodded, encouraging her to continue. "How about race? Black? White? Mexican?"

"None of the above. He's Samoan. Hey, look, I gotta run. I have an appointment."

"Thanks, Ms. Solis. I appreciate it." Jovanic started to move down the risers, then did what Claudia would have called his Columbo move. Turning around, he kept his back to the wall. "Is there *anything* else you can think of that might be helpful?"

Solis huffed her impatience and started down the stairs towards him. "You can't miss him, okay? Just look for the bus with the tribal tattoos on his face."

Randy Coleman dropped into his office chair across from Jovanic, notebook in hand. He pulled a cigarette out of his pocket and stuck it in his mouth.

"What the hell are you doing?" Jovanic asked. Smoking had not been allowed in the building for at least twenty years. Coleman removed it and held it out for Jovanic to see. "E-cig. You oughta try it. I can always tell when you're jonesing for a smoke."

Jovanic ignored the comment.

"Looks like the real thing. It's got the taste, the nicotine, water vapor looks like smoke. See, you get the smoking experience without all the bad shit."

"You sound like a commercial. Put it away before someone sees it and sends you to the time out corner, or whatever the hell they do in kindergarten these days."

"I know, old-timer." Coleman cracked his voice like a shaky old man. "Back in my day, we—"

"Fuck off, Randy," Jovanic interrupted him. "It's your shtick that's getting old. Do you have something for me, or are you just here to waste my time?"

"I've got something on our 'Angel in the dumpster.' Got potential, too."

"Let's have it."

"Remember the apartment building right across the alley from Harvey's?"

"Yeah?"

"The other night when they were canvassing, one of the uniforms talked to a woman who has a friend on the third floor. Seems the friend's ex has been stalking her, vandalizing her car. So, she picks herself up a surveillance kit—couple hundred bucks worth of camera, storage, timer."

Jovanic sat up straighter in his chair, a little zing of excitement buzzing through him as he guessed where his partner was going with his story. Coleman continued, "It's set up to record every night. She points it at the parking lot so she can catch the guy in the act. Instead…"

"She catches our guy?" Jovanic had nursed a faint hope of video *somewhere,* but this was far better than he had expected.

"Well…sort of," the change of Coleman's pitch dashed his hopes. Of course it couldn't be that easy.

"What does 'sort of' mean?"

"The woman's been out of town, got back this morning. She goes downstairs to see her friend for coffee, learns about the body in the dumpster. She freaks—"

"Does this woman have a name?" Jovanic interrupted, getting his pen ready.

"Yvonne Lee."

"Okay, go on."

"So, Lee goes back to her place and runs the video for Tuesday night. At one twenty-two, SUV pulls up by the dumpster and two dudes get out. Mutt and Jeff. Smaller dude opens the dumpster, other dude hauls something out of the back—according to the wit, you can't see what he's carrying, but it's big enough. They toss the package in the dumpster and drive off."

"The three car doors Dumpster Dave heard."

"Yeah—driver, passenger, back door. The body was in the backseat."

"Did Ms. Lee happen to get a license plate?"

"Last four digits." Coleman consulted his notebook. "4731."

"How clear were Mutt and Jeff?" Jovanic asked, rising from his desk. He grabbed his jacket, which was draped across the back of his chair and started to pull it on.

"Not clear enough for an ID, but Lee is copying us a thumb drive."

twentyone

Yvonne Lee, an Asian-American woman, led the two detectives into a second bedroom that had been converted to a home office. The first thing Jovanic noticed when they entered the room was a video camera on a short tripod. It stood at the window, which was ajar, pointed at the alley two stories below.

Lee was talking about her attempts to catch her boyfriend in the act of vandalizing her car. "This is the best idea I could come up with." She led them to the camera equipment. "I figured at least I could catch him going into the parking garage under the building—he has no business there anymore. This setup cost me three hundred bucks."

In her mid-thirties with translucent skin and smoky mascara ringing her eyes, she had the look of a fragile alabaster doll. But there was nothing fragile about the ice in her tone. "When I catch that bastard—and I will—I'll cut off his dick and feed it to him."

Jovanic winced. "You probably shouldn't make those kinds of statements in front of peace officers. It might be interpreted as a terrorist threat. You can go to jail for that."

Lee flashed him an impish grin. "Did that make your manhood shrivel, Detective? What were you expecting, a submissive little old Asian lady? I came to this country young enough to become Americanized."

"Well, I'm sorry about your boyfriend, but your video might help us catch a killer, so maybe that will make you feel better."

"Well, of course I'd be glad to help for that poor girl's sake. I can't believe how disgusting it was—the way those men tossed her in the trash like a sack of rotten potatoes." Yvonne Lee walked to the window as she spoke. She crooked her index finger and beckoned Jovanic to come and look.

He crouched to the level of the camera where the lens poked through the raised window opening. With his eye to the viewfinder, Jovanic found himself looking at the alleyway that passed between the edge of the parking lot behind Harvey's Market on one side, and the apartment building's garage on the other. Any vehicle driving along the alley would cross the path of the lens.

Lee handed him a thumb drive. "I copied the part from 1:30 to 2:00 a.m. I figured you'd want to see if anything else happened after they left."

"We appreciate that, Ms. Lee." Jovanic stepped aside and let Randy Coleman take his place at the camera.

"You know what? It took less than two minutes for them to dump that poor girl. If you didn't know what to look for, you'd think they were dropping off a piece of furniture or, or a rug—something that was too big for their own trash. People do it all the time—leave their crap in someone else's dumpster so they don't have to bother with it. Want me to show you what's on the drive?"

"That'd be great." Jovanic followed her to the glass and chrome computer desk. The monitor was bigger than the TV set he'd grown up with. The thought made him feel old and made him remember Ariceli Lopez's comment about him being a hot grandpa.

Lee plopped onto her chair and tucked a leg under her. She circled the mouse around and the screen came to life. The video was already on the screen, paused. "The website said the infrared would record up to 45 feet at night. You can look at the video on a smartphone, but I was at a conference and I was just too knocked out to check it when I got back to my room at night. Of course, I wouldn't have known what I was looking at anyway, until my neighbor told me."

With a few keyboard clicks, the video started playing. Despite the somewhat grainy quality, the security light on the garage opposite Yvonne Lee's building illuminated the alley well enough to display the shapes of some of the vehicles parked in the lot behind Harvey's. Still, to the casual observer, it would be a challenge identifying the make and model of the SUV that crawled into the frame.

The vehicle came to a halt a few feet from the trash dumpster. Jovanic asked Lee to stop the video. He pointed to the rear brake light. "Chevy," he said to Coleman, who had been a huge car buff long before it became his business to know cars.

"Yeah, it's a Tahoe, I'd bet my left nut on it."

Coleman had spoken in an undertone, but Lee turned and gave him a sharp look. "So, it's okay for you to talk about your nuts, but I can't talk about my ex-boyfriend's dick?"

Coleman blushed. "I apologize, ma'am. That was out of line."

"Oh, puhlease. Now you're insulting me with 'ma'am'?"

"Could you zoom in on the license plate?" Jovanic asked, drawing their attention back to the screen. The SUV was parked at a slight angle, cutting off part of the plate. On the Tahoe, the plate was on the rear bumper. As it was placed higher than on some vehicles, they were able to see the partial number: 4371.

After getting the go-ahead, Lee clicked on Play again. The front doors of the vehicle opened simultaneously on each side. "Stop there," Jovanic said. The vehicle had lifted noticeably when the man on the passenger side exited.

"The size of a bus" was how Jacqueline Solis had described Big Carl, the man who had picked up Angela Tedesco from Bobby Morgan's house on the night of her death. In the early morning shadows and from the distance of Yvonne Lee's third floor condo, Big Carl's features were indistinct. A small hat—maybe a pork pie—perched on his large head might later be used to identify him.

Standing behind Lee, Coleman nudged Jovanic with his elbow. He tipped his chin at the man who had climbed out of the driver's side, and was now frozen mid-stride on his way to the trash dumpster.

Jovanic gave a brief nod of acknowledgment that he had also recognized Robert Morgan. The same asshole who had claimed to be tucked into bed with Ariceli Lopez on the night Angel's body was dumped. That confirmed Mouser's information about the dumpster. The video might not be clear enough to convict him, but Morgan didn't have to know that when they brought him in and leaned on him.

Jovanic directed Yvonne Lee to advance the video a few seconds more. They watched Morgan glance around furtively. When he believed the coast was clear, he raised the lid of the dumpster while Big Carl was opening the back door of the SUV. Carl leaned inside.

It was over in a flash. Carl hauled the body out of the vehicle. He tossed it into the dumpster, as Lee had described—like a cast-off sack of potatoes, of no use to anyone.

Morgan suddenly looked toward the ground. He went into a crouch that took him out of sight for a few seconds.

"He dropped something," Coleman said.

Jovanic made a mental note to send a fingerprint tech back out and check the area in front of the dumpster. They had found no prints on the lid—he must have worn gloves—but if he had dropped something, there was a chance he had left some evidence behind.

Big Carl made a gesture that telegraphed his irritation with Robert Morgan, then climbed back into the SUV. Morgan hurried around to the driver's side. An instant later, the vehicle disappeared from the frame.

To all appearances the scene was just as it had been two minutes earlier. The only difference was, the battered corpse of a sixteen-year-old girl now reposed on a bed of decaying food and other trash.

Yvonne Lee fast-forwarded until several minutes had elapsed and they saw Dumpster Dave emerge from his hiding place behind the low wall.

"I wonder who that guy is," Lee said, as Dave sidled to the dumpster and took a quick peek inside, then dropped the lid and scurried away. He had omitted that part in his narrative when the detectives interviewed him.

Neither detective revealed that they already knew the homeless man. Lee fast-forwarded a few more minutes until Khan Khosa came around the corner unprepared for the gruesome discovery he was about to make.

On their return drive to Pacific Division, Jovanic and Coleman made a few stops around the perimeter of the Venice neighborhood in locations where they knew there were surveillance cameras. Being able to pinpoint the location of the SUV within a few minutes at one of those locations would make it easier to discover whether their suspects had made a stop at an ATM or a gas station on the route in or out of the alley.

The managers at each business they visited agreed to run their tapes within their time frame to determine whether a Chevy Tahoe with the numbers '4731' had visited their location. They would contact them when the tapes were available.

Coleman's next assignment was to check with the DMV, whose traffic cams would catch the SUV crossing an intersection. If luck were with them, Robert Morgan would have run a red light while driving the Tahoe and been photographed. An ID on the owner of the vehicle would be required to run the search. For that to happen, Coleman needed to request a DMV query for all Chevy Tahoes with the numbers '4731' in the plate.

He got the search started in the car. The first thing he learned was that the vehicle was not registered to either Robert Morgan or Alvin Rousch—Viper. Without a surname he could do nothing about Big Carl.

Unlike in other states, vehicle color was not included as part of the California registration process. Jovanic's plea for the department to lobby the legislature for a change in policy had fallen on deaf ears. So it was of no help that they knew the vehicle was either black or dark blue—the only dark colors that were standard with the vehicle—and assuming the SUV had not been painted a custom hue—color could not be used as a search parameter. This irked Jovanic no end.

While Coleman was running his DMV searches, Jovanic checked in with Huey Hardcastle, who was sitting in his car, surveilling Viper's tattoo parlor, from half a block away.

"Any sign of Big Carl?"

"Guy fitting his description showed up at noon," Hardcastle said.

"I guess he wasn't driving a Tahoe?"

"No, man, a Harley." Hardcastle gave a short huff of a laugh. "Size of that guy; looks like a monkey fucking a football."

"What did you get on the plate?"

"Couple of ag assaults, three years at Folsom for possession."

"Name, Huey? What's his name?"

"Carl Latu." He spelled out the Samoan's name.

"Okay, stay on him."

"You got it."

twenty-two

As an ironic joke, Kelly's ringtone was the old Madonna song, *Like a Virgin.* On Thursday afternoon, even before she answered her call, Claudia had a feeling of foreboding that was borne out by Kelly's first words.

"She's split, Claudia. Gone. What the hell should I do?"

"What do you mean, she's gone?" Claudia stared through the kitchen window at the tub of bright red and orange geraniums spilling onto the patio deck, listening with dismay. "What happened?"

"I thought she was still asleep." Kelly sounded ragged with anxiety. "I thought I could take a frigging shower without having to worry about her sneaking off, but damn it, when I came out of my room she was gone."

"You're sure she's not just taking a walk, bumming a smoke off someone?"

"She raided my wallet."

"You're kidding. How much did she take?"

"About eighty bucks, I think. I'm lucky she left the credit cards."

"Oh hell, I'm so sorry. I'll reimburse you."

"I don't care about the money. Shit, Claudia, I can't believe this. You trusted me to watch her, and..."

"Stop right there. This is not your fault. If she doesn't want to be helped, there's nothing you and I can do about it. You'd think she would appreciate a clean bed and a few free meals."

Claudia blew air through her lips. Jamie Parker was not an easy girl to like, but even though she was streetwise, she was still young in years. She wasn't Claudia's responsibility, but after Angel's brutal murder, Jamie's safety weighed on her.

"Did you check the guest room?" she asked Kelly.

"What's to check? She didn't have anything with her. All she left behind was an unmade bed."

"Nothing that could give us a clue what she's up to, where she went?"

"Nope. She didn't even have a purse. There's nothing."

"Could she have called someone to pick her up?"

"I didn't see a phone, but what kid goes without one these days? Even the homeless kids have disposables."

"You have a land line in your bedroom. Can you hit redial and see if she called someone while you were in the shower."

"Hang on, I'll try it."

Claudia listened while Kelly gave her a blow-by-blow account of walking into the bedroom and trying the phone. "Good detective work, Claud, there *is* a number I don't recognize. It's a 310-area code." She recited the number and Claudia scribbled it onto the scratch pad she kept by the kitchen phone.

"I'm going to ask Annabelle if it looks familiar."

"Okay, let me know."

Claudia had another thought. "Jamie's car was still on my street this morning when I drove Monica and Annabelle to school. I'll go down and take a look when we hang up, see if it's still there."

"Dammit, Claudia, I screwed up."

"Seriously, it's not your fault. I'll text Joel and let him know."

"Oh, great. He already hates me."

"No, he doesn't. He's just a little afraid of you. Anyway, *he* couldn't do anything with Jamie, so he can hardly blame you for her taking off."

"Yeah, sure."

"Cheer up. Streetwise kids like her always land on their feet."

Except, Angel didn't.

Claudia hung up the phone feeling less optimistic than her words suggested.

A light glaze of beach sand and dust cloaked the battered old Honda. Shading her eyes against the glare, Claudia peered through the driver side window. She was able to make out a dark, bulky object on the passenger side floor. She went around to the front of the car and tried the handle, surprised to find the door unlocked. It was a testament to her neighborhood that no one had ripped off the backpack in the foot well overnight.

Stealing a furtive glance around to make sure nobody was watching, Claudia took it out. Feeling like a thief, she carried it back to the house and tipped everything out onto the kitchen table.

A pair of black jeans, a tank top. Car keys, a tube of mascara caked black around the twist top, a tube of bright red lipstick. A dozen blue square packets—condoms. A dangerous-looking pocket knife in a sheath. Grains of white powder in a flat piece of aluminum foil, a plastic stirring straw cut in half. Meth? Probably. Jamie didn't have the money for coke. She would have needed a spoon and hypodermic needle for Heroin.

Depressed by the contents of the backpack, Claudia stuffed everything back inside and gave her hands a thorough scrubbing under hot water. A new prickle of guilt stung her. She wondered how Joel would react if she told him what she had just done. Could he use what she had found as evidence of a crime? She was none too sure that arresting Jamie for drug possession would get the girl the help she needed. Claudia had a strong suspicion that she was already too old and too hardened to accept that kind of help.

She called Joel. Straight to voicemail. That meant he was interviewing a witness and unable to answer. Claudia left a brief message. He called back ten minutes later on his way into the station. He had listened to her message and seemed unconcerned about Jamie's defection.

Claudia chose her words with care. "I've got a, uh, hypothetical question for you."

"Okay." He already sounded wary and she hurried on.

"*Hypothetically,* what if someone entered an unlocked car without permission of the owner and removed an item?"

The long pause before he spoke told her that his suspicion antenna was turned up high and he was being just as circumspect in considering how to respond. "The car is unlocked? You're talking about a theft."

"Even if the car owner and the person removing the item know each other?"

"Even if. What kind of item might we be talking about? If the value is more than a thousand bucks, it's grand theft. Otherwise, it's petty theft."

His answer gave her a flutter of relief. "Let's just say—hypothetically speaking—that it was a backpack that contained something like, um, a controlled substance; drug paraphernalia."

"Oh my God, Claudia, tell me you didn't."

"It's hypothetical, remember?" she hastened to remind him.

"Yeah, right." She could practically hear him grit his teeth. "So, what's the question about this *thief?*"

"Harsh word, honey. The question is, if that activity—and finding the drug stuff—were to be reported to an officer of the law, what would happen?"

Once again, the long pause while he thought it over. "There would be some options. The officer could turn in the contraband. Which means he has to take the time to process it, write a report, and submit it as evidence, and that would royally piss him off if there wasn't a good reason to do it. And of course, he would then have to explain where he got it, which could lead to a big problem for the person who 'found' the evidence because she—assuming this 'hypothetical' person is a she—wasn't acting under color of law. You know what that means, right?"

"Yes, of course I know what 'color of law' means. No law enforcement personnel instructed the person to enter the vehicle and take the property. She—or he—did it on her—or his—own."

"Close enough. Of course, if there was just a small amount of the illegal substance, the officer might decide it wasn't worth the effort. He might decide to flush it and forget about it. Or," Jovanic mused thoughtfully, "he *could* seize it as evidence and use it to hang over the owner's head; threaten her with jail if she was withholding important information in some other case the officer was aware of."

"I see. Well, thank you, Columbo, this has been very instructive."

"Yeah, I'm sure it has."

Claudia heard someone in the background speak to him as he entered the police station. He told her he had to go. But not before he issued a warning. "Babe, be careful, okay? I'd hate to have to bail that hypothetical someone out of lockup."

She rang off and poured herself a glass of iced tea, musing on what to do about Jamie's backpack. Maybe just return it to the Honda and lock the door. She could decide later. But before she pushed Jamie out of her head there was one more thing that needed to be done.

Claudia took her tea up to the office and plopped down at her desk. She opened a browser and typed in the phone number Kelly had given her into a reverse directory. It told her that Jamie had called a mobile phone in Venice, no name listed. She was tempted to dial it, but not knowing who would answer, she decided to wait and show it to Annabelle. It might mean nothing at all.

She still had about an hour before it was time to pick up the girls from school. In the event she had missed something important, she wanted to take a second look at Ariceli Lopez' handwriting.

The file she had made for the case was still lying on her desk under a pile of other work that had accumulated throughout the morning. When she opened it, the handwriting gave her the same negative impression as it had upon her first inspection. Red flags leapt off the page. The first thing she noticed was the strange way Ariceli formed her personal pronoun "I." It looked more like a capital D. The significance of that form might not be of importance to the murder investigation, but to Claudia it said Ariceli had problems in her relationship to her parents.

The nasty claw-like shapes on the bottom parts of the g's and y's, which some early handwriting analyst had misnamed "felon's claws," indicated a strong likelihood she was molested in early childhood and then made to feel guilty about it, as if she were the perpetrator.

The large overall size of the writing indicated that Ariceli was not one to avoid conflict. In fact, several indicators—the blunt, heavy ending strokes on words, t-crosses that thinned to a sharp point—pointed to the young woman being antagonistic and fearless about it.

Claudia did not see Ariceli as the type who would step up and be accountable for her actions. She would lie readily if it would get her what she wanted. The lack of upper loops combined with overly rounded writing and strokes that intruded into the oval letters suggested that she lied as a defense, either to save face, or to avoid taking the blame whenever she could get away with it.

Ariceli's motive for lying in her handwritten statement was clear enough: she either knew or guessed what had happened to Angel and she feared that at least some of the responsibility would attach to her. That was not the same as being sorry for any part she might have played in the circumstances of Angel's death. Her ability to rationalize would justify what she was doing and make it okay in her own mind. Her outlook was so unrealistic, she might not even realize it when she was lying to herself.

Playa de la Reina Middle School was on half-day schedule. Claudia stopped the Jaguar at the curb outside the school at one p.m. and waited for Annabelle and Monica. They walked out together, each lugging a backpack similar to the one Claudia had taken from Jamie's Honda. The big difference was, instead of condoms and drugs, theirs held school supplies and the multitude of stuff teenage girls couldn't do without.

After dropping Monica home and waving to her brother from the car, Claudia got out the piece of paper with the scribbled phone number and handed it to Annabelle as they drove away. "Whose number is this?"

Annabelle looked at it and frowned. "Where'd you get this? Have you been snooping in my stuff?"

"Of course not."

"Well, where'd you get it then?"

"Right now, *I'm* asking the questions. Whose number is it?"

"Mouser. Angel's boyfriend."

"I need to know if he picked up Jamie today." From the corner of her eye, Claudia caught Annabelle's surprised look at her.

"She cut out on Kelly?"

"It would appear that way."

"What a bitch."

"Language, Annabelle," admonished Claudia, but secretly, she agreed with the assessment.

"Mouser was mad at her. I totally don't think he would pick her up."

"But he might have?"

"I doubt it."

"Let's find out."

"Mouser's never gonna talk to you, Claudia."

"That's why I need *you* to call him."

"But Joel told me not to talk to him, remember?" Annabelle retorted with an air of self-righteousness.

"I think under the circumstances he'll understand. I just need to make sure Jamie is still safe. Call him, please."

"Right now, with you listening?"

"Yep."

Settling into her pouty face, Annabelle slumped back in the bucket seat and pulled her backpack onto her lap. She dug out her iPhone in its hot pink glitter case and without another word, tapped in the numbers and waited for Mouser to answer.

"Hey. It's Annabelle." A moment later she jerked the phone away from her ear, turning a fierce glare on Claudia. "What're you talking about? I just told them what you wanted me to. Listen—no, wait, don't hang up—Hey, did you give Jamie a ride? Today."

Claudia could not make out what Mouser was saying, but she could tell he was agitated.

"Don't fuckin' yell at me." Annabelle's own voice rose. "Do you know where she is, or not? Fine!" She clicked off the call and tossed the phone into her backpack.

"F-bombs, Annabelle. Not allowed, remember?"

Annabelle's glare heated up. "You set me up. The cops went over to his house and hassled his brother and Ariceli."

"Annabelle, seriously, is that something I would do to you?"

"But you knew he was gonna be pissed."

"I knew Joel and his partner went over there *before* Mouser talked to you. They have to question everyone who knew Angel. And remember, Mouser *asked* you to talk to Joel on his behalf. So, does he have a good reason to be pissed?"

"I guess not." There was a short silence. "Sorry."

"Apology accepted. Look, sweetie, even if he didn't kill Angel himself—and I don't know whether he did or not—Mouser's brother is involved in the murder."

"What do you mean? He hurt her?"

"I don't know anything about that. But if he helped move her body like Mouser told you he did, it's called being an accessory after the fact. It means he becomes part of the crime."

"What do they do to someone who's an accessory after the fact?"

"He could go to prison. I think maybe he could even be charged with the murder."

"Even if he didn't kill the person himself?"

"Yes, even then."

"Damn." It was less an epithet than an expression of surprise.

"Language, Annabelle," Claudia said automatically, feeling like a broken record.

"It's just a word, why does it matter?"

"We've had that conversation enough times that I don't feel like repeating it right now. Did Mouser say anything about Jamie?"

"She called him for a ride, but he didn't have any wheels today and even if he did, she's a filthy skank and he wouldn't piss on her if she was on fire."

Claudia suppressed a sigh. "I'm sorry I asked."

twenty-three

"Hey, Jovanic, who's having the sale on sugar skulls?"

Jovanic turned to the morgue attendant who had just brushed past him. Bone-thin, lank black hair slicked under a hair net, a dark olive complexion, he had a cadaverous look that fit his job.

"What's that, Mario?"

"Your gal there." The attendant jerked his thumb at the nude body of sixteen-year-old Angela Eliana Tedesco laid out on the stainless-steel table. A modesty sheet had been placed over her torso. Her head and upper body were propped on a wood block to give the medical examiner better access. The long blonde hair had fallen away from her neck, exposing the sugar skull tattoo on her shoulder. "Second time I've seen that tat this week," Mario said. "Vic we picked up yesterday has one just like it. Maybe some tattoo parlor got a twofer sale going on or somethin'."

"Are you sure it's the same?"

The morgue attendant gave him a mocking look and shook his head as if in disbelief. "Would I say so if I wasn't sure?"

"Okay, sorry. Who's the other vic?"

Mario nodded his head toward one of several gurneys lined up. Each held a sealed body bag that contained a corpse awaiting post-mortem dissection. "Name's Darla Steinman. Female, thirty-seven, multiple GSW to the chest and head."

Even as he marveled at Mario's talent for memorizing information about the corpses in his charge, the story was ringing bells. The news item that had been playing on TV when he arrived home the evening before. His mind had been deep in his own cases and he had only half-twigged to what Claudia had told him about it. He dredged up what he remembered. "Cheviot Hills, right?"

"Yeah, that's the one."

Jovanic started over to the gurney "Whose case?"

"Detective Flynt caught it. He oughta be in any—oh, here he is now."

Jovanic had a casual acquaintance with the stocky man in a bad suit who had just entered the autopsy room. Colin Flynt was part of the other detective team in Pacific Division.

"What's up, dudes?" Flynt greeted them cheerfully as he suited up in a white gown like the one Jovanic was already wearing. He pulled on a hair net and mask. "You messin' wit my vic?"

"Hey, Flynt," said Jovanic. "Mario says yours and mine have similar tats. Mind if I take a look?"

Mario edged between the narrowly parked gurneys. He stopped at the one he had pointed out. "Not just similar, Detective. Identical."

"This I gotta see," Flynt said. "Busy day for you guys."

"Four homicides, a suicide, and a home-alone," said Mario.

Jovanic followed him to the gurney. Flynt got out his cell phone and flipped screens to the camera app. To ensure proper chain of custody before the attendant opened it, he bent over the body bag and snapped a close-up photo of the lock on the zipper. The photograph could later be used to prove that the bag had remained untouched since entering the refrigerator unit upon arrival at the morgue.

Having completed his photographic record, the detective motioned for the attendant to break the lock and unzip the bag.

RaeAnn, a CSI photographer who worked for the ME, hovered around Mario, documenting every step of the procedure. A few feet away, in anticipation of the arrival of one of the medical examiners on duty, Sandra, another morgue assistant, was preparing to open one of the other pouches. In such a large and busy coroner's office as Los Angeles, whenever feasible, each corpse rated its own ME.

Despite the cold air and the sophisticated filtration system, and despite the paper masks that covered their noses and mouths, the stench of human decay billowed from the heavy plastic as Sandra exposed what was inside. "Poor old guy," she said, muffled behind her mask. "Croaked at home all by his lonesome. Nobody missed him for a few days."

"Holy mother," Flynt exclaimed, making a choking sound. "Glad I didn't eat breakfast."

The foul odor curled into Jovanic's nostrils: something akin to raw meat in a month-old litter box. He knew from experience that even if he did not get close to the corpse, the smell would cling stubbornly to his clothes and hair. Before entering the autopsy suite, he had brushed his teeth with strong peppermint toothpaste and was now chewing clove gum. It helped in most cases. He might have become inured to the stench, but he didn't have to like it. And he was not about to wimp out like Colin Flynt and let everyone in the room know how he felt.

Like any dead animal, even a relatively fresh body like the one he was about to see now, Flynt's victim, Darla Steinman, had its own unmistakable odor.

Blonde, smooth-faced, slim. In death, she looked younger than her thirty-seven years. She had been quite attractive. Except for the hole in the middle of her forehead, which reminded Jovanic of an Indian bindi, she bore a resemblance to his victim, Angela Tedesco.

Maybe it was just that they were both blonde and dead.

Steinman was still dressed in the clothes she had died in. As Mario unzipped the bag further for their viewing, Jovanic could see a sleeveless pink knit top with a ruffle around the neckline. A splotch of dried blood stained the mid-section, where two holes close together told him that the first and second bullets had pierced the heart. That would account for the small amount of blood on her clothing—no pumping action. The third had bored into her skull once she was on the floor. Jovanic visualized her killer leaning over her, finishing the job.

With the photographer continuing to document his actions, Mario cut away Darla's shirt in large sections along the sides. Once the shirt had been removed, it became apparent from the sooty stippling around the entry holes on the shirt, but very little on the skin, that the shooter had been close to his victim—less than six feet away. But what drew Jovanic's gaze was the tattoo at the top of Darla Steinman's right arm.

The sugar skull was slightly smaller than the one Angela Tedesco sported, but other than that, as Mario had insisted, it looked identical.

The CSI tech duplicating his movements, Jovanic took several close-ups of his own with his phone. He also took some at a greater distance to identify the body on which the tattoos were inked.

Two dead women who looked alike. Both murdered in the same week. Identical sugar skull tattoos.

Jovanic did not believe in coincidences.

Two hours later, after the autopsies were complete, Jovanic and Flynt walked across the street to the one excuse for a restaurant in the industrial neighborhood that surrounded the county morgue. Jack in the Box.

"You think we got a serial?" Flynt asked, chomping into a Sourdough Jack. His fingers were shiny with bacon grease and melted cheese.

Jovanic, who had opted for tacos and a diet Coke, shook his head. "Not by the FBI definition. But it's pretty obvious we've got three *connected* killings. Travis Navarette opened a tattoo parlor in competition with Alvin Rousch, AKA Viper. He gets the cocktail."

"And dead," Flynt interjected.

"And dead. Angela Tedesco is connected to both Travis and Viper. According to my CI, she was supposed to hook up with Travis on Viper's orders, but she disobeys and ends up in a trash dumpster. Then we've got your vic, Darla Steinman, with the same tattoo as Angela, shot to death. What've you got on her?"

"The husband—William Steinman—has a prior for domestic battery on her a couple years back. Darla was killed sometime during school hours and he doesn't have a good alibi. He's in pharma sales, on the road a lot. Could have been there at the right time."

"Knowing the kids would find her?"

Flynt shrugged and echoed what Jovanic was already thinking. "Lot of rage, shooting her in the face when she's already down."

"Two years ago, for the battery. How bad was it?"

"He beat her up pretty good—black eye, fractured wrist. Didn't do any time. The judge let him off with AA and anger management diversion. She hasn't filed a complaint since then. *But,* and here's the interesting thing. Dear Darla *did* just file for divorce last week."

"That's interesting. Any weapons registered to Mr. Steinman?"

"Nope."

"How about casings?"

"The shooter picked up two of them. We found one under the edge of a throw rug. Plus the chest wound was a through and through. We caught a break on that; the bullet was in pretty good shape. IBIS got a hit on the round the CSI retrieved. Weapon's a Glock .357 reported stolen two years ago in a B&E." Flynt wiped meat juice off his chin and set the last crumbs of his sandwich in its cardboard box. "What kind of joker leaves a gun lying around for some asshole burglar to pick up?" He sounded personally peeved by the stupidity of the citizenry.

Jovanic wrapped up the second taco and put it on the plastic tray with the trash, his mind going in another direction. He had just remembered that Jamie Parker wore the same tattoo as the two dead women and was wondering whether that meant she was in danger. Did William Steinman have a connection to the two teenage girls' tattoo that was the same as his wife's?

"I'll need to look at the murder book," Jovanic said.

"Knock yourself out." Flynt's greedy eyes were on the taco. "You're not gonna eat that?"

"It's all yours. I've had enough grease for one day." Since getting shot in the gut a few months back, Jovanic had to watch what he ate or suffer digestive consequences.

Flynt unfolded the paper and bit into the shell. He chewed for a moment, then dropped it back in the paper with a look of disgust. "Shit, no wonder you tossed it. Anyhow, stop by my desk later, I'll make you copies of everything we've got, which ain't much so far."

"Thanks. I want to talk to a guy who works for Alvin Rousch, AKA Viper. Gonna have his P.O. bring him in to piss in a cup. That way we'll have him in an interview room and Viper won't know we're talking to him. I'll let you know if anything comes of it."

twenty-four

Jovanic called Carl Latu's Probation Officer and set up the meeting for eight a.m. Friday morning. He then started digging for personal information to use in his interview with Viper's Samoan bodyguard.

With a population of more than 50,000 Samoans in L.A. County, Jovanic already had a passing familiarity with Island culture. He also had a good relationship with Latu's PO, Adam Grant. Grant was ready to bend over backwards to help Jovanic prepare for his meeting.

In "Big Carl" Latu's file, which Grant emailed Jovanic, was a copy of a multi-page letter from 2009 addressed to "Nana" back in the Islands. It had been written while he was incarcerated in Folsom Prison.

Jovanic was well aware that in Samoa, families—parents, children, married children, elderly relatives—live together in separate houses in a compound. Family elders are accorded high status, respected for their wisdom and the history they carry. He made a copy of the letter and faxed it to Claudia with a request for her comments on the handwriting.

The reply came via text message fifteen minutes later:

"Lacks boundaries, poor self-image, follower, strong loyalty. Smart underachiever."

Just as Jack Solis had described it, the Samoan-American's face was inked with a symmetrical black tribal tattoo. It started high on his shaved head and framed angry eyes as black as beetles. Surrounding the broad brown cheeks, the ink met in a point under his chin. Intricate bands wove around biceps that strained against the sleeves of an oversized T-shirt. Knee-length nylon shorts dipped below an ample belly and revealed darkly tanned, ripped calves above white socks and a pair of new-looking athletic shoes.

Carl Latu glared at Jovanic, who stood a few feet from the open bathroom door behind his probation officer. With the two officers in the confined space of the hallway there was barely enough room to turn around. Adjusting his shorts after urinating in a small plastic cup, the big Samoan's body language said he was already uncomfortable and embarrassed. Hell, who wouldn't be? It had taken him a couple of minutes to produce the sample, and Jovanic couldn't help feeling a twinge of sympathy. Not something he would want to do with a cop standing behind him, watching to make sure there were no shenanigans.

"What's it gonna say, Carl?" Jovanic asked the Samoan. "We gonna have a problem?"

The man's gaze was glued to his P.O. as he walked away with the cup to read the results. "Nuttin' for me to worry about."

"You been staying clean? You look kind of anxious."

"No, bro. No probs."

"Glad to hear it. Hey, you've got kids, don't you? How're they doing?"

Big Carl couldn't keep the sheen of pride off his face. "They're good."

"How old?"

But he was savvy enough to know that the detective wasn't going to make small talk with a con without a good reason. "The little one's eleven and Tommy's getting ready to graduate high school. What do you care?"

"Seems like you've had some bad breaks. I bet your boy's glad to have you home."

"He's a smart kid, got himself a football scholarship."

"That's fantastic, man. What's he going to study?"

"Civil engineering."

"That's impressive, Carl. Are your folks back in the Islands pretty excited?"

"What of it?"

Jovanic chewed the corner of his lip, giving him a look of regret. "I just hope you can be there to watch your kid get that diploma."

Carl Latu went very still. "What's that s'posed to mean?"

"I hate to break it to you, Carl, but you've got a whole lot more to worry about than the color in that cup."

"What the fuck you talking about?"

"Then you're okay if I ask where you were on Tuesday night?"

"Tuesday?" Carl looked up at the ceiling, as if he might find the answer there. "Um, I'm pretty sure that's the night I was helping my kid with her homework. She has trouble with her spelling words, you know? I'm no good with numbers, but spelling, I do pretty good." He was talking too much, adding too much detail. Jovanic figured he was buying time while he tried to calculate how much the detective knew.

"Help me out on this, Carl. What does the name 'Angela Tedesco' mean to you?"

Big Carl's gaze flickered, but the movement was so slight Jovanic might have imagined it. "Whozat?"

Jovanic was a half-dozen inches taller than Latu. He moved further into the other man's space so he had to back up against the wall. "C'mon now, Carl. You aren't going to deny knowing Angel, are you?"

"Angel? You said Angela somethin'. Yeah, I know Angel."

"How do you know her?"

"She's just one of them chippies, hangs where I work. They come and they go."

"You still work at Dragon House?"

"Yeah, man. You gotta know I do. What the fuck?"

"You got a beef with Angel, Carl?"

"Hell no, bro. We hardly ever even talk. I leave them girls alone. Don't need none o' that kind of trouble."

"Where is Angel, Carl?"

Staring straight ahead, the Samoan shrugged. "Beats me."

"You sure about that?"

"Yeah, I'm sure."

"Look, I need you to be straight with me. Tell me what happened to Angel."

"Something happen to her?"

"We know you were there, Carl. Bobby already spilled his guts, so you might as well tell the truth." Carl Latu didn't need to know that the gut spilling had been overheard by Bobby's younger brother and reported second-hand to Jovanic by Annabelle.

"That's a batch of bullshit. Bobby wouldn't say—"

"If it's bullshit, you're still in it neck deep, Carl. You know she's dead and you saw it happen. Here's the thing: I don't think you're a cold-blooded killer. I think you're an okay guy who got stuck in the middle of something very bad. Am I wrong about that?"

Carl's lips curled into a sullen pout. "I didn't kill nobody."

Jovanic nodded. "You know what? I'm tempted to believe you. But the problem is, you were there and you did dump the body—we have an eyewitness—and we've got Bobby Morgan. So, even if you didn't kill her yourself, you're an accessory to murder and a few other things, like obstructing justice."

Jovanic had lucked out. The owner of the Handy Wash he and Randy had talked to after leaving Yvonne Lee the day before had left a voicemail while Jovanic was attending the autopsies. The security tape caught Carl

Latu and Bobby Morgan washing and vacuuming their vehicle at 1:55 a.m. on the morning of Angel's death. But Jovanic wasn't going to share with Carl what he had on him.

"I never had nothing against that girl." Carl spoke with the kind of vehemence that Jovanic figured he was telling the truth. "I never touched her. *Never.*"

"Dude. You know we've got you on this."

"I can't—I got nothin' to say to you, bro."

"You're willing to take that fall?" Jovanic pressed him, feeling the other man already weakening. "You're already on probation. You want a murder rap? Think of your kids, Carl. Think of Tommy's face when you miss graduation. And what about your Nana? How would she feel, coming all the way out to California and find her grandson in lockup?"

"Fuck you." Big Carl spoke softly, but the menace came through loud and clear.

Jovanic tapped a finger hard on the massive chest. "No, Carl. It's *you* who's fucked."

twenty-five

Claudia left the witness stand feeling pleased with her testimony. Regardless of how the jury decided the outcome of the case, she was confident she had done a credible job of establishing a foundation for her opinion: that the signatures on the medical sign-in sheets had been written in groups of sittings, rather than on different days as the defense claimed.

The five women and seven men tasked with deciding the multimillion-dollar insurance fraud case had appeared interested and engaged as she explained the elements of synchronous writing. There was a fine line between providing too much information and boring them, and just enough for them to understand what she wanted to get across. She told them how the pattern called 'margin drift' was created, and that when someone signed several times in a row down the page, those signatures demonstrated greater regularity than ones executed at different times, which showed no particular marginal pattern.

Using the wall-mounted TV to project her PowerPoint presentation, she showed photomicrograph enlargements on a screen to establish how the pattern of the ductus would be dissimilar if a pen with such irregularities were to be used, then set down, then picked up and used again at another time. And she demonstrated how ink striation patterns could be formed by imperfections in the ball of a ballpoint pen, or by minuscule bits of lint that collected in the ball housing.

Still, she knew better than to second-guess the jury. Over the course of her career, Claudia had learned through sometimes heartbreaking experience that it was impossible to predict with any certainty how any trier of fact would decide. Sometimes the decisions they made were utterly counterintuitive. But the defense attorney, his shoulders bowed in defeat, had no further questions. He had not retained his own document examiner for his client.

As she passed the counsel table on her way out of the courtroom, the attorney Claudia was working for made her feel good with a surreptitious thumbs up. She pushed through the swinging doors at the back and exited.

Heading to the elevator at the end of the long hallway, Claudia did her best to avoid the gaze of those crowding the benches outside family court. The sound of her heels clicking smartly on the marble floors and her self-satisfied energy seemed to mock the misery of the hapless victims, mostly women. Most of those waiting to request a restraining order were accompanied by small children and babies in strollers. It was all too easy to imagine the violence that had brought them here to petition the judge. And that led to thoughts of Angel.

Joel was fond of reminding her that getting emotionally involved in her cases helped no one, especially Claudia herself. But Angel was different—she was not a case—she had been Annabelle's friend. There was nothing anyone could do for the girl now, except help bring her killer to justice, and Claudia had complete trust that Joel would do that.

Angel's close connection to Annabelle had fired him up in a way she hadn't seen over the past months. He had come too close to death himself a few months ago when his former partner failed to back him up and he was shot. Since returning to the job after two surgeries, Joel had seemed to merely be going through the motions. The work no longer excited him as it had in the past. But with Angel's murder, homicide had come close to home again and re-energized him.

Claudia's mind turned to Jamie. She wondered whether the girl had turned up yet. Kelly had called earlier and reported there had been no word from her.

She sighed. The girl might be a snotty brat, but she had not been born that way. Without doubt, she had lived through an entire catalogue of toxic experiences before turning into a 'strawberry'—a girl who was willing to exchange sex for drugs with anyone who made the offer.

A line from a book Claudia had once read by the psychologist Eric Berne came back. *"People are born princes and princesses, until their parents make them into frogs."*

twenty-six

"I'm hauling Robert Morgan and Carl Latu in," Jovanic said, concluding his update to Tania St. John, the homicide table coordinator. St. John had clawed her way through the ranks, where African-American females had to work ten times harder than their male counterparts to achieve the same levels of success. An attractive forty-year-old, at six-three, with the build of an Amazon, she could stare Jovanic straight in the eye.

The supervisor caught the yawn Jovanic tried to suppress. "Might want to catch a few Zs first," she said pointedly.

He checked the wall clock. Eight twenty-five. He'd been at it all night again, reviewing the three murder books and formulating a plan. His eyeballs were stinging with fatigue, but he knew that if he stopped for a nap now, he would not be sufficiently awake to conduct the interviews with Viper's bodyguards.

"I'm fine," he said. "That's why God invented Red Bull."

"You need to be *on* it with those boys, detective."

"I'll take Bobby Morgan, Randy'll take Carl Latu. Neither of them will know the other is here."

St. John nodded. "You picking them up, or—"

"I gave 'em both wakeup calls this morning and offered a ride, but they opted to come in 'voluntarily.'"

"They don't want you showing up at the tattoo parlor." The D3 stood, signaling the end of the meeting. "We need to get this case wrapped. The bodies are piling up too fast, Joel. This latest one, I'm already getting flack from upstairs."

"Our pretty little soccer mom draws the crowd."

St. John's eyes narrowed. "When our pretty little soccer mom is connected to a teenager in a dumpster *and* an arson victim, it does tend to pull some scrutiny."

"I'm on it." Jovanic left her office and made a beeline for the coffee maker.

Bobby Morgan sat at the interview table in one of the plastic garden chairs the department had purchased from Walmart. They were cheap and easy to hose down and rid of germs, vomit, and whatever other bodily fluids happened to be left over from the latest interview.

Jovanic walked in, freshly shaved, and took a chair across from Morgan.

"Okay, so I'm here." Morgan's chair was tipped back, his legs splayed out in an attitude of indifference. "I didn't have to come."

Jovanic thought about Angel's battered body lying in the garbage and wanted to knock the chair to the floor with him still in it. He forced a cordial smile. "Thanks for coming, Bobby, I appreciate it." For the benefit of the high-definition camera and self-modulating microphone that would record their conversation, he said, "You understand you're not in custody, right? You came in voluntarily, and you're free to leave at any time." What Jovanic did not say was, under the circumstances he had described, he was not required to Mirandize the punk. Which meant he could ask him pretty much anything.

"Yeah, yeah, I got it. So, what's up? You talk to my brother yet?"

Jovanic waited a beat, staring at Bobby until he started fidgeting. He leaned forward. "What's up is, you're going down for murder, dude."

"What? I never fucking killed anyone." Morgan jumped up and strode to the door. "I'm outta here."

Jovanic stayed seated. "Yeah, you can go if you want. But if you leave now, Bobby, it's not gonna work in your favor. I'm here to help you get to the truth. This is your one chance. Take it or leave it."

Morgan hesitated in the open doorway while Jovanic prayed he would not demand to see a lawyer. Finally, Morgan pushed the door shut and dropped back into his chair. "The truth? The truth is I did not kill that chick. I had nothing to do with it, I swear."

"Oh, really? So, you weren't in an SUV in an alley at the beach last Tuesday night, dumping *something?* And you didn't vacuum that SUV at the Handy Wash on Washington?"

Morgan's body twitched in shock. His reaction confirmed that Big Carl had not shared their interview at his P.O.'s office.

Jovanic went on, "You think I haven't talked to somebody already? You think I don't have video of you and Big Carl putting Angela Tedesco in a trash dumpster?"

"You're bullshittin', man. I *looked*—" Bobby Morgan stared wildly around the small room as if looking for someone that might help him.

Jovanic leaned across the table, getting in his face. "Yeah, you looked and you didn't see a camera. But that doesn't mean one wasn't there, picking up every move you made, Bobby. Remember when you dropped your keys?"

It was a guess, and it found its mark. Morgan's eyes moved from side to side as he walked back through his memories of the past few days. The light dawned on his face as he calculated his odds. "Fuck," he said softly. "Fuck me."

"Yeah. It kinda looks like you're screwed, Bobby."

"I didn't kill her. I swear, man."

"Okay, I get that. And you know what? I actually believe it. But the thing is, the girl is dead, and if you didn't kill her, something else is going on here. Obviously, you're involved—you and Carl moved the body. That's conspiracy after the fact." Jovanic spread his hands in a gesture of regret. "So, if I can't prove someone else did it, guess what, dude—it's you, and you're going down for it."

"That's fuckin' bullshit."

"Hey, look, Bobby. If this was just about jackin' some dude's ride, that's a different story. But it isn't that. It's friggin' murder. A sixteen-year-old girl. A girl who was living in *your* house. Don't you get it? You put your sweaty paws on that dumpster; we've got your prints; we've got a witness. That's all we need." Jovanic was lying about what he had, but he could smell the younger man's fear. Watching Bad Bobby melt into a puddle, he figured Morgan couldn't remember whether he'd touched the dumpster or not.

"What if—what if I did know what happened to her?"

"You tell me what you know and let's see what happens from there. No promises, but the truth is the best thing for the investigation." Jovanic rose. "Why don't you think about it. I'll be right back." He turned at the door. "Get you anything? Coffee? Coke?"

Morgan dropped his head in his hands. "I'll take a Coke."

Jovanic left the room and knocked on the door of Interview Room #4, where his partner was conducting the same interview with the Samoan, Big Carl Latu.

Randy Coleman stepped into the hallway, immaculate in a dark suit and snowy white shirt with a blue Hermes tie covered in little horse heads. "What've you got?" he asked.

"Bobby's about to cave. How's it going with Carl?"

"He's sticking with his story. He don't know nuttin' about nuttin'."

"Okay, keep hammering him. Tell him his buddy's giving him up."

"Here's your Coke, Bobby." Jovanic set the red and white can on the table and took his chair as Morgan snapped the top. "So, what's it gonna be?"

Morgan looked up at him with a miserable expression. "You're fucking gonna get me smoked, you know that?"

"Why don't you tell me what happened. Was it Carl? He's a big guy, maybe it was an accident."

"No, man, not Carl."

"He's not really that tough. Look, I'm sure neither of you planned for Angel to die..."

"It was—" He broke off, almost in tears. "Fuck, man, he's gonna have me smoked."

"Who is, Bobby?" Jovanic kept his face impassive, but inside he was giving himself a high five.

"Viper."

"You're between that old rock and a hard place, dude. It's either Viper or the system. How do you think it's gonna look to those twelve people who weren't smart enough to get out of jury duty?"

"What the fuck? I thought—"

"No, you *didn't* think, Bobby. You did what Viper told you to do, and he's gonna leave you twisting in the wind. It's not Viper on that video, Bobby, it's you." Jovanic put on his earnest face, reasoning with him. "Listen to me. He knows you've come down here, or if he doesn't, he's gonna know it pretty soon. You got that, right?"

Morgan's head drooped dejectedly.

"You think you're the first guy who's afraid that telling the truth is gonna get him killed? How many times have you heard of a witness being killed in a murder case? I'm not talking about the organized crime crap they show on TV. Come on, Bobby. How many?"

"I dunno, man, but..."

"It doesn't happen in real life. And when it does happen, it's in those high-profile mafia cases. Let me tell you, Viper is going to be so busy covering his murderous ass he's not gonna give a second thought to you or Carl."

twenty-seven

"He was more scared of Viper than he was of going to jail."

Joel stood in the bathroom doorway watching Claudia brushing her teeth. She glanced up at him in the mirror and took a moment to enjoy the reflection of his well-defined abs. Catching her smile, he reached out to give her rear a squeeze. "M'mmm. Much nicer view than Big Carl's ass."

Bending her head to spit foam and rinse her mouth, she wiggled her posterior at him. "You'll need to do better than that."

"I will," he said with a slow smile. "Promise."

She was still thinking about what he had told her of his interview with the Samoan. "If Big Carl helps you put Viper away, what does he have to be scared of?"

"Viper has a long reach. Remember, it's Carl's job to insulate him. If he rats him out, his life won't be worth shit. But then, there's also the rage of Nana he'd have to face. In his culture, that means a lot. After I was done with Bobby, I came down hard on him."

"What does that mean?"

"It means that if he wants to keep young Tommy out of it, he's gonna have to cooperate." Beckoning to her, Jovanic went into the bedroom. "I want to show you something."

She gave him an inviting smile. "Yeah? You show me yours, I'll show you mine."

"That's an offer I can't refuse. But *first* I have to show you something far less interesting. Remember the homicide on the news the other day, the one in Cheviot Hills?"

"Soccer mom?"

He nodded. "She had the same tattoo as Angel. I want to show you the pictures." Jovanic fetched his phone from the nightstand and started scrolling through the screens as Claudia slipped a long T-shirt over her head and followed him.

"Jamie had the same one, too. But I didn't get a picture of hers." Jovanic turned the phone to face her. There on the screen was a close-up of the glammed-up skull's head tattoo on Darla Steinman's shoulder.

"That's the same tattoo Annabelle got." Claudia handed the phone back. "What does this mean?"

"*What the—*"

"You've been so busy with your cases, we never got a chance to talk. Angel got a tattoo artist she knew to put this same sugar skull on Annabelle."

He slid his thumb across a few more screens. "Here's the one Angel had. Are you sure it's the same?"

"Yes, I'm sure."

"Holy shit. Two women who had this tattoo are dead, and so is the guy who opened up a studio in competition with the artist." Jovanic chewed on his lower lip, contemplating the implications. "Can you tell if these were done by the same artist?"

Claudia handed back the phone. "Email them to me. I'll enlarge them. Tattoo artists don't sign their work, but they have their own individual styles."

Jovanic threw on some shorts and followed her into the office, tapping her email address onto his screen as he went. By the time Claudia woke the dual monitors from sleep mode, his email was already waiting in her inbox. She launched the graphics editing program she used for handwriting authentication cases and opened the two photo files, then enlarged them side by side.

"It's the same as examining signatures," she explained, reciting what she had said so often on the witness stand. "No two are one hundred percent identical, but in most cases, you can tell they were signed by the same hand." She paused, making the switch to what was now on the screens before them. "With a tattoo, you have to look at the style, the quality of the stroke, the colors, the way the design is laid out. This is unusual. Tattoo artists don't like to put an identical design on different clients. They would vary it to some degree."

"This guy, Viper, is using it as a brand he puts on his girls, so he would want them to look as alike as possible."

"Like branding a cow." Claudia gave a shiver of distaste. "But if this is his brand, what's this other guy doing using it on Annabelle?"

"What other guy?"

"His name's Crash."

"You're sure it's the same?"

"I didn't examine it up close, but I'd say it's a fairly good match."

"Can you get her to show it to me?"

"It's not on her shoulder. It's below her hipline."

"Okay, forget that. I need you to take a photo of it."

"Now? She's got school in the morning. You want me to wake her up?"

It was hard enough getting Annabelle up in the mornings without waking her at midnight.

"Babe, this is looking like a triple murder case."

She sighed. "Give me the phone."

As it happened, Annabelle was awake and reading a vampire romance by flashlight when Claudia opened the bedroom door. Shooting her a guilty look, she switched off the light. "I just wanted to finish the chapter."

"Maybe not the best reading material right before bed." Claudia switched on the lamp on the nightstand and sitting on the edge of the bed. "How's the tattoo doing?"

"Scabby." Annabelle sat up on her elbow. "Why are you in my room at midnight asking about my tat?"

"Because Joel needs to see it." Claudia held up her cell phone. "So if you don't mind, I'm going to take a picture."

"That sounds kinda perverted."

"Yeah, right. Joel. He needs to compare it to the one Angel had."

At the mention of the dead girl, Annabelle's eyes got big. "Why would he need to do that?"

Claudia hesitated. "It has something to do with another case. So, if you wouldn't mind—consider it the price of your misconduct—let's get this done and you can go to sleep."

Rolling her eyes in her best drama queen fashion, Annabelle pushed down the bedcovers and hitched up the hem of the T-shirt she was wearing, exposing enough of her abdomen to show the tattoo.

"Ouch." Claudia positioned the lens and snapped several close-ups of the scabbed-over sugar skull. "At least it looks like it's healing properly."

Annabelle gave her the *well, duh* look. "I'm taking care of it. What's the other case about?"

"Just something another detective wanted Joel to look at."

Annabelle flopped back on the pillow and pulled the blankets up to her chin. "You mean somebody else got murdered and they had the same tat as Angel and me?"

Sometimes, the girl was too quick for her own good.

"That's what they're trying to figure out."

"Is he gonna come after me, too?"

Claudia leaned over and gave her a hug. "No, baby girl, there's nothing for you to worry about. But do me a favor and stay away from Jamie and Mouser, okay?"

As soon as the words left her mouth, she regretted them. Annabelle was apt to do the opposite.

After enlarging the photograph of Annabelle's tattoo and comparing it to the others, it became clear to Claudia that although it was a close match to the other three tattoos in content, there were subtle differences in the style, the shading, the colors, the lines. Both showed a natural artistry, but Angel's and Darla Steinman's were done with bolder strokes. Annabelle's had a more finely detailed touch.

"We already knew there were two artists. But why is this guy Crash copying Viper's work? I mean, besides doing Angel a favor, that's a major no-no in the inkslinger world."

Jovanic didn't bother asking how she knew so much about tattoos. He was aware that her experience as a handwriting examiner wasn't limited to handwriting. Anything that constituted graphic behavior was fair game for her considerable skills.

"That's the big question. What do we know about Crash?"

"Annabelle said he was an old guy, but coming from her, that could be anything over twenty-five. He did the tat for sixty bucks."

"In his van."

"Pretty unsavory. Not to mention unsanitary. He gave her tequila, too."

Jovanic's lips flattened in disgust. "Fucking asshole. It's a stretch, but I might be able to pick him up on Child Endangerment. That's a felony, at least it should get him talking about what he knows about Viper. If this Crash guy is copying his work, maybe he trained in his studio, like Travis Navarette." He went over to his desk and booted up his laptop. "Any info on the van?"

"Just that it was white and had no windows; a cargo van, I guess. Must be a million in L.A."

"Shit."

"Something tells me you're not coming to bed anytime soon."

"Sorry babe, let's make my promise an IOU." He spoke absently, his mind already on the investigation. "You might as well get some shuteye."

Claudia planted a kiss on his cheek and left him to it. She was presenting a lecture at an early breakfast meeting in Valencia and could use the sleep. But that didn't mean she wasn't disappointed.

The Internet was the detective's boon. It would have taken days or even weeks to get the same information through department resources, pulling every case from the records. Even getting a summary sheet from the DA would take time. The DA's hourly staff wasn't known for its helpfulness.

Had he not already known the source of Angel's and Jamie's sugar skulls, Jovanic would have accessed the LAPD gang unit's tattoo database to search for the design. Since he did know, he logged onto LexisNexis, the legal database, and did a search for Alvin Lester Rousch AKA Viper.

His search produced records of a slew of charges: extortion, drug possession, arson, even murder for hire. He followed the stories through the *L.A. Times* website and found what he had expected. None of the charges stuck. Viper always had an alibi and no witnesses could be found who were willing to break it.

The articles Jovanic found raised the specter of witness intimidation. Whispers followed Rousch, but never developed into anything useful. Prosecution witnesses evaporated, their once powerful narratives abruptly diluted to useless pap. Once he got into the office, he'd be able to check other programs through a department computer and see whether anything else popped up related to Viper's criminal history that was not publicly available.

Google pointed to a string of articles detailing his involvement with the Skullz motorcycle club, which had flourished under his leadership. Dragon House Tattoos, which he had established some fifteen years earlier, was a known hangout for members of the local branch of the outlaw club—frequent targets of law enforcement for drug and sex trafficking activities. The county jail seemed to have installed a revolving door for the other club members, but Alvin Lester Rousch always walked.

There was an *L.A. Times* photo taken at the L.A. Superior Criminal Courts building on the next block from where Claudia had just testified. Rousch was a man of small stature, but the flat obsidian eyes staring out of his unsmiling face would scare someone twice his size. In fact, Jovanic thought Viper might be the hardest-looking asshole he had encountered over his long career.

By the time he had finished reading about the man's numerous arrests and just as many acquittals, Jovanic knew he was going to work on this case until he put Viper away for the murders of Travis Navarette and Angela Tedesco. Viper might not have hurled the Molotov cocktail through Travis's window himself, but Jovanic knew he had ordered it done. And according to Bobby Morgan's brother, Viper was the one responsible for Angel's savage beating death. He didn't yet know where Darla Steinman fit, but it was too big a coincidence this week that she had a sugar skull that looked like Viper's work, and now she was dead.

He made a few notes about what he had that might goad Bobby and Big Carl Latu into cooperating. When he figured out which of them was the weakest link, that's the one he would lean on. They had both transported Angel's body, which made them part of the crime, but he was not interested in charging them with the homicide. They were just the small fish he would use as bait to catch the big one.

The temptation to join Claudia in bed was almost more than he could resist, even if he was too tired to do more than wrap her in his arms and meld his body against hers. But there was one more search he needed to do before he caved.

Fighting the need for sleep, he typed the moniker, "Crash" into the system, hoping the creep had a record. That would mean at least a last known address and a parole officer.

Annabelle Giordano could be a major pain in the ass, but Jovanic admired her spunk. She had come a long way since Claudia had rescued her from an appalling situation. Even if she had agreed to it, the thought of some prick pouring alcohol down her throat and putting ink on her young skin infuriated him. He would have trouble saying so out loud, but over the past year, she had grown on him.

Of course it couldn't be that easy. Nothing about this case was easy.

A steady dinging jerked him awake. The computer. His face was pressed against the keyboard. He had not even known he'd nodded off. Jovanic dragged himself out of the chair, yawning, and trudged across the office. He had to grab a couple of hours' sleep before he hit the department's computer, where he could access rap sheets, parole information and DMV records.

Meanwhile, the body count was mounting. Travis, Angel, Darla. And now Jamie was missing. She was a piece of work, but he did not want to see her become victim number four. He hoped she was smart enough to stay away from Viper.

Detective Colin Flynt buttonholed Jovanic before he had a chance to start on his second mug of coffee. His sleeves were pushed up, the top button of his dress shirt open, his tie loosened. He perched his oversized ass on the corner of the desk and tapped a file folder he was holding. "I just got a call from a guy, claims he's got something on dumpster girl."

"Why's he calling you?"

"He was calling about my soccer mom. Says there's a connection."

Jovanic sat up straight. "What kind of a connection?"

"He wouldn't say. I'm meeting him at eleven-thirty. The Casablanca on Lincoln. Wanna tag along?"

"Damn straight I do." Jovanic knew the place, a Mexican restaurant themed for the movie. He didn't care about the life-sized Humphrey Bogart statue or the movie memorabilia, but the *Pechugas de Pollo* would get him through the door. "How do you know he's legit? What did he say?"

"Said he was shocked when he saw the Steinman murder on the news. They showed the kids, interviewed Grandma. She's saying the husband did it. Go figure."

"Yeah, that'd be a first."

"Bill Steinman's coolin' his jets in Interview Room 3. You wanna take a run at him? I'm heading there now."

"Sure. I want to know about that sugar skull tattoo on his wife."

Jovanic would have preferred some time to review the Steinman murder book and prepare for the interview, but all he had seen was the victim's body at the morgue. Sometimes you just had to go with what you had. He rose and shrugged into his suit coat. Flynt might dress like a slob, and that could help put the witness at ease, but Jovanic preferred a more professional look.

As they walked to the interview room he asked for more information about Flynt's caller.

"Sounded pretty shook up, wouldn't say much on the phone." Flynt pulled out his notebook. "Name's Shane Oliver, he's—"

"*Shane?* No friggin way."

"What?"

"We're looking for a journalist named Shane."

"You're shittin me."

"I shit you not."

"Well, ain't that a coinkadink."

Jovanic reached for the doorknob. "I don't believe in coincidences."

twenty-eight

William Steinman was the perfect model of a bereaved spouse, thought Jovanic, observing him through the two-way mirror before they entered the interview room. He was seated at the table, linebacker shoulders hunched, head in hands. He looked up as the door opened to admit the two detectives, his face wet with tears. Whether the tears were more for his dead wife or himself was unclear.

"Bill." Colin Flynt reached out to shake his hand. "Don't get up. I'm Colin. I'm heading the investigation into your wife's death. This is Joel."

"Detective Jovanic," Jovanic said, not unfriendly, but keeping some distance. Steinman's warm, moist flesh made him want to wipe his hand on his trousers.

"I didn't do it." Steinman said urgently, not waiting for Flynt to start the interview. "I *know* what that old biddy and the kids are saying, but it's a lie. I would never hurt my wife."

Would never. Jovanic picked up on the trigger words. When a suspect said "I would never," it often meant they had already done whatever it was they were denying. He took the chair across from Steinman. Flynt remained standing over the husband, a posture that gave him the advantage. "Which old biddy is that?" Flynt asked.

Steinman scrubbed his hands across his face, wiping away the evidence of his momentary weakness. He took a deep breath. "You know who I'm talking about, Darla's mom, Marilyn Sanders. She's got the kids brainwashed. I wasn't anywhere close to the house when—when—it happened."

"Is there any reason Darla's mother would say that you did this?"

"Listen, you guys know I got in trouble before. That was a mistake and it was two years ago."

"Why do you think someone would do something like this, Bill?" Flynt asked.

"How the hell should I know? She lets someone in the house and they shoot her. Isn't that what you guys said happened?"

"You think she let them in?"

"Look, Darla never leaves the door unlocked. Ever. She's paranoid about that shit. If someone came through the door, she opened it and let them in."

"So, you think it was someone she knew? Are you aware of anyone who would want to hurt her?"

"No, man. She's just an ordinary mom; she works part-time as a realtor. I mean, she smokes a little weed once in a while, but nothing stronger, and never around the kids." Steinman's face screwed into a deep scowl. "Her mom is always happy to stick her big fat nose in and stay with Ellie and Tim when Darla goes out. Like they need a babysitter at their age."

"How old are they?"

"Em's eleven, Tim's thirteen."

"They're your stepchildren?"

"Yeah, but I've always treated them like they're my own."

Flynt consulted his file. "The information you gave the first officer who contacted you was that you were in Riverside at the time your wife was killed. Is that correct?"

"Yeah, man, that's over a hundred miles from here. I was just getting off the freeway when the cops called me. I was away overnight."

Flynt pulled a two-year-old color photo from the file and dropped it on the table. From his vantage point, Jovanic could see Darla Steinman's puffy face. A multi-hued bruise painted her left cheek; blonde hair pushed behind a torn earlobe where an earring had been ripped out. Her eyes were a contrast in colors—the right one white, the left blood-filled and swollen almost shut. An image of Angel's beaten face and body pulsed in Jovanic's brain and he felt shame for his gender.

Steinman flipped the photo upside down and banged his fist on it. "I told you that was two years ago. I did all the anger management classes the judge ordered, I paid the fine, I did the fucking community service."

"That's a lot of anger to manage, pal. I guess she knew how to push your buttons, huh?" Flynt said.

"I never touched her like that again. You can't hang this on me. I *didn't* kill her."

"Is there anyone in Riverside who can vouch for your whereabouts, Bill?"

"Shit, I don't want to..." Steinman trailed off.

"Gas receipts? Restaurants? Hotel?"

"No, I used cash. Goddammit. It's complicated. There's someone—I don't want to get them involved."

"You were banging some other guy's wife and you don't want her husband to find out."

"Hey, man, Darla filed for divorce. What am I supposed to do?"

"You'll have to give us your friend's name. You know that."

"Aw, c'mon, man. You can't do this to me."

"Mr. Steinman." Jovanic spoke for the first time, pulling the man's attention away from Flynt. "Tell me about the tattoo Darla had on her shoulder."

"The sugar skull? Jesus, she's had that forever. She had it when I met her. Why? What's it got to do with her getting killed?"

"Just checking everything out. She ever talk about where she got it?"

"Nah, man. She used to be a party girl when she was younger, before Tim and Ellie came along. Who the hell cares where she got it?" His expression softened for just a moment. "We had some good times, you know? Back in the beginning. It was her mom who fucked everything up. She's gotta stick her face into my business all the time. She's always saying shitty things about me to the kids, always wants to butt in on our time."

Jovanic leaned back and watched Bill Steinman's agitation grow as he spoke about his mother-in-law. It showed in the way he bounced his knee under the table, the heightening of his color.

"Who else has been beating on Darla, Bill?" Jovanic asked.

"What? Nobody."

"Why'd she file for divorce?"

"I dunno. I guess she found out I was, uh, seeing someone."

"You guess?"

"She did, okay? She found out. She hacked into my email and my phone." Steinman dropped his head and sighed. "What the hell happened? I loved her."

Jovanic didn't care about what had happened to the Steinman marriage. He changed the subject before Bill Steinman could get maudlin. "Who was she dating before she met you?"

"How'm I supposed to know? We're talking, what, eight, nine years ago? She never talked about anyone else."

"Never?"

"No, man. She said the past didn't mean anything. She didn't want to hear about my exes and she didn't want to talk about hers."

"Does the name Viper mean anything to you?"

"Viper? You mean, like a snake?" Steinman shrugged with a small shake of his head. "Should it?"

"How about Alvin Rousch or Crash?"

"Who the hell are these people?" A glimmer of hope crossed Steinman's face. "What are those, gang names? You think *gang members* killed Darla? You know it wasn't me, right?"

Jovanic stood up. Bill Steinman was not his man. His denial had the ring of sincerity. Colin Flynt would continue investigating Darla Steinman's homicide, but Jovanic was going to have to look elsewhere.

Flynt would check into his victim's past; her cell phone records, her contacts in and outside of work. With her work as a realtor, even part-time, there would be plenty to dig through.

Jovanic had enough of his own to work on. His task was to discover how Travis Navarette and Angel Tedesco were connected to Viper. He did not offer his hand this time. "Thanks for your time. Detective Flynt has some more questions for you."

"Hey, wait. Do I need a lawyer?"

Jovanic shrugged. "You aren't under arrest. That's why we didn't read you your rights. You can call a lawyer if you want, but we're just trying to figure out who did this to your wife."

twenty-nine

Jovanic's stomach was growling. The acid from the coffee he had consumed over the morning hours was eating a hole. He flipped back the towel that covered a plate of fresh flour tortillas, happy to munch while waiting for Shane Oliver, the caller who claimed to have information that linked the two female homicide victims.

Recognizing them as cops, the hostess had rushed to seat them in a secluded booth at the back of the restaurant. They had a view of the arched doorway up front. At eleven-twenty the place was empty, easy enough to spot Oliver when he came through the door.

"Be nice if we could solve crimes as easy as ole Bogie." Flynt nodded toward the glass booth near their table. A life-size figure of the actor wore his familiar fedora.

"Maybe if you had his looks."

Flynt gave him the finger. "Fuck you and the horse you rode in on."

The waitress brought their drinks and took their order with a big smile. Jovanic guessed he would have to argue with her to get a bill. Restaurants in this neighborhood liked having cops for customers. It discouraged the riffraff.

Colin Flynt stuffed a second tortilla in his mouth. "Damn, these are good."

Jovanic agreed they were the best he'd ever eaten. Or maybe he was just hungry. He tore off a piece of his tortilla. "Steinman didn't do it."

"Yeah, I know; I just hate assholes who beat up on women."

"Mind if I talk to Grandma and the kids?"

"You think they've got something?"

"You never know."

"You've got a copy of the murder book. Knock yourself out." Flynt checked his watch. "Oliver ought to be here any minute."

"Darla and Angel," Jovanic mused. "Seems unlikely. But stranger things have happened."

"Oliver sounded pretty spooked. Of course, he might turn out to be some schmo with a tin hat who believes aliens are controlling his thoughts."

"Not if he's the journalist we're looking for. Maybe he's got something we can use."

"What's his story?" Flynt chuckled. "Pun intended."

"Can't you do any better than that? My CI says he's been hanging around Under My Skin, doing research for an article about the tattoo culture."

"Maybe he saw dumpster girl get whacked—" Flynt broke off as the waitress approached, arms laden with plates piled high with chicken, rice, and beans.

They ate and chatted about the cases. By eleven forty-five, there was no sign of their witness and Jovanic felt a ripple of unease, a cop's sixth sense warning that something wasn't right. He knew Flynt felt it too, though he didn't say it out loud. His troubled expression spoke louder than words.

By noon, Shane Oliver still had not shown.

"Either he changed his mind and booked it," said Flynt, "or..."

Jovanic got out his phone and started tapping. "Lemme see if Hardcastle's dug up anything."

Flynt returned to Pacific Division to work the Steinman case while Jovanic drove across town to the Cozy Suites motel in Santa Monica. Shane Oliver's sometime editor in San Francisco had grudgingly parted with the information that the journalist was staying at the motel on his own dime, freelancing the tattoo culture story. The editor had refused to divulge any details, even after Detective Hardcastle indicated that they knew from a confidential informant that Oliver had been hanging around a tattoo parlor, interviewing biker members of a notorious club.

"An investigative reporter's no different from you, Detective. They investigate," the editor said. "Shane's a free spirit. Once he gets his teeth into a big story, he'll go off the grid without warning. If you can't find him, he's following up on a lead."

For an economy hotel, the champagne-colored paint on the Old California style building looked fresh, the Kelly-green awnings over the windows crisp and clean. Jovanic found a parking place on the street, then entered and made his way across a short lobby to the registration desk.

A young woman in a light blue shirt, the hotel's logo embroidered on the pocket, stood behind the counter, talking on the phone. She glanced over, acknowledging Jovanic with a smile, and held up one finger, signaling him to wait. He could tell from her side of the conversation that she was talking to a guest. He moved aside his suit coat to let her see the shield on his waistband. Her brows went up and she hurried to end the call.

"What can I do for you, officer?"

"Detective Jovanic, LAPD. You have a guest staying here, last name Oliver?"

The clerk moved over to a computer. Her fingers flew over the keyboard. "Shane Oliver?" She looked up with a slight frown. "He's prepaid through today. It looks like he hasn't checked out yet."

Jovanic gave a pointed glance at his watch. "It's only 12:40."

"Checkout's at 11:00. If he doesn't show up by the time the maid's ready to clean the room, he's gonna get charged for today."

"Would you please ring the room and see if he's there."

"Of course." She picked up the phone and dialed. After listening for a few seconds, she hung up, shaking her head. "No answer."

"Do you record vehicle information?"

"We sure do. I'll write it down for you." The clerk peered at her screen again and grabbed a piece of scrap paper and pen. "He registered a motorcycle, a 2005 Harley."

Jovanic thanked her and excused himself, then went outside to look in the parking lot behind the building. At this time of day there were few vehicles in the lot. The license plate on the gleaming blue and chrome Harley Sportster XL matched the numbers the clerk had written down. The bad feeling grew.

Jovanic returned to the front desk and asked for Shane Oliver's room number.

"I'm sorry, but I'm not authorized to give you that information." The clerk leaned forward. "I thought he looked kinda seedy. Is he in trouble?"

"Not at all."

"Well...I'll have to call the manager."

"That's fine. Please do it."

The manager, a trim young man in a business suit, held out his hand and introduced himself as Jose Preza. "How can I be of assistance, Detective?" he asked, seeming eager to help. Unlike the restaurant Jovanic had just left, having a police detective in the lobby was bad for the hotel business and he knew Preza was in a hurry to move him along.

"I'm trying to locate a guest who's not answering the phone in his room. His motorcycle is parked outside in your lot."

"I see." The manager considered the information, then offered his opinion. "Maybe somebody came and picked him up?"

"I need you to show me to his room, Mr. Preza. And if he doesn't respond, I'll want you to open the door."

"Well, I'm not sure...I think maybe I should call our legal counsel...maybe a warrant..."

Jovanic was at least a head taller than the manager, who was doing his best to stand up straight. He stared the young man down. "A guest's safety might be at stake, Mr. Preza. While you're busy on the phone, this guy could be bleeding out on your carpet. Exigent circumstances don't require a warrant."

The manager's face paled. "Yes, yes, of course. Let me get the key." He hurried behind the desk and programmed a card key for Shane Oliver's guest room while the clerk watched, curiosity oozing from every pore.

Leading the way through a back door, Jose Preza crossed the courtyard and around the pool deck, which was empty of guests. "Mr. Oliver has been staying with us for the past week," he explained as they climbed the outside stairwell to the second floor. "He paid in advance with cash, which is a little unusual. We're not that kind of hotel, you know."

"Do you require guests to show ID?" Jovanic asked.

"Yes, indeed, we scanned his driver's license. It's in the computer if you want to see it. I'd be happy to print it out."

They exited the staircase at a door-lined balcony overlooking the pool. Preza told him that Oliver's room was 215, the third door down.

"Do exactly what I tell you," Jovanic said. "Give me the key and stand over there." He indicated the stairwell they had just exited, took the card key from the manager, and unholstered his weapon.

He moved along the balcony to 215 and knocked hard on the door. "Mr. Oliver?" he called loudly. "Manager."

The silence behind the door felt like the room was empty, but he was not taking any chances. It was less than a year ago that he had taken two bullets and he was not eager to repeat the experience.

With his Glock pointed 45 degrees downwards at half-ready, Jovanic slid the card key through the reader. When the light blinked green, he pushed the door open with his free hand and quickly stepped out of the kill zone.

The door hit the wall with a sharp thwack. Bracing for a shot, Jovanic took a quick peek into the room. Left to right, up and down, a split-second threat assessment before the door could swing back. He caught it before the self-closing piston hinges slammed it shut.

Jovanic stepped inside, every sense on edge. He cleared the living room and bath, then the bedroom, confirming that the suite was empty. He let out a breath and wiped clammy hands on his trousers.

The queen bed was unmade, pillows dented as if recently slept on, comforter spilling onto the floor. The air was stale with the lingering smell of a heavy smoker. A large black duffel stood open on the bed. The journalist had started to pack, perhaps interrupted in the midst of the task.

The dresser drawers were empty. A classic black leather motorcycle jacket hung in the closet. A helmet the same metallic blue as the bike in the parking lot stood on the suitcase rack.

In the bathroom, a Dopp kit on the toilet tank held a toothbrush, toothpaste, deodorant, a partially smoked joint in a baggie. Another baggie contained a handful of undetermined pills and capsules. Was Oliver a druggie, or just playing the part for his research?

In the living room, a laptop was plugged into an outlet on the desk.

"What do you think happened?" The manager spoke from the doorway, staying on the threshold as though afraid to enter the room.

"That's what I'm going to try to figure out."

Jose Preza wrinkled his nose and stepped inside, looked around. "Cigarettes. This is a non-smoking room. He's going to get charged for the extra cleaning."

"Please step back outside, sir."

"Are you gonna take anything out of here?"

"If you want to report these items as 'found property' and turn them over to me, I'll take them off your hands."

"Well—don't you need a warrant for that at least?"

"Not if you're worried about the guest's safety and you believe he's not coming back for his things."

"Hmmmm. Let me go ahead and call the head office on that. I'll see what they want me to do."

"I'll wait for you here."

"Okay, but if you find an ashtray, I need to keep it as proof he was breaking the rules."

The manager closed the door behind him and Jovanic took a video of each room before he touched anything. When he was done, he returned to the laptop and donned a pair of latex gloves he'd brought in his jacket pocket. He touched the glide pad and a screen came up requesting a password.

Damn.

Nothing he could do there. It would have to go to the lab. Were it not for the password, he might have been tempted to poke around a little and see what he could find. But as it stood, his situational ethics went untested.

Assuming Shane Oliver did not return to claim it before they had the opportunity, the techs would make a mirror image of the hard drive and figure out the password before they could comb through it. That way, if the computer later became evidence in a court case, a defense attorney would not be able to accuse Jovanic of having tampered with it.

He returned to the closet and began a systematic search of the leather jacket, unzipping, unsnapping pockets, finding nothing. He checked the duffel, taking out each item and laying everything on the bed. When he had finished, there was nothing of interest in the jumble of T-shirts, underwear and socks. There were a few coins and a wadded up dirty tissue in the Levi's pockets, which made him glad for the gloves.

In the nightstand drawer he found Shane Oliver's wallet. Inside was a thick wad of cash, his driver's license, three credit cards, and a handful of other identification. His room key was not present, but unless he was out taking a walk around the block, which seemed unlikely given that it was well past checkout time, the fact that his wallet was in the room didn't bode well for the journalist. Had someone picked him up?

Jovanic counted almost five hundred bucks, which he spread out and photographed with his cell phone. Behind the cash he found a scrap of paper torn from a legal pad. Someone had scribbled a phone number on it in the 310-area code—Los Angeles.

He tapped in the number for the dispatcher and asked her to find out who the number belonged to. She called back and told him it was a mobile number, which increased the level of difficulty. Thanking her, he clicked off and went for Plan B.

"What's it gonna get me?" Lenny Burton wanted to know. "Tell me why I should kick it to the front of the line."

Lenny worked in the intelligence unit, which gave him access to information using means that Jovanic knew better than to ask about. He and Lenny had a private arrangement that circumvented the need to wait for a search warrant in cases like this one. Jovanic needed to know who owned that cell phone number, and he needed the information now.

"It's your damn job, Lenny," he retorted. "It'll take you five minutes."

"Aw, man. Five minutes? You got any idea of my workload? There's a stack of files on my desk a foot high. Plus, I got no help today—the budget cuts, everyone's on vacation—"

Jovanic cut in. "Quit your whining. My girlfriend's brother has some Dodger tickets he can't use. I can probably get them for you."

The intel man's voice brightened. "Yeah? Good seats?"

"C'mon, Lenny. When did I ever screw you over?"

"True enough, J, you always come through. So, what d'ya need?"

Jovanic had known that once he got his standard gripe out of the way Lenny would come through for him. "Got a missing person connected to a couple of fresh homicides, so I need it yesterday. I've got a feeling this guy is in deep shit."

"Okay, pal, what's the number? I'll get back to you."

Jovanic read it off to him. "Don't take all day, Lenny, okay?"

"You just call your girlfriend's brother and make sure he's still got those tickets. I'll get back to ya."

thirty

Jovanic packed up Shane Oliver's possessions in Oliver's duffel bag. He left a receipt with the manager, planning to drop everything at the crime lab for processing.

He put the duffel and laptop in his vehicle, then phoned Marilyn Sanders, whose name was on his list to call. Darla Steinman's mother was more than willing to grant him an interview at her home in Santa Monica, a few miles from Oliver's hotel.

She lived off Montana near Twenty-Sixth in a beautiful old Craftsman style bungalow shaded in the front yard by two enormous trees. Jovanic didn't know what kind they were, but as soon as he walked between them, he noticed the temperature drop several degrees. Residents of that house would not need air conditioning.

Steinman's mother was standing inside the big picture window, waiting for him. As he came up the brick front walk and climbed the short staircase, she opened the door wide and welcomed him in.

In her navy sheath dress, pearls and high-heeled shoes, she reminded Jovanic of a 1950s TV mom. Despite the tight Botoxed face shared by many older women on this side of town who were fighting gravity, he could see new grief etched there.

Marilyn Sanders invited him inside the pre-WWII era home. Serious money had been pumped into redecorating: Natural wood floors, white-washed walls, minimalist furnishings. Interior walls had been eliminated to create a large open-plan living space that included the kitchen. A French coffee press stood on a marbled counter, scenting the air. She offered him a cup.

Jovanic accepted with thanks and followed her to the counter, where two china cups and saucers had already been laid out.

"Cream? Sugar?" Now that he was here, she was delaying the moment they would begin the interview.

"Black is fine, thank you. I'm very sorry for your loss, Mrs. Sanders."

Her back was turned to him and he saw her shoulders sag a little, her head drooping as if she no longer had the strength to hold it. "The children are staying with me." Her voice caught. "There's no way I'm going to let that monster near them."

"You mean Mr. Steinman?"

"That drunken womanizer. My daughter filed for divorce, but she waited too long. Now it's too late." Marilyn Sanders handed Jovanic his cup. "Have you arrested him yet?"

"We've talked to him and we're checking out his story."

She led him back into the living room and moved to the Italian leather sofa. "Please, have a seat." She spoke a little too loudly and Jovanic wondered if she was trying to cover the sound of her cup rattling in its saucer as she set it on the cocktail table. He could not fault a bereaved mother hands that shook.

Giving her a moment to settle herself, Jovanic sat beside her and took a sip of coffee that was a few hundred times better than anything they brewed at work.

Marilyn Sanders ran her hand through short blonde hair twice, drew a deep breath and let it out. She squared her shoulders and lifted her chin. She was ready.

Jovanic spoke first. "Can you tell me why you believe your son-in-law—"

Before he could finish his question, she broke in. "I thought you people always looked at the husband first. You must know he beat her up before, more than once, though he was just arrested that one time. You don't need to look any further than that. He did it. He killed my daughter."

"Do you know whether Mr. Steinman owned any firearms?"

"Well, he had to, didn't he? He must have got one from somewhere, even if there aren't any registered to him. I'm sure he must know people—gang people, maybe. He shot her three times. Once wasn't enough." Her eyes filled with tears and she pulled a tissue from her pocket. "I'm sorry. I—"

"Please don't apologize, Mrs. Sanders. I can't imagine how difficult this must be for you." Jovanic knew better than to tell her he understood, even though he did. But it wouldn't do any good to tell her that his father had been murdered in a robbery when Jovanic was just a kid. A victim's angry family needed to be allowed their own pain without being expected to consider his.

"It is. It's very difficult." Marilyn Sanders dabbed around her eyes with the tissue and swallowed hard.

He waited a couple of beats. "I need to ask you something that might seem unrelated, but are you aware of your daughter having a tattoo?"

She frowned. "That *skull thing*? My husband and I were furious when she did that."

"Would you happen to know where she had it done?"

"She didn't have it done anywhere. Her boyfriend did it. Alvin something or other. She was sixteen. He was a lot older—maybe in his early twenties. He was the brother of someone she knew at school. That was an *awful* time. I'd rather forget it."

"Awful because—"

"Darla was incredibly rebellious. She was truant from school every other day. We tried putting her in several different private academies, but nothing helped. She used to climb out the window in the night when my husband and I were asleep and take off with these dreadful young men on motorcycles—a gang, I'm sure. We tried everything we knew to stop it, even down to sleeping in shifts to keep an eye on her. I was ready to send her to live with my sister in Ohio." Marilyn Sanders paused to give him a sad smile. "Then there was the big fight."

Jovanic raised an inquiring brow.

Sanders continued. "That Alvin character and another young man—I don't remember his name—they had this terrible fight over Darla. I believe the other one ended up in the hospital with broken bones and internal injuries. And then she decided she wasn't interested and just walked away from both of them and we didn't have to do anything drastic after all."

She gave a big sigh that sounded like regret. "We loved that girl to distraction. She was such a sweet, compliant child, but once she got into her teens, trying to control her was impossible. I believe that's what shortened my husband's life by more than a few years. He died of a broken heart. And now she's gone, too."

"Raising teenagers is always rough," Jovanic spoke with genuine sympathy, thinking of some of the trials he and Claudia had ridden out with Annabelle before she connected with her birth father. And the more recent ones.

"So, why are you asking about that tattoo? It's ancient news."

"Just pursuing some leads, ma'am. We sometimes have to ask questions that might seem irrelevant."

"It was something I'll never forget. Though now, what does it matter?" She sighed again, as if she were having difficulty catching her breath. "I remember that Darla told me Alvin was learning to be a tattoo artist, of all things. He was practicing on her. Can you imagine? Why would anyone want to deface their body that way?"

Her words made him think of the tattoo on Darla Steinman's corpse. The colors of the glamorous skull had been fresh and vibrant, not the faded look of twenty-year-old ink. "You said Darla walked away from these two men after the fight. But would you know whether she had any contact with Alvin later? Maybe got the tattoo refreshed fairly recently?"

"I would certainly be shocked if she had. She was your typical good mother, devoted to her children; always taking them to dance lessons, music lessons, Little League games. Anyway, what's that got to do with Bill murdering my daughter?" She paused, confusion spreading over her face. "Wait a minute, is *Alvin* involved in this?"

"We're looking at a number of scenarios," Jovanic said, which seemed to mollify her. "Are your grandchildren here, Mrs. Sanders? I'd appreciate a few words with them, if you don't mind."

"They're playing video games in the den. It's been a nightmare. Tim came home and found her—but you already know that."

"I just have a couple of questions."

"Is that really necessary? They already spoke with the other detective—Flynt. They don't know anything."

"I understand, but it's important."

When her lips compressed into a disapproving line, Jovanic knew she wanted to refuse, but after a moment she resigned herself. "Please be gentle with them."

"Yes, ma'am, of course."

Darla Steinman's mother rose and left the room, returning five minutes later accompanied by a young boy and girl. Bill Steinman had told Jovanic that they were eleven and thirteen. Typical of his age, the boy was gangly and as tall as his grandmother. His sister stood behind him, half-hiding until Marilyn Sanders made the introductions. She pulled the children to each side of her and put her arms around their shoulders. "Ellie, Tim, this is Detective Jovanic. He's looking into the—what happened to your mother."

Jovanic appraised them as she spoke, taking in the Abercrombie logo on Tim's plaid shirt, the pricey-looking jeans they both wore. As if they were adults, he held out his hand to each of them in turn. Tim, the older of the two, had an unusually firm grip for one so young. Ellie's hand was soft and small inside his big rough one, and he felt her vulnerability like a kick in the teeth. In her yellow cropped tee, decorated with daisies, she was still very much a child.

Ellie plopped onto the sofa and hunched into the corner next to her grandmother, a worried look on her pale face. Tim perched on the edge of a chair opposite, trying to look grown up.

"I'm very sorry about your mom." Jovanic took care that he did not come across patronizing. "I know you've already talked to Detective Flynt about it, and I know it's really hard to keep going over things. But I have a couple of questions I need to ask. Is that okay?" He gave them a moment to nod agreement, then continued. "First, can you tell me, did you notice anything that was unusual, going on with your mom?"

Both blonde heads shook, "No."

"That other guy already asked us that," Tim said with an edge of defiance.

"I understand, and sometimes I have to ask the same questions because I wasn't here when Detective Flynt spoke to you, okay?"

After gaining two reluctant shrugs, Jovanic asked, "Did you ever go someplace with your mom and have to wait out in the car?" In the short silence that followed, Jovanic caught the look that passed between brother and sister. "Hey, guys, whatever you say here, you're not going to be in any trouble. All I'm asking is for you to tell the truth." He smiled and pointed at his white shirt. "If I tell you my shirt is blue, is that true or false?"

Tim's expression indicated that he thought the detective was a moron. "False, *obviously.*"

"Okay, good. I just want you to say what you know that's true."

It came as a surprise that Ellie was the one who piped up first, speaking in a voice so quiet that he had to strain to hear her. "Sometimes, when she would go in that tattoo place, Mom would make us wait outside in the car."

Marilyn Sanders gasped. Jovanic raised a warning hand and she held her tongue with obvious difficulty. "Did you go to the tattoo place with her very often?"

Ellie looked over at her older brother with a question. Tim said, "Not exactly often, like, maybe a few times."

"She always promised to come right back, but sometimes she was gone a long time," Ellie said. "We mostly played video games while we were waiting."

"Do you remember when the last time was that you went there with her?"

"It was last week, on Friday, right after she picked us up from school," Tim said. "Except that one time she let us go inside."

"Yeah? What was it like?"

"It's pretty cool."

"Was mom getting a tattoo?"

"No, she was just talking to the owner."

"She said they were friends," Ellie added, her voice beginning to tremble. "She went to high school with his little brother."

"Okay, thank you. Do remember if anyone else was there besides the owner?"

"Some guys were sitting in the back," Tim said. "They didn't say anything to us, though." His cheeks flushed scarlet. "And there was this girl sitting with them."

Jovanic smiled. "Cute girl?"

Tim shrugged, but the blush remained. "I guess."

"But you didn't get introduced to any of those people?"

"Nope."

Jovanic would have like to show the boy a photo of Angel, but all he had in his phone were post-mortem shots. "What did the girl look like?"

"She had blonde hair and...I don't know. She was a girl."

"Do you know her name?"

"My mom said hi to her," Ellie added. "She said, 'Hi, Angel.' I thought it was a pretty name."

Jovanic's heart rate sped up. He had his connection. "Do you remember anything about the guys, what they looked like?"

Tim scrunched up his face, thinking back. "One of them was super buffed. And he had tats on his face. But we didn't talk to him or the other guys."

"The owner guy gave Mommy some money," Ellie said. "She told us not to tell Bill about going there. She said it was a secret place and only we could know about—"

Tim interrupted angrily. "You shouldn't make us say bad things about our mom."

"You're not saying anything bad, Tim," Jovanic said. "Remember, you're just telling the truth."

Ellie looked up at her grandmother, tears rolling down her face. "Are we being bad, Nana?"

Glaring at Jovanic over the child's head, Marilyn Sanders put a protective arm around her granddaughter and pressed a tissue into her hand. "No, honey, of course not. You're not being bad at all. Just tell Detective Jovanic what he needs to know. He's almost ready to leave. Isn't that right, Detective?"

"Yes, that's right. Just one more thing, kids. Do you remember the name of the tattoo place, or where it is?"

"Um, yeah. It has a big red dragon painted on the window," Tim said. "It's called Dragon House."

Just then, Jovanic's phone signaled a text message. He excused himself and took out the phone, checked the screen. Serendipity. Lenny had come through.

Jovanic was on his way to the crime lab, wondering what Darla Steinman's cell phone number was doing in Shane Oliver's wallet, when he took a call from Jose Preza at the Cozy Suites.

"I thought you'd want to know, Detective." The manager sounded excited. "The maid was changing the linens in Mr. Oliver's room. She found something under the pillow."

thirty-one

"Let me get some gloves." Claudia led Joel into her office and took a box of disposable exam gloves from a drawer. "I know you don't want my prints on it," she said, taking out two pair.

"You're such a pro," he teased, setting the paper bag containing Shane Oliver's notebook on her desk.

"I learned from the best, Columbo."

Claudia sat down behind her desk, and eased her fingers into the stretchy gloves, then reached for the bag and pulled the top open.

They had eaten a late dinner while he gave her a broadbrush summary of his day. They had then climbed the stairs together to Claudia's office. He wanted her take on Shane Oliver's journal, which he had picked up from the Cozy Suites. It measured around six and a half by nine and a half inches and was bound with a black cardboard cover.

"Have you read it yet?" asked Claudia.

"Not yet, just flipped through a few pages. It's a work journal, notes. The last page was dated yesterday. Too bad it's not like the movies—a big clue, telling me where to find him."

"How inconvenient. There should be a big neon arrow in the book, pointing to Angel's killer."

"We pretty much *know* who the killer is. We just need the evidence to tie him to the crimes." Joel came around behind her chair as she opened the book and rested his hands on her shoulders and began massaging the tight muscles. "You're all knotted up."

"M'hm. All this upset with Annabelle—Angel, then Jamie disappearing. It's been getting to me. Ohhhh, that feels good." His firm thumbs made little circles as they inched up her skull. His fingers raked her hair, making it hard to concentrate on the handwriting in the journal. She made an effort to pull her focus onto the page.

The journal paper was unlined. Shane Oliver's writing was small and highly simplified, a mixture of print and cursive. Letters that were joined had quick, clever connections. Many words were written at high velocity, which resulted in a thready, undefined look and impacted the legibility, making it hard to read. Some notes were written at an extreme uphill slant, others straight across the page.

Claudia, who had not yet read what was written there, looked up from the journal and started describing her first impression of the writer's personality from his handwriting. "He's very intelligent; a quick, facile type of thinker. He's articulate and he's got a talent for jumping from one thing to another without dropping the ball. He's also damned unpredictable—kind of an action junkie. It's hard for him to make a commitment. He likes to leave everything open-ended, in case something better comes along and he wants to change his mind."

"That would support what his editor said, but that doesn't mean he left the hotel willingly. He left his computer behind; his wallet, his notebook. I checked back with the manager after I left the crime lab. Nada. No sign of him."

"Well, for sure he's a smooth talker, so let's hope he can talk himself out of whatever it is that he's apparently gotten into. Any idea what might have happened to him?"

"Yeah, unfortunately, I do. We know he's been developing a story about tattoo parlors. But he's an investigative reporter, so that means the story isn't what it looks like on the surface. He'll have been asking a lot of questions, digging up whatever shit he can find, which maybe certain people would rather keep buried." Joel leaned over and pointed to something written on page one. "Viper's name keeps popping up—Alvin Rousch. Remember, Angel's boyfriend, Mouser, told Annabelle that Shane was hanging around Dragon House, which Viper owns. *And* Viper is the guy who put his mark—the sugar skull—on Darla Steinman, who's now dead."

"*And* on Angel, who's also dead. And on Jamie, who's missing."

Claudia shuddered, thinking of the sugar skull tattoo on Annabelle's skin, thankful that even though the artist had copied his design, Viper was not the one who had put it on the girl.

"Then there's my firebombing victim, Travis Navarette," Joel continued. "It's all happened too close together. Three homicides connected. That can't be a coincidence. And now Shane Oliver may have dug up something too dangerous for him to know. Maybe he saw or heard something he shouldn't have."

Claudia voiced the question that was nagging her. "I wonder what a soccer mom like Darla was doing at the tattoo parlor while her kids were waiting outside in the MommyMobile."

"Probably not having milk and cookies. Maybe she was just getting that old tattoo refreshed. Plenty of women get tats these days."

"Her mom told you she dumped Viper when she was about sixteen, didn't she?"

"Yeah, after 'the big fight.'"

"Why would she start up with him again now? Maybe this is nothing new. She might have been seeing him for years."

"Flynt's going to take a closer look at Darla." Joel's fingers gave her shoulders a final squeeze. He dropped his hands and went to the office door. "Viper is at the center of all the strings. I just need to find a way to pull them all together."

Claudia stretched her neck from side to side, already missing his touch on her skin. "I'm worried about Jamie, too."

"I have no doubt Jamie's back on the street, looking for her next fix." Joel rubbed his eyes and yawned wide. "Girls like her learn how to survive."

"Angel didn't."

"She hadn't gotten down to that level of desperation yet." He yawned again, wider. "I'm gonna hit the shower and head back to the office. Don't wait up for me."

"Okay. I'll scan the journal so I can keep working on it."

After Joel left, taking Shane Oliver's journal with him, Claudia sat at her computer and opened the PDFs she had made of the seventeen pages. She had scanned them in color at high res, which ensured that she had the next best to original quality.

Like a diary, most pages had a date written at the top. The first was dated a week earlier. Starting on page one, she read through the notes Oliver had scribbled in black ink, most in his own personal shorthand. There were a few lines to a page, as if he wanted to remind himself of a general topic, leaving plenty of room to add more notes later.

Under the heading "Dragon House," he had made a list of names. Alvin Lester Rousch—Viper—topped the list, followed by Robert "Bad Bobby" Morgan, "Big Carl" Latu. Several other names were new to Claudia.

Next to the unfamiliar names, Oliver had drawn a bracket connecting them, and the word "Skullz," which she recognized as the name of the motorcycle club Jovanic had told her hung out at Dragon House.

A few pages later was the heading "Under My Skin," with Travis Navarette's name underneath, and the note "Trained at DH." Folded into that page was an article cut from an *L.A. Times* print edition published two days ago about the firebombing of the tattoo parlor, and Travis's horrific death.

Claudia pulled out her keyboard drawer and opened a Google browser, then typed in "Skullz." Several articles came up with stories about various crimes that had put members in the media spotlight. She wondered whether Shane Oliver had gotten too close to some of the gang's illegal doings while hanging around Dragon House.

On page nine of the journal an underlined note read, "Inkslingers Ball," and a date, underneath was written "Darla Steinman" and a new name, "Gerald Harris."

Back to Uncle Google.

With a little research, Claudia discovered that the Inkslingers Ball was a body art and piercing convention scheduled for the upcoming weekend at the Pomona Fairgrounds. She guessed that Shane Oliver had planned to attend.

Clicking on the two-minute video posted on the convention website, she was bemused by the spectacle of a Mohawk-haired young man demonstrating the sharpness of a series of razor blades. He sliced a sheet of paper in half before swallowing the blades whole, then pulling them back out on a string.

Charming.

Claudia picked up her phone and gave the voice command to call Joel. Since it was late, chances were, he was alone in the office.

"How would you like a drive out to Pomona this weekend?" she asked.

"What's in Pomona?"

"The Inkslingers Ball. It's in Shane Oliver's journal."

"The tattoo expo?"

"You already know about it?"

"It's held every year at the Fairgrounds."

"Have you read the journal yet?"

"I'm working three homicides, babe. Oliver's editor says he's probably chasing a wild hare, so the journal isn't a high priority right now."

"I think he planned on going to the convention. So, I was thinking, it might be a good place to get some intel on Viper." She paused. "And maybe the guy who inked Annabelle will be there."

"I had a feeling there was more to it." Jovanic chuckled. "If you get your lovely little paws on that guy—like Mr. T. used to say, *I pity the fool*. Damn, I'm dating myself."

"So, what about Pomona?"

"Okay. If there aren't any other leads to develop here, it could be a good idea."

"We can take Annabelle and have her point out the guy if she sees him—Crash."

"You know she'd rather eat glass than go to a tattoo convention with us old fogeys."

"Don't let her hear you say that. She'd eat it just to spite us."

"You're probably right about that. Keep up the good work, Grapho Lady."

Shane Oliver had penned a brief chronology of Viper's life: Born in Victorville, California; father convicted of the murder of his mother, a hooker. Moved in middle school to live with paternal grandparents in Santa Monica. He had not listed a criminal history for Viper, but if he had a juvenile file, it would be sealed.

Darla Steinman's printed name appeared as the heading of a page in which another carefully folded paper had been tucked. This was a printout of another *L.A. Times* article. The date on the article was twenty years earlier, so it had come from the newspaper's archives.

It detailed the vicious beating of a twenty-two-year-old male named Gerald Harris, Jr., who had been hospitalized with serious injuries after an altercation with Alvin Rousch. Reports indicated that the two youths and their friends had arranged to meet in a deserted parking lot at Palisades Beach late one night, a tire iron on one side, a knife on the other. Rousch had sustained superficial knife wounds; Harris, broken bones and a head injury.

Both men refused to press charges and declined to speak with police. With no stated victim, there was no crime to prosecute, and no additional ink was dedicated to the story.

Claudia was not surprised by what she had read. Jovanic often complained about similar situations where those involved—most of the time gang members—didn't even bother to lie about what had occurred. Pride, fear of reprisal, or in some cases an intent to later visit their own retribution on the other party, kept them silent.

Wondering how long Harris had been hospitalized and whether his injuries had been life-threatening, Claudia Googled his name, along with some of the other pertinent information. Nothing else came up on him, so she gave up and resumed her examination of the journal.

Travis Navarette rated a page to himself, along with two more folded articles. One reported on a break-in at Under My Skin during its opening week two months ago. There had been some minor vandalism, credited to "probable juvenile activity." The second was an account of the fatal firebombing last Tuesday, which mentioned the earlier crimes and suggested a possible connection.

Shane Oliver's scribbled notes were cryptic and difficult to decipher, but Claudia figured that what looked like a checkmark might be a capital "V" for "Viper." She was aware that Jovanic suspected Viper of ordering the arson, and it appeared that Shane's own investigation was taking him in that direction, too. If Viper had caught on, it wasn't much of a stretch to imagine that Shane's life might be in danger.

It was nearly one a.m. and she was still at the computer when she heard Annabelle's bedroom door open. A few seconds later, the sleepy-faced girl padded barefoot into the office and flopped on the sofa, drawing her knees and arms into a fetal pose.

Claudia got up and covered her with the afghan she kept folded over the armrest. "What's up, sweetie pie? Trouble sleeping?"

Annabelle closed her eyes and opened her mouth in a long yawn. "I *was* asleep. Mouser woke me up."

"What did he want?"

Snuggling under the afghan, she opened her eyes halfway and looked up at Claudia. "He wanted to talk about Angel."

"In the middle of the night?"

"He doesn't have anyone else he can talk to. He was so sad. I felt sorry for him, even if he is kind of a jerk, so I just listened for a while."

"That was kind of you, sweetie, but I hope he doesn't make it a habit. You should turn off your phone at night."

"One more day of school," Annabelle countered. "Then it's Saturday. I can sleep in."

"Any news from Jamie?"

"I asked Mouser about her. She left out of town with some guy. She was trying to get Mouser to pick her up and give her a ride over here to get her car, but he said no. He still thinks it's her fault Angel's dead. Jamie told him if he didn't come for her, she was gonna have to go with this other guy, and she didn't want to. But he didn't give a rat's—he didn't care. He hung up on her."

"Her keys are downstairs in her backpack. I didn't want to leave it out in her car in the open," Claudia said, rationalizing her actions to herself. "Did he say who the guy was or where they were going?"

"Nope." Annabelle yawned. "Is it okay if I sleep right here, Claudia? Even when you go to bed?"

"Sure." Claudia touched her hand to Annabelle's cheek. "Sleep well."

For a few minutes she sat at her desk, watching until the girl's breathing evened out and she sank back into a dream world where her friends were not murder victims.

Claudia sighed, thinking of Jamie taking off for parts unknown with a strange man, and offered a quick prayer for her safety. She was not religious, but it made her feel a little less helpless, as if she were doing *something*. All Jamie had to do to retrieve her car keys was knock at the door. Hopefully, not in the middle of the night.

Claudia printed out the scanned journal pages and laid them out on her desk, going over each one again. She paused at the Inkslingers Ball entry. Whether Joel was able to break away or not, she resolved that she and Annabelle would go to the tattoo convention on Sunday.

thirty-two

Jovanic was filling his coffee mug when Flynt ambled over with the fresh-eyed look of a man who had enjoyed a full night's sleep.

"You look like shit," Flynt said. "Pull an all-nighter?"

Jovanic rubbed his chin and felt the rough stubble under his hand. "Yeah, Flynt. While your fat ass was snoring like a baby, I was doing your work for you." He took a sip of his coffee. It was weak and lukewarm, but he wished he could mainline it. "You find anything new on Steinman?"

"As a matter of fact, old buddy, I did turn up something pretty interesting." Flynt grinned like the Cheshire cat. "Turns out Susie Homemaker has an old vice sheet."

Jovanic's brows shot up. "Serious?"

"Nailed for a 'b' when she was nineteen; got probation."

"No shit. And she's been clean since then?" Jovanic let his skepticism show. He wondered whether Darla's parents were aware of the prostitution charge. It might be what Marilyn Sanders had referred to that she believed had hastened her husband's death.

"Straight and narrow." Flynt shrugged. "Didn't get caught again, anyhow."

"Who was she working for?"

The grin widened. "You're gonna love this. She spent a lot of time at Alvin Rousch's tattoo studio, but they could never make anything stick."

Jovanic whistled under his breath as he thought about the implications. Darla Steinman had renewed and maintained her ties to Viper. And it appeared she had kept the association secret from her family. So, where did Shane Oliver fit?

Jovanic was sitting at the table with Robert Morgan, struggling to stay alert, when someone from dispatch knocked on the interview room door and rousted him. A call had come in. He left Morgan writing out his statement on a yellow legal pad and stepped into the hallway, glad of the opportunity to stand up and stretch.

A body had been discovered under the Santa Monica Pier. There was no ID, but from the description, Jovanic instantly knew whose body it was. In the victim's pocket was a scrap of paper with the phone number for Pacific Division scrawled on it, along with his and Colin Flynt's names, and a plastic room key from the Cozy Suites Hotel.

Jovanic took a good, hard look at the picture on the driver's license in Shane Oliver's wallet. The journalist was forty-seven, five-eight, one-sixty. He pulled up Oliver's Facebook page on his phone.

The sole photo was a three-quarter view of a man standing by the motorcycle that Jovanic had seen parked in the Cozy Suites parking lot. Oliver wore jeans, motorcycle boots, and a T-shirt that showed off full-sleeve tattoos on both arms. Dark glasses concealed his eyes. His hair, which was largely covered by a black baseball cap worn backwards, was scraped back into a ponytail. He looked the part of a biker and it was easy to imagine him fitting into the Skullz scene at the tattoo parlor.

Fuck.

Shrugging into his jacket, Jovanic ruminated on what might have led the man to his death. He stopped at the 7-Eleven on Lincoln and picked up a liter of Coke, then drove the quick five miles up to Santa Monica Pier, a sick feeling roiling his gut along with the overload of caffeine. Four homicides in one week, all connected to Alvin Rousch, could not be a coincidence.

If he could convince the D.A. that Bobby Morgan's statement would stick, he would be halfway home. But Viper's history of slithering out from under serious charges reminded Jovanic that it would be stupid to presuppose a slam dunk. Any weak points in the case would have to be shored up to make it immune to attack. That meant making sure they had good evidence that corroborated Bobby's story about Angel. Preferably Carl Latu's testimony. The case had to be airtight before he took it to the D.A.

Shirley Lorraine, the coroner's investigator, drove into the parking lot next to the Santa Monica Pier right behind Jovanic. At ten-fifty a.m. on a Friday, the place was already pretty packed.

In most cases Jovanic would have arrived long before the coroner's office and be checking out the scene while he waited for the investigator to come and take possession of the body. He caught up with Lorraine as she climbed down from her SUV and swung into stride next to her. He knew better than to offer help with her bag. Shirley Lorraine's independence was legendary.

"You got a homicide hotline?" he asked. "How'd you get here so fast?"

"On my way back to the office from another scene—a hit and run. I heard this one on the radio. I was closest, so I said I'd take it. Hey, I heard they found your name on the vic."

"Yeah. I've got a pretty good idea who it is."

They walked across the lot, Shirley rolling her equipment bag behind her, and badged their way through the yellow tape. Jovanic told her about Shane Oliver's call to Colin Flynt the day before, and his failure to show up for their appointment at the Casablanca restaurant.

"It was pretty obvious he didn't just go out for a stroll. It was past checkout and he left everything in his motel room. Except his cell phone. I didn't find it in the room."

"Easy ID if it's on him." Shirley Lorraine shook her head gloomily. "I knew I should have called in sick this morning; almost did. I was gonna just veg and watch *Good Morning America.* But noooo, I get a whole string of DBs to process."

Jovanic knocked elbows with her. "Look at it this way, Shirl, your day's going a whole lot better than theirs."

"When did you become Mr. Optimism?" She grinned up at him. "At least I don't have to go looking for the lead on this one. Don't go anywhere, hotshot."

A few yards away across a swath of sand, a group of uniforms stood waiting for them. The marine layer still shrouded the city of Santa Monica, a depressing pall that seemed fitting to Jovanic as they approached the access to the area underneath the hundred-year-old pier. The ocean made an eerie sighing sound, as if it were mourning the inhumanity that had brought them all there.

The patrol officers parted for the two investigators and allowed them to make their way under the pier. Shirley Lorraine took a pair of vinyl gloves from her bag and snapped them on with a cheery, "Hey, fellas."

She didn't need to introduce herself to the seasoned veterans who had responded to this call. They were acquainted from many such scenes.

While she spoke with the first responder, Jovanic took a look around. He crossed the perimeter tape and stepped onto the wet sand, glad he wasn't wearing his best shoes. It was obvious that the tide had washed away any trace evidence they might have collected, but he watched where he walked anyway.

He already knew from the call out that an early morning treasure hunter searching the area with his metal detector had stumbled across the body half-hidden behind a wooden piling. Far from the parking lot entrance, it would not have been seen otherwise and could have washed out to sea without anyone being the wiser. The treasure hunter was sitting in a patrol car being interviewed by Detective RJ Scott, who would transport him to the police station to take a formal statement.

Shirley Lorraine pulled back the tarp that covered the body. A faint odor of decomposition wafted upward as they looked down upon what remained of the man Jovanic identified from his driver's license as Shane Oliver.

The victim's right shoulder was in the sand, his legs bent behind him, indicating that he had fallen backwards and made no effort to catch himself. He was wearing a leather vest, black jeans, and the boots Jovanic had noticed in his Facebook photo: lace-ups with a buckle and strap across the front, a series of dangling chains across the heel.

His hands were bound with grey duct tape. Only Oliver's left profile was visible. He had been punched in the face. "Need to get the toolmarks expert to make a mold." Jovanic crouched to get a closer look at the deep wound on Oliver's cheek. "It looks like some kind of pattern. The suspect was probably wearing a ring. Maybe we'll get lucky and match it."

"Takes a really big man to hit a guy when he's restrained." Shirley got down on her knees and rolled the body. The vest flopped open revealing a black T-shirt with a silk-screened skeleton on a motorcycle across the front. It bore an oddly prescient slogan "Everybody Dies."

She pointed out three holes in the leather vest, close together over the heart. "Medium bore. Probably a thirty-eight."

Jovanic did not question her. She had an uncanny sense for ammo. He knew that if the first bullet had hit Oliver in the heart, like Darla Steinman, it would have immediately stopped pumping and there would be very little blood. Whatever there was had been washed away by the waves. As frustrating as the lack of trace evidence was, he knew they were lucky that jammed up against the piling as it was, at least the body had not been washed out to sea with the tides.

How long had Shane Oliver been lying there? More than twenty-four hours if he had been brought here before Jovanic got to his motel room. He considered the possibility that the killer had kept the journalist some-where else until after dark the night before, beating out of him how much incriminating information he had gathered and what he had done with it.

"No phone," Shirley concluded after going through his pockets. "Maybe the suspect dumped it."

"Or took it with him." It should be relatively simple to get Oliver's phone number and get a warrant to trace it.

"That'd be sweet. Criminals can be so stupid."

"He was on his knees. The shooter was standing over him."

"Yeah. He fell back on his butt, then keeled over onto his side. You can see livor mortis where the blood pooled in his face. He's already out of rigor." Shirley's eyes scrunched as she did the math. "This time of year, the ocean's about 50 degrees at night. If he's been here through at least two high tides, that would slow decomp."

She ran her expert eye over the victim, then rolled him onto his stomach, looking for any other wounds. "One's a through and through." She showed Jovanic where a bullet had gone straight through Oliver's chest and exited the back of the leather vest.

Making a quick calculation in his head, in his mind's eye he traced the bullet's trajectory. He started looking for shell casings in the sand. "I'm gonna go ask to borrow our wit's metal detector," he said after coming up empty. If RJ had finished interviewing their witness—

Shirley Lorraine interrupted his thoughts. "Oh man, are you one lucky D."

"What've you got?" Jovanic followed her pointing finger to a bullet that was almost entirely embedded in Oliver's left boot heel. A surge of energy went through him and pushed the fatigue to the background. "Holy shit, Shirl! If Claudia wouldn't kill me, I'd plant a big wet one on those rosy lips."

The coroner's investigator grinned. "Never mind Claudia. I'd have to file a sexual harassment grievance."

Jovanic got serious. "You're gonna let me take the boot straight to the lab, right?"

"Sure. Help me get it off him."

Jovanic left Shane Oliver's boot at the ballistics lab with an urgent request for results, though it was Friday, so nothing would happen with it until next week. He met up with Randy Coleman at a McDonald's.

"Did you get Bobby Morgan booked?"

"Yeah," Coleman said. "He was whining about Viper putting a hit on him, so they gave him his own cell at Van Nuys. He'll be okay there for a few days. If we cut him loose on Tuesday, he won't have to go to County."

"Bobby makes a better witness than he does a suspect and we've got bigger fish to hook. I'll ask the D.A. to offer him an immunity deal if he testifies. I think he'll go for it. What about Big Carl?"

"Still working on him. He's chillin' at the station. Once he knows Bobby caved, no reason for him to keep his mouth shut."

"With Bobby's statement and the video we got from Yvonne Lee as corroborating evidence, the D.A. should be ready to file paper on Viper by Monday." Jovanic took a bite of his Big Mac and chewed thoughtfully, letting his mind work out a question that had been pestering him all morning like an annoying tickle just out of reach.

"What?" Coleman asked. "You've got that look. What's the problem?"

Jovanic shrugged. "It just doesn't feel right. Viper's kept a low profile for a lot of years. Now, four homicides in one week, all with a clear connection to him."

He set his sandwich back in its box and took out a pen, started making a list on a napkin. "First, Travis Navarette—competition—gets firebombed. Then Angel gets done in a drugged-up rage because she disobeyed him. Then Steinman. Why her? Looks like she's been working for him for years. What happened that set all this off? Shane Oliver digs around and gets too close to *something,* we don't know what, so he has to go." Jovanic looked at the names he had block printed on the napkin. If he turned it over, he knew he would see the heavy pen strokes had bled through to the next layer. Claudia never disparaged him for his printing, but she often encouraged him to use cursive writing. She said it would help him get in touch with his feelings.

Like he wanted to do that.

Coleman said, "No coincidences, right? Maybe Darla saw what happened to Travis or Angel. Maybe she talked to Oliver about it."

"Her name is in his notebook." Jovanic dunked a fistful of fries into the mound of ketchup he'd squeezed onto the paper tray cover. "But if Darla's been servicing Viper's clients all these years, she knows he's no boy scout. Why turn on him now?"

"She's got kids, doesn't she? Maybe him beating a teenage girl to death was her limit."

thirty-three

"I don't want to be seen with him." Annabelle's lip stuck out in a sulky pout. Much of the 50-mile drive from Playa de la Reina to the Pomona Fairgrounds had passed with her resisting the idea of looking for and confronting the man who had inked the sugar skull on her fifteen-year-old skin. Now she was turning her disfavor on Joel, who had driven separately in the event something broke on one of his cases and he needed to make a quick exit.

"I thought you two were getting along," said Claudia.

"Everyone will know he's a cop. He walks like a cop. He *looks* like a cop."

"And you know people here who are going to look down on you for being with a cop?"

"They don't have to *know* me."

"Well, if we run into this Crash guy, I think it's good for him to know you're with a cop. Shake him up a little. What does he look like?"

Annabelle heaved a big, fed-up sigh. "I don't know. Old. Skinny. Crappy teeth." She gave a little snort. "Actually, *missing* teeth. He doesn't have any in the front."

"What color is his hair? How long is it?"

She thought about it before answering. "Kinda grey, in a long pony-tail."

"That description includes about a third of the population here."

In spite of herself, Annabelle giggled. "I'll tell you if I see him."

She opened the passenger door and immediately began to complain about the heat. According to the digital thermometer on the roof of a bank building, it was 106. Claudia groaned, too. After spending the better part of an hour in the air-conditioned Jaguar, the sun beat on her bare shoulders like the fires of hell.

Joel stepped from his Jeep in the adjoining parking space and stretched. Despite the oppressive temperature, he was wearing Levi's. To cover an ankle holster, Claudia guessed. Having taken the day off, he was unshaven. His beard, always quick to grow, shadowed his jaw in a sinister way that she found incredibly sexy.

The sleeve of his black T-shirt covered his left bicep, where he wore his father's name—Bennis—on a banner over a police shield. There was an innate distrust of cops in the tattoo culture. No point rubbing it in their faces.

Catching his gaze across the tops of their vehicles, the eye roll Claudia gave him said it all. "What's the plan?" she asked as he walked around the Jeep.

"Take a look around, see what's up."

"Should we be elsewhere when you talk to Viper?"

"When are you going to get him for killing Angel?" Annabelle cut in before he could respond.

Joel put up a restraining hand. "Don't worry, we're working on it."

"I heard you tell Claudia he always gets away with everything."

"Don't you know you're not supposed to eavesdrop?"

"You shouldn't let him get away with it. He *murdered* her." Annabelle's expression darkened. "He should *die* for what he did."

"Trust me, kiddo, I understand how you feel, and—"

"But how can you just let him go free after what Mouser's brother—"

"It's being handled, and that's all you need to know right now," Jovanic interrupted her. "We're not gonna talk about it here."

"But I want—"

"*Enough,* Annabelle," Claudia said firmly. "Let's get inside. Your nose is already getting sunburned."

Aghast, Annabelle put her hand up to cover the offending organ. She hurried ahead of them, her ire at Viper's evasion of justice evaporating in her urgent need to avoid a possible red nose. Even her mortification at being forced to suffer the company of a cop seemed to have disappeared.

He shook his head in exasperation as they followed her to the ticket booth. "You sure she's gonna be okay here?"

"Not really. But we can't pretend nothing happened."

"You know I can't discuss an open case with her."

"Of course I know that. I'm not saying you should. Just that it's not going to stop her from processing what happened, however she processes it."

She could feel his impatience, but her protective instincts always kicked in when it came to Annabelle, and he knew better than to interfere. When they caught up with her a moment later at the ticket booth, Claudia gave the girl a long look. Not wanting to start an argument with Joel, she refrained from saying what she was thinking: that since Angel's death, the PTSD flare-ups worried her.

Annabelle had witnessed the ruthless murder of someone she cared about. Such a memory would not leave a child her age unscarred; more so a child whose mother had also been violently torn from her early in life. The feverish light she'd noticed in the girl's eyes had made Claudia hyperalert for acting out. Since Angel's reappearance in her life, her progress had stalled.

Joel paid their admission fee at the gate and each of them held out their hands in turn for the ticket-taker's stamp. They joined the throng of fairgoers inside the grounds. Pushing through the doors of the hangar-like building, the trio entered the Inkslingers Ball Tattoo and Body Piercing Expo.

They walked into a wall of noise, a pulsing cacophony that reverberated throughout the building. Even Annabelle clapped her hands over her ears. It took several seconds for Claudia to realize what they were hearing—a drumbeat. The sound was everywhere. The poor acoustics made conversation impossible. Joel slipped an arm around her shoulders and motioned her toward the drums.

They made their way through rows of exhibit spaces, through the crush of human canvases. Body art ran the gamut from understated hearts and flowers to full body suits that covered arms and legs and torsos. Relatively few were like Claudia, a blank slate where their skin showed.

In many booths tattoo artists seated on low stools worked on their customers out in the open. Scattered between booths, vendors sold tattoo supplies and equipment or goth jewelry. Stalls displayed racks of T-shirts with silkscreen slogans such as, *"Respect: you get what you give."*

Claudia kept her eyes peeled, looking for an artist who fit Annabelle's description of Crash. Most of the working males were on the younger side, or had dark hair or shaved heads or wore do-rags. She discounted the ones who looked like lowriders, but the biker types got a second glance. Some of them might be members of Viper's gang, the Skullz.

The name of each tattoo studio hung from a curtain on the back panel of its booth. She looked for the Dragon House logo. Jovanic's heightened vigilance bristled like invisible armor. Claudia could feel it. Annabelle was right. Even with the scruffy stubble, he couldn't help carrying himself like a cop. She smiled to herself, glad of it. His presence always made her feel safer, and that had nothing to do with the fact that he was carrying.

As they neared the back of the building, through the circle of spectators she could see feather headdresses rising high above the crowd—dancers in Aztec tribal costume kicking and whirling. Dozens of bells on their anklets jingled to the warlike beating of the drums. The percussion pounded harder, faster, building to a crescendo until the air was vibrating with the sound.

Claudia felt Joel squeeze her arm. A slight jerk of his head brought her attention to Annabelle, whose rapt gaze was focused on one of the dancers. Her face was made up like a sugar skull—thick dark smudges around the eyes, black stitches drawn across the lips as if she were dead. Very like the sugar skulls tattooed on Viper's girls. Like the one Crash had put on Annabelle.

"God, I hope she doesn't decide to copy the makeup," Claudia murmured in Joel's ear.

"Say your prayers, babe," he whispered back, squeezing her arm. "I'm gonna look around, talk to some folks and see what I can find out. See you in a few."

He slipped away, leaving them to watch what remained of the performance.

When it was over, afraid they would become separated in the packed aisles, Claudia grabbed a handful of Annabelle's T-shirt, surprised at the lack of resistance. Annabelle was enthralled with everything going on around them.

They wandered up and down the aisles, pausing to admire some of the artists at work. Claudia mostly people-watched, amusing herself by guessing what the handwritings of attendees might look like based on the tattoos they wore. It was an idle game, as people were too varied to guess with any accuracy. Chances were, most of them printed in one form or another, rather than using cursive. At least, that was what she had observed in a book she'd read called *Permanence.* There was a photograph of each subject with a handwritten note detailing the reason for the tattoos worn by the writer.

Annabelle wanted to stop at one of the jewelry booths where there were rows of sterling silver sugar skull earrings on display. These were more traditional, unlike the glamorous style of her tattoo. She gazed wistfully at the jewelry. "If they had some like my tat, I'd buy them."

"Don't you think one sugar skull is enough?"

"There's no such thing as too many sugar skulls." Annabelle's impish grin drew a smile from Claudia.

The jewelry vendor, a girl in a tiny black mini dress, sauntered over and started pulling items from the case to tempt her potential customer. She set out boxes of earrings on top of the glass case.

She couldn't have been much older than Annabelle. The two began an animated conversation about piercing gauges. Claudia moved off to the side to give them some space.

"Looks like you're gonna have to get out your pocketbook," a woman said from behind her.

Claudia turned. The speaker was seated on a stool in the next booth. Her tattoo table was currently vacant. A second female tattooist was coloring in a large piece on a woman's back.

Unlike some of the tacky, overdone women Claudia had observed at the event, the one who had spoken was a knockout. She was the "sexy and she knows it" kind who drew admiring glances from both genders. Perfect body. Blonde-streaked black hair half-covering one eye in front, shaved short in back. High cheekbones, peach-colored skin that glowed.

Red and black hearts, skulls, and diamonds decorated the finely inked lacework that covered her arms from shoulders to knuckles.

"She's got her eye on something." The woman was watching Annabelle pore over the jewelry with the vendor.

Claudia half-turned so Annabelle couldn't hear her. "No jewelry for her today. She's in big trouble. She sneaked out and got a tattoo."

"How old is she?"

"Fifteen. And he knew it."

"Boyfriend?"

"No. A much older guy."

"Not one of ours." The woman shook her head with certainty. "Nobody here would do it underage without getting consent from the parents."

"This guy did it in the back of his van."

The woman raised a winged brow. "That's seriously fucked up. Who is he?"

"He goes by Crash. Ever hear of him?"

The woman thought about it for a long moment. "Uh uh. He wouldn't be popular around here—give the rest of us a bad rep." She held out a slim hand covered with tattooed roses. "I'm Raven."

"I'm Claudia."

Raven grinned, showing a perfect set of gleaming pearly whites. "I snuck out plenty at that age, but I didn't get any ink until I was legal. My daddy would have totally whaled on me."

"I know what you mean," Claudia agreed. "But her friend had a particular sugar skull and she just had to have one like it. The friend's was done by an artist named Viper. Maybe you know him?"

"Course I do—Dragon House. We're like family here, we all know each other. The reputable salons, anyway—not some dumbass who works out of his van."

"Is Dragon House here?"

"They're on the other side." Raven waved vaguely to the far side of the building, where Claudia's travels had not yet taken her.

"I thought I'd talk to Viper, since this Crash guy seems to have copied his piece. Maybe he knows him."

Raven stared at her as though she were crazy. "You do not want to do that, sistah. I can tell you right now, Viper would be none too happy to hear someone's copying his work."

"You mean he doesn't believe imitation is the sincerest form of flattery?"

"Uh, no. In this business, imitation is forgery."

"Okay, I get that. I'm a handwriting analyst, so forgery is something I understand very well."

"A *handwriting* analyst? Seriously? You mean, if I sign my name, you can tell me all about myself?"

"Not *all* about yourself, but a little bit." Claudia rarely agreed to do a quickie analysis, especially on just a signature. But maybe if they got a little friendlier, Raven might provide some information about Viper she could take back to Jovanic. That would be even better than learning about Crash.

Grabbing up a flyer and a pen lying on her equipment cabinet, Raven turned it onto the blank side and got to work. She took her time drawing her name in purple ink, adding a twinkling star as the i dot and another at the end of "Raven." She handed it to Claudia with obvious pride.

The showy flourishes were more like a drawing than a natural signature. Because the style acted like a mask, attempting to conceal, rather than reveal, the writer's true nature, handwriting analysts called it "persona writing."

"This is a constructed signature," Claudia said. "It's not the real you. What it tells me is, you want to come across as strong and powerful and sexy—which of course you are—but inside, you feel kind of small, like maybe there's something lacking. You use your outer appearance, your image, to compensate for what you think is missing."

As she finished, Raven was staring at her, openmouthed. "Omigod, that is *so* true. How did you know that?"

Claudia gave her a knowing smile. "It's my job to know it." She pulled a business card from the purse slung over her shoulder and handed it to her. "In case you ever decide to have a whole analysis done."

"Wow, thank you so much; I'm gonna do that."

"You're welcome. So, Viper—"

"Well, like I said, he's not here today. He was here yesterday, but I heard he's got some troubles."

"Troubles?"

"Yeah, one of the girls who worked for him. She got herself killed."

Claudia didn't think she was talking about Angel. She took a chance. "You mean Darla?"

Raven's eyes widened. "You knew Darla?"

"I heard the cops don't know who did it. Have you heard anything?"

"Nobody's talking about it." Raven shook her head. "You just can't tell with some of these guys. You do everything you can to protect yourself, but maybe one of her customers followed her home. She got popped right in her own house."

"She worked for Viper for a long time, didn't she?"

"On and off since high school, whenever she needed extra cash. We used to party together back then. Thought we were the shit, makin' it with the older guys." While she spoke, Raven the businesswoman kept an eye on passersby, no doubt looking for paying customers.

Claudia, recognizing that their conversation time was limited, improvised as fast as she could. "Was that when Gerald Harris was around, too?" she asked, recalling the name from the article in Shane Oliver's journal.

Raven shot her an odd look. "That crazy dude? Wow. I haven't thought about ol' Gerry in forever. He and Viper used to be like, best buds. 'Course, Viper wasn't Viper back then. He was just Al. And Darla was this juicy little piece of tail and both of 'em wanted some of it."

Raven's gaze took on a far-off look. "I tried telling her she shouldn't mess with those dudes, but she wasn't about to listen. She started gettin' crazy on both of 'em. Then it was *on,* girl. War, with a capital W. In the end, Gerry got beat down so bad, he was—" She pointed to her head and made a twirling motion. "Never the same after that. So, how'd you know them?"

"Oh, you know, same crowd, but I'm a little older than you and Darla."

"I think—" Raven broke off as the artist at the other table hailed her.

"Hey, Tab. Customer." A man had stopped at the booth and was looking pointedly at Raven.

Without a backward glance at Claudia, Raven put on a big smile and went to work.

Joel texted her to meet him at the concession stand. While the three of them chowed down on hotdogs and ice cream cones, Claudia reported on her conversation with Raven and Joel groused that he wasn't having any luck getting anyone to talk. Annabelle felt the need to remind him that it was because everyone could tell he was a cop.

Ignoring her, Jovanic put his mouth close to Claudia's ear. "I want you to come with me to the Dragon House booth," he spoke in a voice low enough that only she could hear. "You and Annabelle are going to be my props."

"Your what?"

"I'm gonna act like I'm taking pictures of you, but I'll actually be aiming at the guys in the booth behind you."

Claudia laughed. "A reverse photo bomb?"

"Exactly. I want to see who Viper hangs out with, get some pics. Get him to talk, get a little rapport going."

"By rapport, you mean rattle him?"

It was Jovanic's turn to grin, only his had a vulpine quality. "Hey, if my presence causes him to do something he wouldn't normally do, that's not on me."

"Except according to Raven, he's not here today."

Jovanic gave a philosophical shrug. "Let's see who is."

Two youngish men were manning the Dragon House booth. Both wore wifebeater T-shirts that displayed their full sleeve tattoos. One was busy working on a woman who was face down on his table, naked aside from a string bikini bottom. He was outlining a black and pink lotus design that started on her spine and wove across her back, down her hips. The other man was sitting on a stool, staring into the distance.

Claudia positioned herself and Annabelle to the side of the men, as if posing for a photo. Pretending to capture the scene, Joel focused his viewfinder to the area behind them. Giving him a big, fake smile, Claudia told Annabelle to smile, too; not surprised when the girl just stared at him with her patented 'I'm so freaking bored' sigh.

Joel clicked a few pictures and put his phone away, then casually approached the seated man. He wore a striped Ivy cap pulled low over suspicious eyes. Large bore holes along his ears graduated in sizes from smaller on the rim to one-inch circles in the lobes. A ginger chin curtain jerked their way, asking a silent question.

"Hey man, how's it goin?" Jovanic said.

The man grunted, but he got up and came over to them. "Whassup?"

Jovanic pulled Claudia close to him. "My girlfriend's thinking about getting her first tat."

"Yeah?" The eyes narrowed to a squint, checking her out.

"She's interested in getting a sugar skull."

"That so?" The man pointed to a thick portfolio that lay open on a folding table. Raw sketches of tattoos on one page, photos of the finished product on the facing page. "Help yourself, see if there's something you like."

Claudia started paging through the book, pointing out some of the flowery designs to Annabelle, who was more interested in the darker patterns. With one ear tuned to Jovanic's conversation with the man, she heard him ask if Big Carl was around. Since Big Carl was still in custody, she knew he was just trying to get the guy talking.

"What do you want with Carl?" The artist asked.

"Just wanted to say a friendly hello."

"Ain't here."

"How about Bobby. He around?"

"Nope."

"No Viper, either, I bet?"

"Ya just missed him."

Jovanic shook his head like he couldn't believe his bad luck. "Serious? I missed all of 'em?"

"Viper left about thirty minutes ago. Went back to the shop."

"Okay, dude, thanks." Jovanic turned to Claudia. "Find anything you like, babe?"

"The one I wanted isn't in this book." She looked at the guy. "I have a pretty specific sugar skull in mind."

"If we showed you a picture, would you be able to copy it?" Jovanic asked.

"Sure. We can do anything, bring it on."

"I got it right here." Jovanic got out his phone and accessed the post-mortem photos he had shot of Angel in the trash dumpster. The one he selected displayed the dirty green rim in the foreground and the sugar skull that covered her upper arm. He turned the phone to show the artist.

Ivy cap glanced at the screen. He took a step backwards as if he had been punched. "What the *fuck?*"

Jovanic turned, taking Claudia and Annabelle with him, and walked away.

They had exited the exhibit hall and were headed to the parking lot when Annabelle's phone sounded. She checked the screen, shrugging that she didn't recognize the number.

"Hello?" Annabelle listened with a scowl, then shoved the phone at Claudia. "It's for you."

"For me?" Claudia took the phone and held it to her ear. "Hello?"

"It's me, Jamie."

"Where are you? We've been worried."

"Can you come get me? I'm scared. This dude is kinda whack."

A vein in Claudia's temple started throbbing. It felt like a *déjà vu* experience, reminding her of the time Angel had called her late at night, asking for help, and she had said no. "What happened? Are you safe right now?"

"I ditched him when he went out back. I'm at the 7-Eleven gas station."

"Where? What city?"

"I'm in bumfuck Lancaster." Her previous indifference had been replaced with a whine. "I hadda come. He said he'd give me a ride and I didn't have any place to go. I didn't know he was gonna come all the way out here."

Lancaster was located in the high desert, at least a hundred miles north of Pomona.

"Why did you leave Kelly's house? You could have stayed there for a few days."

"Yeah, that wasn't gonna work. Anyhow, my car's over by your place. I went to get it, but someone stole my keys and shit out of it."

"Your backpack is in my house. All you had to do was knock on the door."

"It's *your* fault I don't have my wheels. You have to come pick me up."

Catching sight of Joel's face, which held a scowl as deep as Annabelle's. Claudia held up a finger to let them know she would not be long. Picking up Jamie in Lancaster was the last thing she wanted to do, but the truth was, she had taken Jamie's keys, which meant she was at least partly responsible. "We're in Pomona. That's almost a two-hour drive."

"But I already tried everyone and my battery's getting low on my phone." Jamie heaved a dramatic sigh. "Guess I'll have to hitch a ride back to Venice."

"Wait. Don't do that. Give me the address."

The girl recited the street corners where the gas station was located. She added, "There's some weird guys looking at me. I'm gonna go in the store and wait. Hurry up, okay?"

Claudia clicked off and handed the phone back to Annabelle, whose face was still screwed into an angry glare. "She wants you to go get her?"

"Yes. She says she's scared of the guy who gave her a ride up there."

"She's not scared; she's just using you because she doesn't want to be there."

"You're too old for your own good," said Claudia, with a feeling that Annabelle was probably right. She turned to Jovanic. "If we called the cops up there—"

He was already shaking his head before she finished her sentence. "They're not a taxi service. She's seventeen, she went with the guy willingly. She apparently left him under her own steam. Under those circumstances, the cops aren't going to do anything."

"Cops are useless," Annabelle muttered under her breath.

Claudia ignored the remark. "Looks like I'm stuck, then. Good thing we brought both cars. C'mon, Annabelle, let's go."

"No way."

"What?"

"I'm not going. She snitched out Angel and got her killed. I don't want to ever see her again."

"In that case, you'd better apologize to a certain cop for your rudeness. Maybe he'll be nice enough to give you a ride home."

"You're really going to go get her?"

"Looks that way."

Joel threw up his hands in a gesture of disgust. "Jesus, Claudia. She got herself there. Don't you think she could find her own way back?"

"You're choosing her over me?" Annabelle's voice caught on her words. Before she could prevent it, Claudia grabbed her and gave her a hug. "That's a choice I don't have to make, and if I did, of course I would choose you, silly girl. But right now, you have another ride home. Her keys are in our house. I don't want to be responsible for her hitchhiking."

She turned to Joel and pressed a quick kiss against his lips. When he didn't kiss her back, she almost reconsidered. But it was too late, she had promised Jamie. "Can I count on you two not to kill each other on the way home?"

There was no answer.

thirty-four

Annabelle maintained a stony silence, for most of the ride back to Playa de la Reina, seething over what she saw as Claudia's betrayal. How could she prefer that skanky bitch? Jamie thought she was such a hard ass. She wouldn't have gone with the dude if she was scared. Annabelle was serious about what she'd told Claudia—Jamie was just manipulating her to get a ride, and Claudia had fallen for it.

She was pretty sure Joel would rather not have been forced into taking her with him, but there was no way she was gonna sit in the same car with Jamie, not even if she had to walk all the way home. It was bad enough having to ride in the Jeep. Her anger with Joel for not arresting Viper was tearing her up inside. The cops knew he was a stone-cold killer. Why didn't they do something about it?

A little voice inside her head whispered that she and Angel had never been best friends, and that Angel had left her alone in Crash's van, but that didn't matter. The cops should have beat Viper to death, the way he had done Angel.

Joel's words came back: Angel was strangled.

Annabelle's stomach lurched. Without warning, her vision went black. Her fingers and the palms of her hands tingled as heat rose up her neck and into her cheeks. She quickly turned her face to the window, struggling not to let it show. She was counting on Joel not noticing how her breathing was getting shallow and faster. He had the radio jacked up loud on a seventies station and was singing under his breath to some song that sounded like *'Me and Mrs Jones,'* so she figured she was safe.

Dr. Gold and Claudia had explained to her what post-traumatic stress disorder was—like when soldiers went to war and saw abominable things, and when they came home, they kept getting flashbacks. Dr. Gold had given her treatments for it and she had improved over the past few months. The nightmares, which used to come almost every night, had been getting fewer and farther between. But since Angel—

Guilt and remorse clogged her throat, but it was not Angel's face she saw. The scene looped and looped like a horror movie until she wanted to scream for it to stop. She told herself it was just a memory imprint; that what she was seeing was long past. But to Annabelle, every time the movie ran in her head, it was as real as if it were once again unfolding in front of her.

Why had she not tried harder to stop him? She had jumped on his back and beat her fists against his head, but he had been oblivious, throwing her off as if she were of no more consequence than a fly. Snatching the leather belt Annabelle had lovingly made in art class he had looped it around his victim's neck...

She jammed her fingers into her ears, but she could not block out the cries for help, the sounds of struggle as he twisted the belt tighter, tighter. She could still hear the choking sounds weakening into gasps; the killer's panting. Her own whimpers.

"Hey, are you okay?"

She suddenly realized that Joel had turned off the radio and was darting concerned looks at her between watching the freeway traffic. What had she done to bring his attention to her? Annabelle gulped a deep breath and tried to sound casual. "I'm fine."

"You sure? I thought you yelled something."

"I guess I fell asleep."

"Nightmare?"

He sounded sympathetic, and she glanced at him under her lashes. Even though she was mad at him, she really liked him a lot. But she couldn't share what was going on inside her head. She went for offhand. "I guess so. I don't remember."

Joel reached over and gave her knee a pat. "I know it's been the pits for you, kiddo. I'm doing everything I can to fix it. Just hang in there. It's all going to be okay."

"Angel's dead. It's not okay for her."

"You're right about that. All we can do is try to get some justice for her."

"Doesn't seem like it."

He kept the radio turned off for the rest of the ride, but neither of them had much to say to the other after that, and the awkward silence dragged until he pulled into Claudia's driveway. "I'm gonna go change and then I'm going to watch the game. Do you have something to keep you busy?"

"I'm not a child, you know," Annabelle replied in her most adult manner. "I'm almost sixteen. You don't have to babysit me."

While Joel went upstairs, she got herself a soda and carried it up to her room. The horrific images refused to get out of her head. Only this time, the victim she saw was Angel.

Annabelle stretched out on her bed and tried to focus on the *Twilight* book she was reading, but it was impossible to concentrate. Eventually, she gave up and put the book back on the nightstand. She tried to think of something fun that she and Monica could do together, but that didn't work either because the bad thoughts kept intruding. Thoughts she had been struggling unsuccessfully to banish. Thoughts about Viper, a man she had never met, but who seemed to have taken over her mind.

He can't get away with it.

He needs to pay for what he did.

He has to pay.

I'll make him pay.

Around and around the thoughts went, like horses on a carousel in a never-ending circle.

She pictured herself walking into the Dragon House tattoo parlor. The man she visualizes as Viper looks at her and all he sees is a fresh piece of young ass like Angel and Jamie. Someone to dominate and use however he wants.

She pulls a gun out of her backpack and his jaw goes slack, his eyes widen with terror. He starts to beg, "*Please, don't shoot me. I'm sorry. I'm sorry!*"

But she pulls the trigger anyway. There's a loud bang and he falls down. She straddles his lifeless body, pulling the trigger again, shooting him in the heart. Then, with a feeling of intense satisfaction, she walks away.

Her room was a little darker when she opened her eyes and looked at the time on her phone—4:05. She must have dozed off for real. Claudia would be back in a couple of hours with Jamie. *Ick.*

She lay there for a little while longer, trying to decide what to do next. She imagined all over again what she would like to do to Viper. And as she pictured it, piece by piece, a plan began to formulate.

She could hear the game going strong downstairs, but Joel was not yelling at the TV as he often did. Annabelle jumped up off the bed, trembling all over, partly with fright at what she was contemplating and partly with sheer excitement.

Moving silently down the staircase until she could see across the room, she leaned over the banister. He was sacked out on the couch, snoring loud, gusty breaths. With the brutal schedule he'd been working over the past week, then the long drive back and forth to Pomona today, she knew he had to be exhausted. Good. That suited her fine.

She ran back upstairs, careful to avoid the squeaky treads, and got her backpack.

The door was open to the bedroom Joel shared with Claudia when he wasn't at his own apartment, which was most of the time. Even though she knew he was sound asleep in the living room, Annabelle entered on tiptoe.

His gun was in its holster on the nightstand where he always left it on his side of the bed. Claudia didn't like him leaving it in the open, but his response was always the same: he needed to have it within easy reach, and besides, there were no little kids in the house.

She knew it was a Glock 9mm because Joel had showed her how it worked. They'd had the Big Talk about how she must never touch it, and she had promised. And of course, Claudia made sure Annabelle heard about it every time there was something on the news about some little kid with irresponsible idiots for parents who had accidentally shot himself or someone else. Or someone had gone crazy and shot up their school or a movie theater or a mall. As if *she* was that stupid or crazy.

Next to his holster where Annabelle knew she would find it, was Joel's key ring. She closed her fist around it so the keys would not jangle and scooped it up.

It was hidden behind the pants hanging on the lower rail, but Annabelle knew there was a small safe on the floor against the back wall of Claudia's walk-in closet. Claudia made no secret of it, or the fact that she loathed its contents. But after some of the dangerous situations she had landed in since they'd met, Joel had insisted she have a weapon of her own—a 9mm semiautomatic that he called a baby Glock. Despite the cute name, Claudia had accepted it only under loud protest.

With the door open, the closet was semi-dark, but Annabelle didn't want to turn on the light. She was shaking like Jello on a plate, but once she fitted the special key into the safe's lock, it turned like it was supposed to.

She lifted the lid and reached inside. Her fingers found the leather holster and curled around the weapon. She had not made any promises about *this* gun.

It was heavier than she had expected. She knew it was already loaded, so she would not have to worry about getting the bullets into the magazine. Leaving the lid of the safe open so she wouldn't have to use the key again later when she returned the weapon, she made sure the clothing on the railing concealed it and crept out of the closet.

Before she had time to give a second thought to what she was doing, the gun was in her backpack, Joel's keys were back on the nightstand, and she was on her way downstairs.

The ease with which she had accomplished the first step of her plan emboldened her to take the next one.

Joel was no longer snoring, but his rhythmic breathing told her he was sound asleep. Pretending to herself that she was invisible, Annabelle stole past him to the kitchen. Jamie's backpack was on a chair. Taking the car keys, she left through the back door, closing it quietly behind her.

Around the side of the house, then down the street, where the old Honda sat, gathering dust. Lucky for Jamie, she had missed the street sweeper, Annabelle thought sourly. Too bad she didn't get a ticket.

Because she was not yet sixteen, Annabelle didn't qualify for her driver's license. She had a provisional permit, though, and had practiced driving the Jaguar plenty of times with Claudia. Before that, when she was twelve her fake father had taught her to drive his golf cart on the private road around his Malibu estate so she could run errands for him. Still, she had to be mondo careful not to get stopped. Claudia would be furious if she got a ticket for driving without a license. Or stealing Jamie's car, which reminded her of the times she and Angel had gone joyriding with their gangsta friends, before Claudia came into her life. Thinking of it all, she realized with surprise that she didn't miss those days one bit. Besides, going to juvie was not an experience she wanted to repeat.

Being several inches shorter than Jamie, the first thing Annabelle had to do was figure out how to move the seat up to allow her feet to reach the pedals. Then the engine gave a little sputter when she turned the key in the ignition, as if it wasn't going to start. *No!* There wasn't time to hot-wire it like she'd watched her former homies do.

Fingers crossed, she tried again and it sounded a little stronger this time. Maybe the battery had run down after sitting for a few days. The third time, the engine turned over and came to life. The gas gauge showed almost empty, but Dragon House wasn't far. There *had* to be enough gas to get there and back. She hadn't brought any money with her.

Now that she was in the car, moving the gear shifter into Drive, Annabelle felt as calm as the water in the canals down by Venice Beach. She knew where Dragon House was located because Angel and Jamie had told her. Lincoln near Rose in Venice. It would take maybe ten minutes to get there.

Last time, she had failed to save someone she cared about. Today she was going to make up for that failure.

Annabelle checked the rearview mirror. She remembered to look over her shoulder and check behind her before pushing her foot on the gas pedal and pulling away from the curb.

The curving hill that led down to Culver Boulevard seemed even steeper than usual, as if the incline had become almost vertical just to scare her. Conscious of the sheer drop just past the low railing on the other side of the road, she drove slowly, one foot hovering over the brake until she reached the bottom.

It only took a minute, then she was passing Tyler's Coffee House and making a right onto Culver. Her heart started thumping again and she was grateful traffic was pretty light as she drove the half-mile past the Ballona wetlands and turned left onto Lincoln.

It was a little farther than she expected, but with its red dragon roaring across the front windows, Dragon House Tattoos was easy enough to spot. Annabelle parked Jamie's car on the street around the corner from the studio and turned off the engine.

Oh my God. What the fuck am I doing?

What the cops should have done.

She was here. She was going to do it. With a stealthy glance around to make sure nobody on the street was watching, she opened her backpack and checked inside. There was the revolver, its short black grip molded to fit the user's hand. It kinda looked like a toy, but anyone with half a brain could see it was definitely not that. Annabelle was positive it looked real enough to scare Viper into the confession she intended to record.

Before leaving the house, she had checked her phone to make sure the battery was charged all the way. Now, before climbing out of the Honda, she accessed the Voice Memo feature and got it ready to record.

As she rounded the corner, for one heart-stopping moment, Annabelle wondered whether the shop might be closed this late on a Sunday. Then she reminded herself that the Dragon House artists at the Expo had said Viper had left to go back to the shop.

She pushed on the glass door and it opened. Inside, although the lights were on, there was a feeling of darkness. Annabelle got an impression of tattoo art papering the walls, and framed photographs of customers who had come to Dragon House to get inked.

Her focus sharpened. The space was divided into four cubicles. Each cubicle had its own metal tool chest like the kind auto repair shops use, a rolling stool, and a chair that looked like it belonged in a dentist's office.

A man was sitting in one of the chairs with his eyes closed. When Annabelle walked through the door, he was on his feet in an instant, and coming toward her.

"What can I do for you, young lady?" he asked in a sort of growl.

"I—I'm looking for Viper." She sounded small and weak in the cavern-like space.

The man, who had the hardest, meanest face Annabelle had ever seen in her life, was not how she had pictured him, but she knew who he was. He looked back at her, unsmiling, and asked, "What for?"

He was a smallish man, not nearly as tall as Joel. Not even as tall as Claudia. But standing over Annabelle, he wore an attitude that was badder even than her fake father, who was a criminal. Viper moved closer and she could feel his interest in her.

She made herself think of what he had done to Angel. When she answered, she was pleased to hear she sounded stronger. "Uh, because um—because I want to get a tat and I heard Viper's the best around."

"You did, huh? Well, you heard right. But you gotta be eighteen to get work done in this shop, and *you* are not eighteen."

Conscious of the heavy gun in her backpack, Annabelle stood up straighter and jutted her chin. "Jamie and Angel aren't eighteen."

The rest of him remained immobile, but the man's eyes narrowed to slits in his leathery face. He reminded her of a snake and she suddenly understood why he was called Viper.

"What do you know about them?" he demanded.

"Angel's my friend. She showed me her sugar skull and I wanted one and…" She trailed off, her heart threatening to beat a hole right through her chest.

"Yeah? What makes you think I'm gonna ink *your* tender young flesh?"

"They said you might if I—" She could not make herself say the words. "If I was nice to you."

He gave her a long look. "That so? And just how nice are you prepared to get?"

She forced a sly smile onto her face. "I really, *really* want a sugar skull just like theirs."

"There's one way you can get that, and it starts with a blow job. How's that sound, teenybopper?"

Annabelle wanted to throw up. "Sounds fine. Can we do it now?"

"You're in a big motherfuckin' hurry, aren't you?"

"Well—I borrowed someone's car, and I have to get it back."

Viper went to the front door and turned the lock, then flipped off the lights in the shop, leaving it in shadow. "I'll think about it while we go for a little test drive."

Beckoning her to follow, he disappeared through a door near the far wall of the shop. Annabelle trailed him as though she were sleepwalking. The plan was working just how she had intended, but her mind had gone blank and she was moving on auto.

"You're not wearing a wire, are you?" Viper asked, sitting back on a black leather couch in the back room.

"A—a wire?"

"Lemme check." He reached out and grabbed her by the waistband, yanked her to stand right in front of him. There was nothing sexual in the way he ran his hands over her body, moving them across her chest, under her arms, up the inseams of her jeans to her crotch. He did it expertly, like he had done it many times before, but that didn't make Annabelle feel any less violated.

When he was convinced that she was clean, Viper began to unbuckle his belt. Annabelle, who had let her backpack fall to the floor when he grabbed her, picked it up and put it on the other end of the couch. She reached in and pressed the record icon on her phone.

Viper watched her digging in the bag. "What the fuck are you doing?"

"I just need to get something."

"You don't need anything to blow me." He unzipped his jeans and brought out his penis, which was already getting hard. "Get over here. On your knees."

But Annabelle already had hold of the Glock. When she withdrew it, her finger was on the trigger. She took a step back and pointed the gun at Viper.

"What the fuck?" For an instant, he looked shocked, the way he had in her fantasy. But then—she could not believe it—he laughed. "That's a nice piece for a little girl like you. Where'd you get it?"

She stretched the weapon in front of her, the way she'd seen it done in TV shows. The gun was shaking hard and she held both hands around the grip, trying to steady it. "It's going to shoot you if you don't tell me what you did to Angel."

Viper scowled. "Who says I did anything to Angel?"

"I *know* what you did. I just want to hear you say it." Sadness and anger welled up, blurring her vision with tears, but she couldn't spare a hand to wipe them away. She blinked several times to clear her eyes. "How could you do it? How could you treat her like garbage?"

"She *was* garbage." Viper held out his hand, making a "gimme" motion. "C'mon now, be a good little girl and put the gun down before you get hurt."

His mockery angered her. She would *make* him take her seriously. "You always get away with shit." Annabelle had to fight to keep the quaver out of her voice. "You're not going to get away with it this time. Say it. Say you killed her. Go on, *say it!*"

"You little shit, who the—" He flew off the couch and lunged at her. Before she could react, he grabbed her trigger hand.

There was a loud explosion and Viper went down.

thirty-five

"I have to get up," Jovanic said, spooning Claudia closer and putting the lie to his words. Drying perspiration cooled his skin and he breathed in her warmth. Over most of the last hour he had savored every inch of her with the passion of a lover separated for a year, rather than just a week of extra heavy-duty rotation. He had kissed her awake at five a.m., apologizing for spending the evening dead to the world, then doing his best to live up to his promise to make up for it.

She snuggled against him with a small groan of protest. "No, stay here. It feels too good; you can't leave."

Resting his hand on her hip, he pressed his lips into the warm space between the base of her neck and her shoulder, tasting her with the tip of his tongue. Claudia reached up and gently raked her fingers through his hair, caressed his cheek. Pressing a last kiss into her skin, Jovanic tore himself away and sat on the edge of the bed. He leaned over, resting elbows on knees, trying to clear his head and talk himself into the mood for work.

"I've got to get to the office and see where we are with the trace on Shane Oliver's phone. If we get lucky, the killer kept it."

"Wouldn't it be nice if it led you right to his front door?"

"That it would," he agreed. "Hey, I thought I heard Annabelle vomiting last night. Is she okay?"

Claudia turned onto her back with a yawn. "Poor kid. She said it was the hot dog she ate at the expo. I think she's still mad at me, too, for picking up Jamie. She wouldn't let me in her room when I got home, she said she was too sick to talk."

Jovanic stood up and fixed the blanket over her. "She'll get over it now that Jamie's out of the picture."

"Yeah. As soon I handed over her keys and backpack, that chick was gone without so much as a 'thanks for the ride.'"

"Waste of your time and gas, babe."

"I know, you told me so. Yada yada. But at least my conscience is clear." She watched him enter the closet to select a dress shirt and tie. "By the way, I didn't get a chance to tell you who the guy was that took Jamie to Lancaster."

He came out with his clothes and laid them over a chair. "You were too busy riding me like a circus pony."

"Bucking bronco is more like it," Claudia said with a self-satisfied smirk.

For a half-second, Jovanic considered jumping back into bed. It wasn't the sex, which was spectacular. He just wanted to be close to her in a way that he couldn't remember ever feeling before. He shook his head like a dog shaking off water.

"Mmmmm. Okay, gotta stop that or I'll be late for work. So, tell me, quick. Who was the guy?"

Claudia propped herself on an elbow. "You won't believe this. The guy who gave her the ride is the guy I was looking for at the expo. Crash."

Rummaging in the drawer for a pair of socks, Jovanic turned to look at her. "You've got to be freakin' kidding me."

"I was *so* pissed. I wanted her to show me where he lived, but she claimed she didn't remember how to get there. I know she was lying."

"What makes you so sure?"

"Her lips were moving."

"Aw, you're such a cynic. Sweet little Jamie, a liar? I can't believe it."

"Har har. She'd just walked from his place to the 7-Eleven. When she wanted me to give her a ride back here, she claimed her battery was dying, but she spent most of the ride on the phone, trying to score. At least she didn't find any drugs in her backpack. I flushed them."

Jovanic stuck his fingers in his ears, "Lalala. I did not hear that."

"Hear what?" Claudia quipped. "How was your ride home with Annabelle?"

"Mostly, I got the silent treatment." He grabbed a pair of boxers from the dresser and headed for the bathroom, pausing at the door. "I was listening to the radio. All of a sudden, she yelled something. Claimed she was dozing and had a bad dream, but I don't think so."

"It's the PTSD again. Time for her to have another session with Zebediah. She'll talk to him."

"Good move." He turned on the shower, then thought better of it and peered hopefully around the door. "Come scrub my back?"

Joel ran down the back steps carrying a bulging plastic garbage bag and hurried along the side of the house. He opened the Jeep and in the passenger door, scooped up the collection of cups and bits of leftover trash from several days' worth of food on the go.

When the vehicle's interior was as clean as he could get it without a trip to the car wash, he dumped the debris into the big garbage can he had wheeled out front the previous evening for the weekly pickup. It was a minor miracle he had remembered to do the chore. Dizzy with fatigue and after several beers, he hadn't even bothered with dinner before falling into bed. If someone had held a gun to his head, he could not have kept his eyes open a moment longer.

"Hey, Joel."

He turned to see their neighbor, Marcia Taylor, jogging up the street with her German Shepherd, Flare.

"How's it going?" Jovanic asked, leaning down to pet the dog, whose tongue was already busy licking the back of his hand.

Marcia reached into her pocket and pulled out a phone in a pink plastic case. "Annabelle apparently dropped this by your house. I picked it up on my way out this morning. How many times does this make?"

"I've lost count. Maybe she needs to think it's gone for good."

"Yeah, maybe—"

At the same moment, Jovanic's own phone rang. The ringtone was one he had assigned to his team members. He excused himself and Marcia continued on to her house.

"You won't believe this," RJ Scott announced when he answered the call.

"Try me."

"Our guy, Alvin Rousch? Admitted to Regional last night. Somebody shot him. I just saw it in the newspaper."

"Is he still alive?" Listening to Scott, Jovanic slipped Annabelle's phone into his pocket and went around to climb into the Jeep.

"Serious, but he'll be okay. He's not saying who did it, though."

"Those assholes never do. On my way."

Fifteen minutes after receiving Scott's call, Jovanic was at Marina del Rey Regional Hospital and Trauma Center, waiting to see the surgeon who had removed the bullet from Viper's abdomen. Taking Annabelle's phone out of his pocket, he toyed with the idea of checking out who she'd been talking to. Claudia would tell him not to invade her privacy, but in his view, a fifteen-year-old in his care didn't enjoy the protection of privacy laws. Especially a fifteen-year-old like Annabelle Giordano, who had to be the most exasperating and, he had to admit, endearing, kid he had ever encountered.

He wanted to know whether she was still in touch with Mouser after he had forbidden the contact. Jovanic dragged his index finger across the screen, surprised to see that the last app Annabelle had accessed was Voice Memos.

What had she been recording? The time stamp showed 4:43 pm yesterday. His recall of the time they had arrived home from the tattoo expo was a little hazy, but he thought it was around 3:15. After that, Annabelle had gone up to her room while he watched the game—slept through it, anyway.

Something was not adding up. How could she have made a voice recording at 4:43 if she had dropped her phone outside at 3:15? Had she gone somewhere while he was asleep? She had been sick later in the evening when he got up to take a leak.

He was still thinking about it when a doctor in blue scrubs and a pink paisley surgical cap entered the waiting room and approached him. "Detective Jovanic?" She offered her hand. "I'm Dr. Redfern, Dr. Feldman's surgical resident. He asked me to come and speak with you. You're here about Mr. Rousch?"

"Yes. How's he doing?"

"He came through surgery just fine. In fact, he's already out of ICU and in Recovery, but it's going to be a little while before he's ready to answer questions."

"Can you tell me anything about what happened?"

Dr. Redfern consulted the electronic tablet she had brought with her. "He called for an ambulance himself at five-seventeen last night and reported that he'd been shot." She glanced up. "He was pretty lucky. The bullet just missed the stomach, or it would have been a lot worse."

"What else did he say?"

"He didn't identify the shooter, if that's what you're asking." She checked her screen once again. "He was shot once at close range, with a .380. Like you cops carry."

"I hope you saved the bullet."

"Of course. I'll see that you get it if you'll leave me your contact information."

Jovanic handed her his card. "Okay if I see him?"

"Won't do you any good, he's sedated, and he's going to be in significant pain when he wakes up. Give him at least till this afternoon."

Having suffered a similar wound himself less than a year earlier, Jovanic understood all too well about the pain. He told Dr. Redfern he'd be back later when her patient was able to talk. He had just reached the elevator when she called him back.

"Hey, Detective, I just remembered something that might be useful for you."

He strode back over to her. "Yes?"

"It was in the notes. One of the EMTs indicated that when they picked him up—apparently, he was attacked where he worked, in a tattoo parlor. He didn't say who shot him, but he did say something that indicated the shooter was female."

"What did he say?"

"Something like 'the bitch shot me.' I'll ask the charge nurse to find out who the EMT was so you can talk to him."

"Thanks. I'd appreciate that."

Jovanic took the elevator down to the lobby wondering what the chances were that the shooter might be Jamie Parker. Rousch had called 9-1-1 at five-seventeen. Would that leave enough time for Jamie to grab her car from Claudia's street and get to the Dragon House and shoot him? The trouble was he couldn't think of a reason why she might. She had protected Viper when Jovanic interviewed her. And Jamie had professed no love for Angel, so there was no revenge motive.

On the way across the hospital parking lot, he called Claudia and asked what time she had brought Jamie back to the house.

"We got here around 7:00. Why do you ask?"

"Someone shot Viper last night and it may have been a female."

"*What?* Why would Jamie shoot Viper?"

"Beats the hell out of me. Just looking at possibilities. Anyway, 7:00 puts her out of the frame."

"I'd starting checking ex-wives if I were you."

"Yeah." He climbed into the Jeep, trying to ignore a troublesome nagging in his gut. Something he didn't want to explore. "How's the kid doing?"

"I'm worried about her. She wouldn't get out of bed this morning and she tried to hide it, but I heard her crying. An upset stomach shouldn't last this long. I hope it's not food poisoning."

"Make sure she stays hydrated."

"I will. If she's not better tomorrow, I'll take her to the doctor. It might be the stress over Angel. It's brought back everything that happened before."

"Let me know if you need help."

"Thank you, Joel. You are so—" she hesitated. "I love you."

He hesitated for just a moment, too, before his response, "I love you, too." The words never came easy, but he felt them rooted deep in his heart. He and Claudia were like two blind people groping for each other in the darkness. He was hopeful they were getting closer.

"Hey, before I forget," he said, "I've got Annabelle's phone. Marcia found it outside."

"I can't believe she lost it again. That's at least the fourth time. As sick as she is right now, I doubt she'll miss it."

They said their goodbyes and rang off. Jovanic sat in the Jeep, trying to connect with what was bothering him. Something was working its way up through his subconscious, but was not yet close enough to the surface to identify.

He phoned Randy Coleman and told him about Viper getting shot, then asked whether he'd had any luck in getting the warrant for a trace on Shane Oliver's cell phone.

"Yeah, but the phone company's dragging their heels," said Coleman. "We should have something by noon. I'll let you know."

"What about next of kin for Travis Navarette?"

Randy asked him to hold on. Jovanic heard his partner calling to someone else, then come back on the line. "Yeah, it just now came in. His father's name is Gerald Harris. Travis was using his mother's maiden name. She's deceased."

"Why does that name sound familiar? Gerald Harris."

"You want me to send somebody out to do the notification? Or just have the locals do it?"

"Wait a sec. I got it. Gerald Harris is a guy Viper put in the hospital twenty years ago."

"Huh. How's that for coincidence?"

"Yeah, Randy. Big 'coincidence.' What the fuck's going on here?"

Coleman paused, apparently running through his head what Jovanic had just told him. "So, the Gerald Harris who got beat up by Viper is the same guy whose son got firebombed?"

"That's what I'm saying. Hold off on the notification. Get the team together and meet me at The Firehouse."

While he was waiting outside the restaurant for the other detectives, Jovanic took Annabelle's phone from his pocket and accessed the Voice Memo screen again. Claudia would admonish him that listening to what she had recorded would be like reading someone's diary.

The thought of Claudia made him smile. He had watched her defenses crumble over time as she grew to trust him and accept the fact that he was not going to hurt her. The weekend before this crazy week began, he had gone to a jeweler in the mall and bought an engagement ring. His uncertainty about her answer was all that held him back from offering it to her.

Jovanic sat there in the Jeep, visualizing a couple of scenarios where he took the plunge and actually asked her to marry him. With half his mind busy on thoughts of Claudia, he idly tapped the arrow that started the voice memo playback.

A coarse male voice sounded loud and clear: "You don't need anything to blow me. Get over here. On your knees."

Jovanic sat up straight, his attention riveted to the voice on the phone. He listened with dawning horror at the mocking laugh and the man's damning observation: "That's a pretty nice gun for a little girl like you."

And then, unmistakably, Annabelle's trembling voice trying to sound tough. "It's going to shoot you if you don't tell me what you did to Angel."

Hardly daring to breathe, Jovanic listened to the entire episode. He heard every word of Annabelle's abortive attempt to scare a confession out of one of the meanest thugs in Southern California. Viper's shout of protest. The deafening blast of a gunshot.

The long silence, then Annabelle's whimper. "Omigod, omigod, omigod, I killed him. What am I gonna do? I didn't mean to kill him. Omigod."

thirty-six

Joel barreled up the back steps and entered the kitchen, where Claudia was pouring herself a cup of coffee. She swung around as he entered, her face lit with pleasure that turned quickly to alarm.

"Where is she?" Jovanic demanded.

"What's wrong?"

Not trusting himself to speak, he pushed past her, taking the stairs two at a time. Claudia called after him, but his mind was racing. He went into their bedroom and made straight for the closet. "Shut the door," he said tersely, knowing she was right behind him.

"What's going on?"

He could see she was frightened, but Jovanic could not offer her any reassurances when he was scared stupid himself. "Where's your Glock?"

"In the safe, of course. Why?" She repeated her question: "*What's going on?*"

Jovanic was already inside the closet, his keys in his hand. He had chosen to place the safe there because it was inconspicuous and unlikely to be spotted by someone who didn't know to look for it. Claudia stood in the doorway behind him, watching mutely as he yanked the cord that switched on the light. He shoved aside the neat row of trousers and skirts that concealed the heavy locked box. Crouching on his heels, he turned the key and opened the lid.

The Glock was right where it was supposed to be, looking as innocuous as a deadly weapon could look. He prayed that its presence meant he was mistaken, but he knew better. His mouth was dry as he took the gun from its hiding place and straightened. Claudia backed up, pale and wide-eyed, giving him room to exit the closet. The questions on her face were palpable, but she didn't ask them again.

Removing the semiautomatic from its holster, he pointed it at the floor and pressed the release. Knowing what he would find, he slid out the magazine and checked it anyway. One empty slot, one in the barrel. His face burned as the blood rushed to his head.

"Holy fuck."

He snapped the magazine back into the receiver and moved past Claudia, the Glock still in his hand. She reached out and tried to grab his arm, but he shrugged her off and wrenched open the bedroom door.

Jovanic strode along the landing to Annabelle's room and without bothering to knock, slammed open the door. Annabelle shot up in bed with a squeal of fright.

"What the *hell* did you do?" In his tone was a seething storm of barely contained fury. "Look at me, Annabelle! *What did you do?*"

She hunched behind the covers, squeezing her eyes shut, trying to make herself small enough not to be seen. "Claudia, help me!" The muffled voice barely rose above a squeak.

Jovanic leaned down, eyes blazing, and ripped the blanket away from her face. "She can't help you this time. You fucked up a little too good this time."

"I'm sorry, I'm sorry. Don't yell at me."

"You think this is yelling? I haven't even—"

"Stop it, Joel!" Claudia's urgent appeal came from behind him. "Can't you see you're scaring her? You're scaring me, too."

He turned the fury on her. "Oh, I'm scaring her? Well, guess what—she *needs* to be scared. She'll be a lot more scared when her ass lands in jail. I could lose my goddamn job because this—this—" Struggling for control, he bit his tongue on the epithet that wanted to fly out of his mouth. "She friggin' *shot* my suspect with the gun I gave you." He held up the Glock for emphasis, enunciating each word with precision, making sure Claudia comprehended what he was saying.

She sank down on the bed. "Oh my God."

Annabelle started sobbing. "I didn't mean to. I was just gonna scare him, but he grabbed it and—and—"

The words were garbled, but clear enough to take their meaning. She scooted back against the headboard, shrinking as far away from Joel as she could get. "I didn't mean to kill him, I didn't. I thought—if he would just tell what he did to Angel he would get into trouble and they would make him p-p-pay."

Jovanic was well aware of how to use his height and imposing build to his advantage when he wanted to spook a suspect. He was not deliberately using those assets now, but he knew how intimidating he must seem to the girl in the bed, and he was beyond caring. It took every ounce of restraint he could muster not to grab her by the shoulders and shake her like a rag doll.

"Put that gun away, Joel, and stop glaring like that." Claudia's strained voice finally penetrated the red mist clouding his vision. "You're angry and with good cause, but it doesn't help for you to stand over her like King Kong." She pushed at his legs. "Back off."

The adrenaline surge that had propelled him from the restaurant parking lot was starting to ebb and his hands were shaking. Jovanic took a few steps away from the bed and sat on the dainty white wicker chair at the study desk. He knew he looked ridiculous perched there, but he had to steady himself, regain control of his emotions.

"I can't believe this. Annabelle." Claudia's tone was pitched high with anxiety. "You promised us…"

"I only promised not to touch *Joel's* gun." There was a touch of her old defiance, despite the tears running down her cheeks. Claudia reached over to the box of tissues on the nightstand and passed her a handful. She turned to Jovanic. "When did it happen?"

"While I was taking a nap yesterday before you got home. She took your Glock, got herself over to the tattoo parlor, and shot him."

"Stop calling it *mine*. You know I never wanted it."

"Okay, it's *my* fault she shot him. I guess I should be grateful she didn't take *my* gun." Jovanic fished the cell phone out of his pocket and held it up by its pink shell. "And did I mention she recorded the whole stinking incident?"

Annabelle gasped. "How'd you get my phone?"

"You dropped it outside again, *sweetheart*." He didn't use the word as a term of endearment. "Lucky for you, Marcia found it."

"You took Jamie's car." Claudia interjected. "I *knew* it wasn't parked right. It was out from the curb and further down the street. Tell me what happened."

"I just walked in the door. He was there by himself."

"Nobody else? No customers?"

"Both his bodyguards are in the slammer," Jovanic added, the bitter, angry edge still tinging his words. "His other artists were at the expo. She picked a quiet time of day. Couldn't have been more perfect. Clever girl," he added sarcastically, tapping icons on the phone.

Viper's recorded voice filled the room. The tension, already thick in the air, ratcheted another notch higher. Annabelle curled into a tighter little ball and turned toward the wall, pulling the covers all the way over her head again.

When she heard Viper order the girl to her knees, Claudia gasped something inaudible. Seconds later, the gunshot exploded. The look of shock on her face stabbed Joel with remorse. He had not intended to take out his anger on her.

Annabelle sobbed even harder. "I didn't mean to kill him. I swear I didn't. Don't let them lock me up, Claudia." Her arm snaked out from under the covers and grabbed onto Claudia's hand. "I was just going to scare him, I swear. He grabbed the gun and it went off, and—"

With a big sigh of surrender, Jovanic relented. "You didn't kill him."

The bedcovers came down as far as her eyes. "What—he was lying there on the floor, he wasn't moving. There was blood all on his shirt."

"Yeah. But after you left, he started moving and he called 9-1-1. They dug the bullet out of his belly, and he's going to live."

Relief flooded Claudia's face. Then reality hit. "Do they know she shot him?"

"He doesn't know my name," Annabelle chimed in.

Joel wouldn't look at her. "He doesn't have to. It'd be easy enough for the investigators to figure out who you are if they connect a few dots. But he won't tell them anything. It's a matter of honor for someone like Viper. He would never admit to being shot by a fifteen-year-old girl."

Claudia sat on the sofa in her office watching Joel pace the long room. A half-hour after the showdown with Annabelle and they were still going at it head-to-head. She felt as though she had stepped into an alternate universe—one where this cold, unforgiving homicide detective was a stranger to her.

She got a flashback to their first meeting when she had seen him this way before. She had been a witness at a crime scene where Jovanic was the lead detective. They'd got off on the wrong foot, but the early tension between them had morphed into a flirtation that grew into something important.

Over time, Claudia had started to believe she could let down the barriers she had erected long ago, that she could kiss her well-earned commitment phobia goodbye. She had come to believe that Joel wouldn't hurt her. But now, looking at the stony set of his jaw, the rigid line of his mouth, she was no longer so certain.

"What good would it do to lock her up?" she asked in a tight voice, frustrated by his refusal to bend.

"The world might be a safer place," he retorted with brutal detachment. "What do you think is going to happen when it comes out that she shot him with a gun I bought, Claudia? That she used my keys to open the safe? That the gun was loaded? Do you think my sergeant is going to pat me on the shoulder and say, 'no problem, we'll just forgive and forget?' If that's what you think, you're dead wrong."

"But you didn't know—"

"You think they'll care that I didn't *know?* Or that she claims she didn't mean to shoot him? I should have *already* called and reported it."

"You can't do that! You heard the recording. It was accidental."

"Yeah, I heard the recording. The guy says she's got a nice gun, then she shoots him. She stole a car, drove without a license and threatened a guy with a loaded gun. Does that sound like an accident? What's a judge supposed to do with that?"

"You can't let her go to juvenile hall. She tried to kill herself last time she was there."

"It's not up to me, and you know it."

"Yes, it is."

He stared at her, looking incredulous and more hurt than she could imagine. "You *can't* be thinking—"

"You said yourself that Viper will never tell."

"And you think he won't come after her? Remember what happened to Angel."

"I thought you were almost ready to arrest him. We can keep her safe 'til then."

"Claudia, listen to me and listen good. You're talking about crossing a line here. That bullet will go into IBIS. If we were to cover up a major crime, which is what you're talking about, this gun can never be used again. It would come back to the slug they took out of Viper."

"Then make it go away somewhere it'll never be found. I hate the fucking thing."

"I took an oath to uphold the law. Now you want me to break it?"

"Of course I don't want you to. But Joel—"

"She might keep quiet now, but who's to say she won't shoot off her mouth somewhere down the line?"

"She couldn't. She'd be implicating herself."

"Annabelle needs to come clean, for her sake and mine. I'll still be in trouble, but at least I'll know I did the right thing. It won't do her any good to grow up having this on her conscience. She's under sixteen and he didn't die. She won't be charged as an adult. With a good lawyer—"

"Her father's coming home next weekend. We won't have to deal with it anymore."

"Are you serious? We'll be dealing with it for the rest of our lives." Jovanic shook his head. "I can't believe we're even having this conversation."

He picked up his coat from where it lay across a chair and started for the door. "I have to go back to the hospital and check on Viper." He didn't look back at her. "Don't wait up. I'll stay at my place tonight."

thirty-seven

Jovanic drove to the hospital and shut off the engine, feeling sick to his stomach. So few hours ago Claudia had been in his arms, giving herself to him without reservation. Now there was a wall between them a yard thick and a mile high. From where he sat, he was not sure he would ever be able to breach it. Or even whether he wanted to.

He had been a cop for more than twenty years. A good cop. That didn't mean he had never bent a rule or cut a corner, but what she was asking him to do went far beyond cutting corners.

Claudia was the love of his life. He wanted to grow old with her, to take care of her and shield her from the crazy and dangerous situations she all too frequently got herself into. He could understand her attachment to Annabelle, and if he hadn't exactly welcomed the girl's intermittent presence as part of their picture together, he had reconciled himself to it. But his dreams of the future had never included Claudia asking him to cover up a serious crime.

Disillusionment shot through him like a cold poison invading every cell of his body.

If he swept this criminal misdeed under the rug, what else might Annabelle do? The girl was a loose cannon. If she got away with it this time, would she feel empowered to go further the next time something made her angry? Jovanic knew that he would never be able to trust her again. Christ. She could blackmail him if she wanted to.

He was screwed. Whatever decision he made, it would always be there between him and Claudia, a sharp thorn of resentment rubbing a hole in their relationship. Either he would go against his principles and resent her for it, or he would not and she would resent him. He thought of the engagement ring in its blue velvet box hidden in his sock drawer. It felt like a purchase made in vain.

He had virtually moved in at Claudia's house. He couldn't remember the last time he had spent a night at his own apartment. The only time he went there anymore was to pick up mail and pay the rent. But tonight, he intended to sit on a bar stool at Cowboys for a few hours and make a big dent in a tequila bottle. When he was well and truly blitzed, he would go to there and sleep alone in his own cold bed. Picturing the night without Claudia snuggled against him, his heart plummeted even further.

His phone beeped, signaling a text from Randy Coleman:

You want the Lancaster sheriff to notify Gerald Harris re Navarette, or wait?

Jovanic stared at the message, his mind clicking like a computer, running the data.

Gerald Harris lived in Lancaster.

"Crash," the artist who put Viper's tattoo on Annabelle lived in Lancaster.

Travis Navarette was Gerald Harris's son.

Harris has a twenty-year-old grudge against Viper, who beat him so badly that he sustained a head injury and broken bones.

Travis was killed in a firebombing presumably engineered by Viper.

Using his phone, Jovanic accessed the DMV database and pulled up Harris's driver's license picture. And as he sat there gazing through the windshield, fitting the pieces together, something in the parking lot caught his notice.

A white cargo van had drawn up in the red No Parking zone next to the hospital entrance. The driver's door opened and a man jumped down. From where Jovanic sat, the man's face was not fully visible, but he could see the rangy frame, the long, greyish ponytail. According to Annabelle, Crash drove a white cargo van and sported a ponytail.

Under his breath he muttered, "Harris."

He climbed out of the Jeep, trying to look casual. He wanted to run, but that would alert the man he now believed to be Gerald Harris aka Crash. Jovanic strode fast in his direction, but Harris, walking like he was in a hurry, was already disappearing through the hospital front doors. The slight bulge in the back of his jacket made Jovanic quicken his pace, but he was too late. As he entered the lobby, the elevator doors were just sliding closed on his quarry.

With Harris's son dead and his old nemesis Alvin Rousch lying in a bed in this building, there was no good reason for Harris to be here. Instinct told Jovanic he was on a mission of vengeance. There was no time to stop and ask for Rousch's room number at the front desk, no time to wait for the elevator to return.

Jovanic spotted the stairwell door. He slipped through and ran up two flights, glad he had quit smoking. At the third-floor landing, he took a moment to catch his breath before stepping into the hallway where he had met with Dr. Redfern that morning. There was no sign of Harris.

Turning left, he started down the corridor, opening doors, looking into rooms.

"Hey, can I help you?" A male nurse in blue scrubs hurried up to him, a look of concern on his face.

"Where's Alvin Rousch's room?" Jovanic demanded.

"Are you family?"

Jovanic opened his coat to let the nurse see the shield on his belt. "I'm a police officer and there may be a dangerous person on the floor."

The nurse looked him up and down. Jovanic's business suit, his neatly trimmed hair and authoritative manner seemed to convince him. "He's in 310." He was pointing behind him.

Quietly, Jovanic told him to call Security. A few seconds later he heard the coded call over the PA.

He drew his Glock and pointed it at the floor. Keeping to the wall, he moved fast down the long, curving corridor, praying no one stepped out of any of the rooms. The nursing staff would have heard the security code and be preparing for lockdown.

Even before he reached Viper's room, he could hear the sound of an angry raised voice. Getting down into a crouch, he began to edge his way to the half-open door. If Harris heard him and turned, his eyes would be trained at head height, not down low, which would give Jovanic the advantage.

"Come on, motherfucker, open your goddamn eyes," the voice rasped. "I want you to see what's coming to you."

Jovanic rapidly crossed the entry. Still in a crouch, he eased the door open just wide enough to see into the room. A glance inside showed him the foot of the bed and Gerald Harris standing next to it, his back to the door. He was holding a gun and it was pointed at Viper's head.

All the years of training and experience coalesced into that laser-focused moment.

Jovanic backed out and straightened up. Leaning his cheek on the wall, he brought the Glock up to shoulder height and held it on the door jamb. With his dominant left hand holding the gun and his right hand steadying his wrist, Jovanic pressed the back of his right hand to the jamb.

Protecting his face, exposing only as much as he had to, he brought his head away from the wall and peered over his hands. He gave a loud shout. "Drop the fucking gun, Harris; Police. Don't fucking move. Don't turn around. Drop it! Drop it!"

Somewhere along the corridor, someone screamed. Jovanic, figuring it was a panicked patient, ignored the sound and held his stance.

Inside the room, Gerald Harris never moved. He spoke calmly, as if he had been expecting this confrontation. "This time, he killed my boy. I got nothin' left."

Jovanic took it down a degree. "Slowly put the gun down, Gerald. No sudden moves or I'll drop you right here." His finger was already on the trigger, squeezing. "Fucking do as I say. Do it *now.*"

In his peripheral vision Jovanic was aware of movement; people running in the corridor behind him, putting themselves in the line of fire. He knew he would have to calculate his next move at lightning speed. He raised his voice again. "Drop the gun, Gerald."

Gerald Harris brought up his weapon. He pulled the trigger once and started to turn toward the doorway. A half-second later he was dead.

thirty-eight

Claudia couldn't stop crying. She had locked herself inside her bathroom with a full box of tissues and was rapidly running through them. When Annabelle knocked on the door after the first hour, timidly asking if she could do anything, Claudia wasn't even able to answer.

It felt like someone had died. Joel was gone and she had a terrible dread that he would not be coming back. When he'd told her he would be spending the night at his apartment, he had walked past without looking at her, as if for him, she no longer existed.

Lobbing the soggy tissue clutched in her fist into the trash basket with a dozen others, Claudia plucked a fresh one out of the box. It was unlike her to weep and she hated the sense of vulnerability it gave her. Even her skin felt raw and exposed, like a bad sunburn that was unbearable to touch. When had she become this weak person?

She knew the answer. It had happened gradually as she let herself love him. The fatal mistake was believing it was okay to open up and welcome him in. She pressed her face into a towel so Annabelle would not hear a fresh round of sobs.

Annabelle. The daughter she would never have. She huffed an ironic laugh at herself. She was nobody's mother. She knew better than to blame herself for the child's actions—Annabelle already had a long history of neglect and abuse before Claudia came into her life—but that she had so completely stepped outside the bounds of what was right was a bitter disappointment. Claudia had wanted to believe that the influence she exerted was stronger than that.

Who was she fooling? She pulled herself up from the toilet lid and leaned her hands on the vanity, gazing in the mirror at her puffy face and bloodshot eyes. In one day, she had failed two of the people she loved most in the world. She had seen the betrayal reflected in Joel's stunned expression. It ripped through her all over again, a dagger to the heart. He believed she had chosen Annabelle over him. A sharp flash of anger shot through her. Why couldn't he see that the girl needed protection?

Why hadn't *she* seen that she should protect *him?*

A new torrent of tears welled up and spilled over. The anger she felt was directed at herself. The sadness was that she had done no better than Annabelle in keeping a clear perspective.

Joel was right. It would do no good to protect the girl from the consequences of her actions, even though they were well-meaning. What if Viper had been killed? There were stories in the news every day of kids being criminally tried as adults because they had committed horrendous crimes. Was that how she should be viewing Annabelle—as a criminal?

No. She had her faults, but Annabelle had a good heart. She *wanted* to be good and she had worked hard on herself over the past couple of years. She had made excellent progress, too. Until Angel.

Having given in to her misery for long enough, Claudia ran cold water into the sink and splashed it on her face. Her friend Ann Cunningham would give her the advice she needed.

Ann was a criminal defense attorney Claudia had met through Kelly Brennan. They had worked together on a couple of forgery cases and Ann had a record of winning. Around the courthouse, her colleagues had coined a new term for the district attorneys who unsuccessfully opposed her. They called it *getting Cunninghammered.*

Ann would take Annabelle in hand and figure out what they could do to protect her, and Joel's job, too, if he would allow it. Of course, in his view, defense attorneys were lower than bottom feeders, so chances were small that he would.

Claudia patted her face dry, blew her nose one more time, and took a deep breath. One thing she knew for sure—her life without Joel Jovanic would be a dark and lonely place. Would he accept a plea of temporary insanity? Or was the damage she had done to their relationship too profound to heal?

She went along the landing to Annabelle's room and knocked on the guest room door. When there was no answer, she knocked again. "Annabelle, let's talk about it."

Still no answer. With a sinking feeling, she opened the door onto an empty room.

thirty-nine

Traffic whooshed past as Annabelle trudged east on Jefferson Boulevard, the same road along which she had driven Jamie's car yesterday on her way to scare Viper into a confession. Less than twenty-four hours ago and life as she knew it had once again taken a horrible turn. She was getting to be a pro at fucking things up.

There was no sidewalk, only a scrub verge on the edge of the wide road. Some of the drivers honked at her as they passed, the backwash of hot air from the big trucks nearly blowing her off her feet. She wished one of them would slam into her. Maybe she should step off the verge and into the road. She was such a screwup. She deserved to die. Nobody would miss her.

Claudia's voice whispered in her head. *"I would miss you."*

Annabelle told herself that she didn't merit the love of someone like Claudia. But knowing that Claudia did love her was the thing that kept her from flinging herself into the path of the cars rushing by.

At the beginning of the Ballona Creek Bridge the road narrowed. The verge on which she had been walking disappeared altogether until she got to the other side. Maybe it was because she felt as though she were in a dream that the danger factor didn't bother her. It was the thoughts of how she was going to make it in jail that made her shiver. But she couldn't stand knowing that her stupidity had caused a rift between Claudia and Joel.

She'd heard them in their bedroom this morning after they left hers. They had been arguing about her fate. And Joel was going to get in trouble because of her. She had heard him say he was going to sleep at his apartment, too. He never did that. As long as she had known them, every night he came home to Claudia's house and slept there, with Claudia. They loved each other and she, Annabelle, had ruined everything.

Shame at her culpability sent a hot flush into her cheeks. In her desperate need to avenge Angel she had not given a thought to the consequences her actions could bring down on other people. It hadn't occurred to her that brandishing a loaded gun, even without intending to use it, could lead to someone getting shot. And that someone getting shot with Claudia's gun would get Joel into serious trouble.

Annabelle had been plodding along for most of an hour, her wretchedness growing with every step, when she reached the bridge that spanned Pacific Coast Highway. At least the narrow bike lane on the PCH Bridge made it a little less unsafe to walk at the edge of the road. She figured Centinela, the last street to cross before she reached her destination, was still over a mile away.

Joel had kept her phone with its damning recording, and it was Claudia's spare that rang in her pocket at least three times. Annabelle didn't answer it. She didn't want to say where she was going. Claudia would try to stop her and she was afraid she would be persuaded. The five-mile trek was the beginning of her punishment. She didn't even allow herself to listen to music as she walked.

She was glad her legs were beginning to ache. She welcomed the blister she could feel forming on her little toe. By the time she got to the blocks of apartments that stood between her and the Pacific Division Police Station where Joel worked, Annabelle felt like she'd been walking forever.

It had only been a few days since the last time she was at the police station, when Claudia had dragged her and Jamie there to give their statement about Angel. That time, Joel had met them at the back door and escorted them inside. They'd had to walk past a couple of losers handcuffed to a low bench in the middle of the walkway. This time was different.

Annabelle moved between the cement bollards that stood at the head of the walkway at the one-story brick building. She passed the row of vending machines outside the entry, where she could see through the door to the lobby. An old guy was standing at a long white counter, talking to a uniformed cop on the other side. Beside the cop, a lady was sitting at a computer, with a phone at her ear. A row of plastic chairs filled with depressed-looking people was lined up along the wall, looking as pathetic as she felt.

Her feet felt glued to the sidewalk, but she had no choice. She had to prove to Claudia that she was not just a selfish little bitch anymore. At the end of October, she would be sixteen. It was time to start taking responsibility.

Annabelle straightened her spine and sucked in a big breath and pushed open the heavy door. She got in line behind the old guy, who was leaning on the counter, griping about his neighbor.

The woman at the computer hung up the phone, but her gaze swept right over Annabelle like she wasn't even there. She called out a name, and one of the people in the chairs, a skinny young woman with a black eye, shoved past Annabelle and went up to the desk.

People came and went and the cops behind the counter continued to ignore her. Because she was a kid, Annabelle guessed resentfully. Should she go up to the counter, or continue to wait? She shifted from one foot to the other, getting antsy. Beginning to lose her nerve.

She started thinking about the days she had spent in juvie. Angel was the one person who'd treated her like a human being in that nasty, scary place. Angel didn't deserve to be dead.

Annabelle was afraid she wouldn't be able to live through another confinement. Last time she had cut herself with a piece of broken glass after she got out. She pulled down the long sleeves of her T-shirt, conscious of the scars that still stood out against the pale skin of her wrists. That little adventure had been followed by a week in the psych ward. A lump clogged her throat. It would have been better if—

A startled voice shook her out of her reverie.

"*Annabelle?*"

forty

For an instant, Joel Jovanic's heart skipped. What the hell was Annabelle Giordano doing in the lobby? *If something had happened to Claudia…*

Ignoring the curious stares of the woman at the front desk and the uniform talking to a citizen, he went around to the door that separated the lobby from the detective squad bay and beckoned Annabelle to follow him.

He led her to one of the small interview rooms and sat her down on one side of the table, while he took the other chair. Normally, he would have remained standing to show who was in control, but he felt bad about the way he had acted this morning, scaring her the way he had, despite the fact that she had earned it, and more.

"What are you doing here?" he asked, afraid to hear the answer.

"Please don't break up with Claudia." Annabelle's voice was shaky, tears threatening. "I'm gonna tell them I stole the gun and you guys didn't know anything. She's been locked up in the bathroom all day, crying and crying, and I feel like shit. I know it's all my fault." Finally, she ran out of words and hung her head.

Hearing that, Jovanic felt like shit, too. He had never known Claudia to go on a crying jag. Knowing that he was the cause of her tears made him want to crawl into a very deep hole. He looked across the table at Annabelle and found that this morning's anger had drained away. Maybe he was just too tired to hang onto it. Or maybe the bullet he had put into Gerald "Crash" Harris's head had given him perspective on what was important.

"Viper is dead. Crash killed him in the hospital."

"What? *Crash*—"

"They knew each other a long time ago and they were enemies. Crash had a son named Travis—"

"You mean Travis who knew Angel?" Annabelle interrupted.

"Yeah. He learned to tattoo at Viper's shop. We'll never know for sure, but my guess is he probably grew up hearing from Crash about how much he hated Viper. I think maybe he trained at Dragon House and then set up his own shop to try to take business away from Viper in revenge for his father."

"Did Viper burn down Travis's place?" Annabelle asked.

"I think he did. And when Travis got killed, Crash decided to get *his* revenge." Jovanic didn't tell her about what he now believed was collateral damage—Darla Steinman and Shane Oliver. Connecting what Steinman's mother had told him with what Claudia discovered at the Inkslingers Ball, he was not surprised when the ballistics report showed that the same gun had killed both Steinman and Oliver.

He had developed a theory that Crash either went to Darla for help in getting at Viper and she'd rejected him, or he had simply shot her in revenge over their old rivalry. He then went after Oliver for the same reason, or believing that he held incriminating evidence. With both Viper and Crash dead, they would never know for sure.

As much as Annabelle had already suffered, Jovanic wanted to spare her those details. "Crash must have seen on the news this morning that Viper was hospitalized. It's easy to call and find out what room someone's in. I just happened to be there when he arrived."

"But Travis got killed last week. Why did he wait so long?"

"Viper always had bodyguards around until last Friday. They're in custody right now."

"What happened to Crash? Did you arrest him?"

"I was too late. He shot Viper and I had to shoot him."

Annabelle's hand went to the place on her abdomen where Crash had put the sugar skull tattoo on her. "Is Crash dead, too?"

For a half-second, Jovanic was back in Viper's hospital room doorway, his gaze fixed on Gerald Harris's gun hand. There had been no time to think before squeezing the trigger. Once Harris started to turn, his reflexes had taken over. Before he could register the sound of the discharge or the bullet hole in Harris's cheek, the other man dropped like a rock. Then all hell broke loose.

He looked at the teen with sudden understanding. Considering all she had suffered in her young life, maybe she wasn't doing so badly after all. He nodded. "Yeah, Crash is dead, too. So, that puts this matter to rest and you can go home."

Annabelle looked confused. "What do you mean?"

Exhaustion pressed down on him. If he could have laid his head on the table and closed his eyes right then, he would not open them for a week. He loosed a big sigh. "I mean that nobody here is going to want to hear your confession. With both these guys dead, the file is going to be wrapped up and nobody will want to unwrap it. They won't care who shot Viper first, and they sure as hell won't want to do the paperwork because it's not going anywhere. Under the circumstances, the D.A. won't prosecute you. There's nobody left to press charges."

He could have had her write up a statement and hand it in at the front desk. But the truth was, the person in charge would thank her for her honesty—wink, wink—and drop it in the trash can as soon as she was out the door. They would roll their eyes and comment on sexy little attention whores who'll do anything to get on the front page of the newspaper. They would not notice that Annabelle would rather not call attention to herself, or that she was trying to clear her conscience. Their motivation would be to clear their desks.

Annabelle's lips pressed together in a tight line, as if determined to hold back her tears. Jovanic got a little choked up himself. "It's gonna be okay, kiddo. What you did was totally wrong, even though it was for a good reason. And now, you've tried to make it right, so at least you learned something. You're going to have to see Dr. Gold about what happened, and you're going to have to keep going until he says you're okay. And then, let's put it behind us."

A big fat tear spilled over and dribbled down Annabelle's cheek, landing with a splash on the tabletop. She quickly brushed it away and wiped her wet fingers on her jeans. "I l-l-love Claudia. I didn't mean to hurt her."

Jovanic reached out and took her hand in his. "She loves you, too. Don't ever think otherwise, Annabelle."

She nodded and asked in a small voice, "Are you going to break up?"

Jovanic looked at her long and hard before giving her his answer. "Kiddo, I don't know."

forty-one

Thursday evening

Claudia took a quick peek in the rearview mirror and checked her makeup. The eye drops had done their job and though the skin around her eyes was still a little puffy, most of the evidence of her two-day crying jag was camouflaged under a light application of highlighter, makeup, and blush.

On this, the third day since she'd heard from him, Joel had texted and asked her to meet him at Shanghai Red's for dinner. She had nearly dropped the phone. His silence since the shooting at the hospital—which she had learned of, to her horror, on the news—had persuaded her that she was never going to hear from him again. Her feeble attempt to begin rebuilding the walls around her ego had already begun.

In those days since he had left her house, Claudia's world seemed to have shifted and crumbled. Even Annabelle was strangely quiescent following her disappearance after the Big Confrontation, as she had come to think of it. But she had refused to say where she had disappeared to and Claudia could not find the heart to press her on the subject. Then Monica invited Annabelle to stay for the last few days before her father came home from Canada. Claudia gladly let her go.

Not having to put up a cheerful front for the girl's sake was a relief, but having neither Annabelle nor Joel in the house made it a very lonely place. In a half-hearted attempt to take her mind off Joel and the burden she had placed on him, she made a stab at dealing with some of the work that was piling up on her desk.

A woman had sent the handwriting of her abusive boyfriend, wanting to know whether he was dangerous. Claudia wanted to shake her. In light of the hateful way the man addressed her in the handwritten letter, she should not need a graphologist to answer that question. However, the woman's own handwriting, which Claudia required when doing a third-party analysis, demonstrated her need to be a 'good girl.' That meant a pleaser who failed to recognize the boyfriend's behavior as abusive and call a halt to it.

Staring at the specimen, Claudia's mind was a blank. The red flags for danger in the man's handwriting were clear, but with every attempt she made to start writing the analysis, Joel's face floated in front of her. Putting her fingers on the keyboard and typing the words seemed to exceed her current abilities. Despite his attempt to cover it up, she had seen how much she had hurt him that day. With every fiber of her being, she wished she could reel the words back in.

Then his text arrived and Claudia began to wonder whether he had chosen the site of their very first formal date as the place to formally end the relationship.

What kind of clothes were appropriate for an imminent breakup? Her pride refused to allow her to dress as provocatively as she would like. It would be humiliating if he thought she was trying to manipulate him into staying with her. She settled on a rose-colored cowl neck shell under a soft black knit cardigan and pants.

On her way down to the garage, she argued with herself over perfume. Jovanic loved the Opium scent she often wore for him. Before she reached the Jaguar, she ran back upstairs and compromised with a light spritz in the hollow of her neck.

Arriving at Shanghai Red's in Marina del Rey, she turned the Jaguar over to the valet. Her nerves were getting the better of her as she paused on the little bridge over the koi pond, struggling to center herself. A school of the big colorful fish swam over, gathering in an expectant group below her, doing their best to look hungry. Claudia wished she had some offering to drop into the water, but the koi were destined to be disappointed. She sighed. Disappointment was the theme of the week.

Standing there in the gathering dusk, she tried to prepare herself for the coming meeting, but the tranquil beauty of the waterfall and the twinkling lights strung on the wooden rafter above the walkway could not touch her anxiety. Finally, gathering her wits, she left the hopeful koi behind and continued on to the restaurant.

Joel was already in the lobby, standing by the fireplace. He looked serious and ill-at-ease. Not a good sign, Claudia thought. But her stomach flipped the way it always did when she saw him and she had to remind herself not to reach out for him.

He made no attempt to kiss or touch her. His manner was as formal as if he were about to interview a suspect. "Thank you for coming," he said. "I wasn't sure you would."

Claudia tried to smile, but her facial muscles seemed frozen. "You've been very quiet."

"I've been doing a lot of sleeping. And thinking."

Uh-oh, here it comes.

The hostess called his name then, and handed them over to their server, who led them to a back room that overlooked the marina. The lights in the condos across the water were just beginning to come on, reflecting gold on the water. As irony would have it, they were seated at the very table where they had sat that first night. Claudia had been nervous then, too.

But that had been the jitters of excited anticipation. Pretty much opposite to the way she felt now. What was she going to do without him?

Jovanic ordered a glass of pinot noir for each of them and the server left behind an awkward pause. Claudia had no idea what to say, so she just waited. He seemed unsure, too.

"Do you remember the first time we came here?" Jovanic asked at length, as if reading her mind.

"Of course I do."

"A lot has happened since then."

"Yes."

He cleared his throat. "Like I said, I've been doing a lot of thinking."

"And sleeping," she echoed his earlier comment.

"I was pretty out of it. It's amazing how sleep—and the lack of it—can affect one's perspective."

"No doubt," she agreed, managing a wry smile. "How has it affected yours?"

"I need to apologize for yelling at you the other day, and for the things I said. I'm not going to make excuses. I'm just sorry."

Claudia shook her head. "You don't have to—it's me who owes the apology. I put you in an unfair position. I've talked to Ann Cunningham, my lawyer friend, and she's willing to take Annabelle's case if she ends up having to go to court."

His perceptive slate grey eyes caught hers and held them. She tried to fathom what emotion they held, but he could be as impassive as a sphinx. Not wanting him to read her pain, she dropped her gaze to the menu in front of her, but she left it closed.

"You're an enigma, Claudia."

That was ironic.

She glanced up and was still unable to read him. "How so?"

"We've been together for more than two years. You say you love me. You've shared your most intimate secrets with me. We've had some disagreements, but usually we've ended up on the same page."

She thought she knew what was coming, and she shrank from it.

"I thought we were getting closer," Jovanic went on. "But this thing with Annabelle. We weren't on the same side. All of a sudden, we weren't a team anymore. Instead of 'us,' it was you versus me."

"I know. I got scared."

"Scared of what?"

Claudia paused, gathering her thoughts. "It felt like—stepping off a cliff. I know Annabelle needs me, but..." she broke off.

"But you're not sure of me? You think I won't be there to catch you?"

"It's foolish, I know. You've *always* been there. Even when I acted against your advice."

"Acted against advice—you?" His familiar wry grin broke her heart. "When could that have been?"

"Hmm, let me think. There was that time when you came to Las Vegas when Annabelle got kidnapped..."

"Uh huh. And I do seem to remember a certain trip to New York."

"Yep, that too." She refrained from reminding him of last spring at the cult compound. At least that one had not required air travel. Claudia felt herself blush as she realized how many times he had come, if not to her rescue, to be there for her in the aftermath of the dangerous situations in which she had placed herself. She had come to count on him *always* being there. Now, though, looking into the face she cherished and seeing his expression as serious as she had ever known it, she began to absorb the possibility that he would not be.

Jovanic stuck his hand into his inside pocket and took out an envelope. "I have something I need you to look at."

Claudia's mouth went dry. "What is it?"

"Some handwriting."

She stared at him, baffled by his timing. "You want me to look at some handwriting right now?"

"M'hm. It's a tough case, and it's driving me crazy." He handed the envelope across the table. "This is really important, so give it your best shot."

The envelope was unsealed, the flap tucked in. Inside was a folded piece of paper. Unfolding it, Claudia saw right away that the handwriting was Jovanic's own block printing and signature. *He's breaking up with me in a note,* she thought bitterly. At least he hadn't done it by text message.

Then she read what he had written:

My Dearest GraphoLady, will you marry me?

THE END

This case is closed—but escape can be its own kind of risk.

When violence reaches too close to home, Claudia is forced to reckon with the reality that expertise and good intentions don't guarantee protection. The boundaries she once relied on have proven fragile—and rebuilding them won't be simple.

Still reeling from a brutal courtroom attack, Claudia Rose leaves home in search of distance and control, only to find herself drawn into danger far from where she expected it. The experience sharpens her instincts even as it unsettles her sense of safety, forcing her to confront how easily trauma can follow, no matter how far one runs.

Claudia's story continues in *Outside the Lines,* Book 6. Turn the page to continue reading.

Outside the Lines

Monday Morning

Sylvia Vasquez opened the back door and peeked out. The Señor would be angry if he knew she had not picked up the mail since Friday. He'd warned her about mailbox thieves and instructed her to clear the box every day as soon as the mail carrier left. But Sylvia had been too busy enjoying the weekend with her new man to care about her employers' mail. They were out of town again and would be all week—they wouldn't know the difference.

She stepped outside in her ratty bathrobe and worn slippers. The neighbors wouldn't see her this early and the morning fog provided cover for a quick run to the box.

Sylvia unlocked the steel security gate that led to the alley and opened the mailbox flap. It took a second to register the mass of crumpled toilet tissue crammed into the box as she reached for the stack of catalogs and magazines, letters on top. That boy across the street, no doubt. Tonto adolescente!

With an irritated "tsk," she grabbed a handful of tissue and felt something hard. Before she could wonder what it was, a flash erupted and a bright tongue of flame shot out. The box exploded with a loud crack-bang in a cloud of blue-black smoke. Fragments of black metal and masonry flew into the alley.

The blast of searing heat sent Sylvia staggering backward. For a moment, she couldn't make sense of what she was seeing—blood pulsing from the stumps where her index and middle fingers were supposed to be. She stared at her hand.

The acrid reek of gunpowder burned her nostrils. Dogs barked, the sound hollow and far away in her ringing ears.

Where was her abuela's ring? Where were her fingers?

Unbearable pressure squeezed her rib cage like the coils of a giant python, robbing her of the breath to scream for help. Her eyes rolled back in her head. Her galloping heart gave a terrible lurch.

Sylvia Vasquez dropped to the ground.

The pounding in her chest abruptly ceased.

two

The marbled courthouse hallway was as silent as a held breath.

After waiting on the cold, hard bench for ninety minutes to testify in the Danny Ortiz trial, Claudia's mind was as numb as her backside. She'd gone over and over her exhibits until she was sick of the sight of them, and the handwriting on the tablet screen no longer registered in her brain.

The final witness from the morning session—a weapons expert—had been held over the lunch recess and was now back on the hot seat. Endlessly.

Down the hall, a courtroom door opened and two attorneys stepped out. They weren't part of the Ortiz case; they were dueling over some other hapless defendant's fate—bail or no bail, or a reduction in prison time—for someone facing LWOP, twenty years might sound palatable.

Claudia watched the minor drama unfold, glad for the distraction. She was fully confident in her opinion, but the worries were always there in the back of her mind: what if she forgot something important? What if she flubbed it? And the big one: could she convince the jury? Her stomach clenched as it always did before she got on the witness stand.

A text dinged. Joel Jovanic, her fiancé. He'd made dinner reservations at their favorite restaurant. Claudia sent a heart emoji back and slid the tablet into her briefcase. She stood and straightened her skirt, strolled the long hallway, and when no one had come out looking for her, returned to the bench and waited some more.

By the time the DA's investigator finally appeared and said they were ready for her, it was 3:15.

Jesse Alvarez was a burly, dark-complexioned man from Belize who loved to make people laugh. The week before, when Claudia had met with him and his boss, Paul Feynman, he'd cracked a couple of lawyer jokes that left Feynman shaking his head. Today, the humor was gone from his eyes. There was nothing remotely funny in the trial of a cop killer.

She grabbed her briefcase, took a deep breath, and followed Alvarez through the heavy oak doors into the packed courtroom. Aware of curious faces turning toward her, Claudia made her way through the gate that separated the gallery from the counsel tables and the bench.

The District Attorney, always seated closest to the jury, carried the burden of proof and was expected to be the ultimate champion of Truth, Justice, and the American Way.

The spectators were split into two sharply divided camps. Seated behind the D.A. were the grieving family and supporters of the undercover cop Danny Ortiz was accused of executing in cold blood.

The rows behind the defendant and his public defender, Alison Smith, were occupied by hard-looking young men sporting shaved heads and prison tattoos. Their chola girlfriends, clad in skintight Levis, wore penciled-in eyebrows that made commas over heavily rimmed blue-shadowed eyes.

Claudia took the oath to tell the truth and mounted the witness stand. The unforgiving lens of a television camera stared at her from the back of the courtroom. Mindful that the slightest slip would be broadcast to the entire Southland, she carefully set aside a half-full cup of water left by the last witness and reminded herself not to swivel in her seat.

"State and spell your name for the record." The clerk must have said those words at least a thousand times, and her bored tone proved it. As Claudia recited her response, the defendant, who had been doodling on a legal pad, looked up and caught her eye. The loathing in that dead black stare chilled her to the bone. If Danny Ortiz could have shot poison darts at that moment, she would be one dead handwriting expert.

Judge George C. Abernathy glanced down at Claudia from his lofty perch. "Good afternoon, Ms. Rose."

She smiled and nodded. "Good afternoon, Your Honor."

She had testified before Abernathy more than once and was aware of his reputation: a hard-nosed hang-'em-high jurist—the kind of judge the prosecution prayed for and the defense dreaded. He was broad across the chest in his black robes and had a ring of white hair on his mostly bald head. Add a long white beard to the bushy brows and he was Santa without the ho-ho-ho.

Claudia's role in the proceedings was to authenticate the handwriting in a letter that took credit for the killing of Detective Hector Maldonado, whose cover had been blown during a drug buy. Danny Ortiz was accused of forcing the detective to his knees and shooting him twice execution-style, then dumping his body in an East Los Angeles alley.

Ortiz's public defender had supplied him with a conservative blue Oxford shirt intended to avoid the prejudice an orange jail jumpsuit might have raised. For the same reason, the defendant was neither cuffed nor shackled at the defense table.

A member of the 7th Street Crue, his gang moniker, "Li'l Dude," was ironic. There was nothing little about Ortiz, who stood five-ten and weighed in at two-twenty. The ink on his neck was mostly hidden under his shirt. The same wasn't true of the crude prison-house tattoos on his face: devil's horns on his forehead, two blue teardrops below his left eye—the gangbanger's badge of honor for multiple kills.

The high-profile nature of the case meant three deputies were stationed in the courtroom, rather than the standard two: a custody officer near the door to the holding area, a second at the back door leading to the judge's chambers. An elderly female deputy manned the desk where attorneys from other cases could quietly ask questions while court was in session.

Judge Abernathy surveyed his courtroom, his gimlet eyes resting on the attorneys. "Are we ready, Counselors?"

The District Attorney rose. "The People are ready, Your Honor."

In an election year, this case would be a good win for Paul Feynman. He had already conducted a press conference on the courthouse steps, assuring the public that the cold-blooded execution of a police officer deserved nothing less than his personal attention.

Alison Smith, the public defender assigned to the case, rose as well. "The Defense is ready."

The judge nodded. "Mr. Feynman, please proceed."

The D.A. buttoned his hand-tailored, charcoal-grey pinstriped suit coat and bid Claudia a good afternoon. His slightly doughy pink cheeks, sensuous lips and thick neck reminded her of the actor Alec Baldwin. He even wore the actor's hairstyle—salt-and-pepper, slicked straight back.

"Thank you for coming today, Ms. Rose. Would you please tell the jury your occupation and what that means?"

Aware of the red eye of the TV camera blinking at her, Claudia faced the jury box.

The jury did a fair job of reflecting the L.A. melting pot. In the back row, two young Hispanic women and a twenty-something Anglo in a UCLA sweatshirt all held steno notebooks at the ready—no electronics allowed in the courtroom. Three grandmotherly types were likely defense picks who might feel compassion for Danny, even in the face of the heinous crime with which he was charged. A youngish Black woman in a business suit sat next to two middle-aged men in T-shirts—one Black, one Hispanic. An elderly man, who Claudia guessed was Filipino, had already nodded off, chin on chest. In the front row, a rail-thin Asian man in a cardigan wore the spaced-out gaze of a computer geek. At the other end sat his polar opposite: an obese, middle-aged white man in shirtsleeves and tie.

A jury of Danny Ortiz's peers? Gang members didn't get picked for jury duty.

"I'm a forensic handwriting examiner," Claudia said, speaking clearly into the microphone. "I compare disputed handwriting to known samples—exemplars—and offer an opinion about who wrote it."

"Thank you," said Feynman. "I know you've been practicing in this field for quite some time. Would you kindly tell the jury about your background and education?"

There was a fine line between reciting the many pages of her curriculum vitae that detailed what made her an expert in the field, and listing enough of her credentials so that the jurors' eyes didn't glaze over. Making sure to look at each member of the panel in turn as she spoke, Claudia kept the narrative moving. Along the way, the DA injected questions about papers she had published, conferences where she had spoken.

At the end, Alison Smith made a weak objection to her qualifications, but Claudia had testified in more than fifty cases. There was no chance the judge wouldn't qualify her in this one.

"Overruled," said Judge Abernathy. "Ms. Rose may testify."

Feynman thanked him and turned back to Claudia, "Sometimes you are retained as a jury consultant, isn't that right?"

"Yes, in those cases I use handwriting analysis to help my client select jurors."

"And in such cases, you're analyzing *personality*, is that correct?"

"Yes."

"Did you use personality analysis in the case we are talking about here today?"

"No. My assignment in this case was to compare handwriting for purposes of authentication."

"Please tell us more about what you were asked to do."

"Certainly. Your office provided me a handwritten note that's known as a "kite." She spoke directly to the jury. "A kite is contraband communication that's passed between jail inmates. In this case, there's an unsigned note, and I am told that the defendant denies having written it."

"Ms. Rose, do you see the Court's exhibit book on the table in front of you?"

She would have to be blind to miss the fat, black three-ring-binder whose contents had been entered into evidence before she took the stand. Over the course of the next thirty minutes, the DA walked her through the documents in the binder. First, the pages that contained the questioned handwriting, followed by the exemplars that represented Ortiz's true, known handwriting.

At last, he asked, "Have you formed an opinion as to whether the questioned writing is genuine or not?"

"Yes, I have."

"And what is your opinion, Ms. Rose?"

Claudia sat straighter in her chair. "It's my opinion, to a professional degree of certainty, that both the known and the questioned writing *were* written by the same hand."

Everyone knew it was coming—this was what she was here for. Still, her words brought a hush to the courtroom, as though it were she who had pronounced the death sentence.

three

Feynman paused to give the jury a chance to soak in what she had said. Then he asked, "Have you prepared some demonstrative exhibits for the jury?"

"I have." Claudia turned to the judge. "May I step down?"

The judge gave permission and she left the witness stand, not surprised by the subtle shift in the energy of the room. Visual cues held attention better than simply talking at people.

Feynman's assistant had loaded her presentation, and Claudia stood in front of a large TV screen, remote in hand. Even the sleepy juror sat up when the first exhibit—the kite Danny Ortiz denied writing—came into focus. The damning words tumbled across the page from edge to edge without respect for margins, the rounded letters slanting strongly to the left.

Early in the investigation, Jesse Alvarez had run up against a brick wall in his search for samples of Ortiz's handwriting that Claudia could use for comparison. The defendant had refused to provide additional exemplars, citing the law against self-incrimination. There was only one exemplar available—a form he had filled out while in jail. She'd had to tell them that the form, being hand-printed, was unsuitable for comparison to the kite, which was written in cursive.

It wasn't until months later, a packet of handwritten letters surfaced—letters Danny Ortiz had written to an ex-girlfriend on the outside.

The girlfriend, who described him as "a piece of shit nastier than a cockroach," couldn't have been happier to turn them over to the prosecutor's office. To Claudia, it felt like an act of providence.

Examining the new evidence, Claudia found a few minor differences, but enough significant similarities to reach a conclusion. Even if there had been no other commonalities, there was a rare distinguishing feature present in both samples: the bottoms and sides of letters contained a distinctive type of gap—a result of the pen being lifted from the paper for a microsecond. The lift made it appear as if a tiny section of ink had been erased. There was no question in Claudia's mind that the girlfriend's letters could be used to identify Danny Ortiz as the writer of the kite.

She wouldn't be testifying about his personality, but it was impossible to ignore what the handwriting told her: Danny Ortiz was emotionally immature and had no more than average intelligence. A strong need for approval and rebellion toward authority figures might have stemmed from unsatisfactory bonding with his mother. Add to that an utter lack of morality, a short fuse, and zero self-discipline—an explosion was inevitable.

The jurors were alert and interested as Claudia explained the exhibits. The first exhibit was one of Danny's letters to his girlfriend. He had written that he loved her and she'd "better never fucking forget it." He begged her to please start loving him the way she should, that his life was all about her.

From the corner of her eye, Claudia could see the defendant squirming in his chair. Forcing herself to ignore the distraction, she clicked to the second letter. "Fuck off and dye!!" it began. "You stupid lying fucking hoe."

She was pointing to the radical changes in size and slant changes in the document when Danny Ortiz shoved his chair back and started to rise.

The two bailiffs stepped away from the wall, hands resting on their weapons. Alison Smith, who was half Ortiz's size, seized his arm and yanked him back down. He shook her off and slumped back in his chair, spewing a string of profanity directed at Claudia.

Judge Abernathy banged his gavel and jabbed an angry finger at the public defender. "Can you keep your client under control, Counselor, or do I need to have him restrained?"

Smith leaned down, whispering urgently in Danny's ear. He gave a sharp nod, but Claudia saw that his face had paled and he was breathing rapidly.

"My apologies, Your Honor. Uh, my client was embarrassed at, er, having words, which were written in anger—"

The judge's expression darkened to a thundercloud. "Do I look like I care *why*, Counselor? There will be *no* further outbursts. *Do* I make myself understood?"

His gaze swept the defendant's supporters, who had begun muttering to each other, voicing their outrage. "*Quiet!*" Abernathy roared. "Or I'll have the room cleared." He turned back to the public defender, who was visibly trembling. "Ms. Smith?"

"Yes, Your Honor."

"Then sit down and let's get on with it."

At the judge's nod, the bailiffs stepped away from the defendant and returned to their positions. Smith resumed her seat, her cheeks red. "Thank you, Your Honor."

The exchange left Claudia feeling sorry for the public defender, who looked young enough to have passed the bar exam within the last couple of years. How had Alison Smith landed a trial opposing the high-profile district attorney himself? Had she pissed off the Chief Public Defender who knew this case was a no-win? Or was her boss showing confidence in her by giving her a big chance?

Gathering her wits, Claudia continued, glancing over at the jurors from time to time. She was pleased to see them nodding, their expressions rapt as they followed the red dot of her laser pointer. They didn't appear to notice, as she did, that Ortiz continued to glower at her while she highlighted the similarities between the documents.

She returned to the witness stand, preparing for the defense to take a run at her.

Alison Smith got to her feet for cross-examination. Medium height and thin, she wore an off-the-rack navy suit. Her wispy blonde hair, held back in a bun, could have used a brush. Despite her harried appearance, though, she stood straight-backed and spoke in a firm voice. "Ms. Rose, did you at any time meet with my client?"

"No."

"You did not personally take a handwriting sample from him?"

"I was told he had refused—"

Smith broke in. "So your answer is no. Is that right?"

"That is correct."

"And all you have is an angry ex-girlfriend's word that the letters she submitted were written by my client. Isn't that right, Ms. Rose?"

"No."

"No?" Smith echoed, then made a rookie mistake that gave Claudia the opportunity to score an important point with the jury. "Then how do you know those letters were written by Mr. Ortiz?"

"His inmate number is on the return address and his signature, which is consistent with other signatures on jail documents, is on the letters. The handwriting on the envelope is also consistent."

Ignoring the titter that rippled through the courtroom, Smith pressed on. "But an ex-girlfriend could have had someone else—"

Feynman objected. "There's been no offer of proof anyone else wrote the letters."

"Sustained. Do you have anything else, Counselor?"

"No, Your Honor, thank you. Nothing further." Smith took her seat.

Claudia's testimony needed no rehabilitation, so Paul Feynman passed on the opportunity for redirect. She had been on the stand for a little less than ninety minutes.

Judge Abernathy glanced at the clock, his lips twitching in an almost-smile, no doubt pleased that the afternoon session was coming to a close a little early. He turned to Claudia. "Since there are no further questions, Ms. Rose, you are excused."

"Thank you, Your Honor." Claudia slid her paperwork back into her briefcase, her mind already on her dinner plans with Joel. She shot a glance at Feynman, wondering whether he wanted her to stick around. His head was bent toward Alison Smith, who was urgently whispering in his ear. Maybe the public defender was ready to cut a deal for her client.

Abernathy began thanking the jury for their day's service and instructing them not to discuss their opinions with anyone.

As Claudia stepped down from the witness stand, one of the gang-bangers in the gallery jumped up, his hands forming a gang sign. He pointed at Claudia and shouted, "Better watch your back, *puta!*"

The judge rapped his gavel. "Bailiffs, get that person out of here. I'm holding him in contempt."

Claudia froze in place as the two deputies pushed through the gate to the gallery and dragged Ortiz's still-cursing homie past her to the lockup.

The door slammed shut behind them.

That's when Danny Ortiz leapt out of his seat and rocketed across the defense table.

Acknowledgements

For the first time in the series, much of this story is told from the point of view of Claudia's romantic partner, Detective Joel Jovanic. Having no personal experience in law enforcement, I assembled the best team of experts ever. Derek Pacifico's Homicide School for Writers was a great help, and consulting with him personally added an extra layer of veracity. He also had some great ideas, which I shamelessly "borrowed." Detective Heather Gahry, who, like Jovanic, works at LAPD, added many important and helpful insights and I thank her, too, for the interesting and enjoyable lunches we shared. Scott Silveri offered the unique perspective of a police chief, and my former critique partner, retired LAPD detective Bob Brounsten, answered all questions, except why they call him The Bad Bob (one day, I will find out).

From the title, you may have guessed that this book has a tattoo theme, and there could be no better help on that score than input from my talented older son, Erik Lowe, who is himself a tattoo artist (https://www.facebook.com/Tattooguy6ooo). He took me to a tattoo convention for atmosphere, and offered several times to ink me up, which I politely declined. I did, however, twist his arm until he drew exactly the right sugar skull for the book.

It was a great pleasure to once again work with editors Kristen Weber and Ellen Larson. And as always, my deepest thanks to longtime critique partners who make me a better writer: Robert Bealmear, Bruce Cook, Gwen Freeman, Barbara Petty. And to my dear friend Raul Melendez, who may have left our group, but readily makes himself available whenever I get stuck and need an idea. I always appreciate his willingness to share.

About the Author

Sheila Lowe is the author of thirteen novels, including the award-winning Forensic Handwriting series and the Beyond the Veil paranormal suspense series. She is also a real-life forensic handwriting expert who testifies in court cases. In addition to writing stories of psychological suspense, she writes nonfiction books about handwriting and personality. Her memoir, Growing From the Ashes, details her journey from a strict religious cult to spiritual freedom following the murder of her daughter. She lives in Southern California with Lexie, the Very Bad Cat.

To sign up for the newsletter: www.sheilalowebooks.com
For information about handwriting analysis: www.sheilalowe.com

facebook.com/SheilaLoweBooks
twitter.com/Sheila_Lowe
instagram.com/SheilaLoweBooks
bookbub.com/authors/sheila-lowe
goodreads.com/sheilalowe
linkedin.com/in/sheilalowe